# THE CALL FOR FINIS:

## PRIDE

## A.J. TORRES

*The Call for Finis: Pride*

This is a work of fiction. Names, characters, places, and incidents either are the product of the author's imagination or are used fictitiously. Any resemblance to actual persons, living or dead, events, or locales is entirely coincidental.

Cover Art by Odette A. Bach
Cover Text by Milica Popović
Chapter Header Design by Evenstar Books

## Content Warning/Trigger

Out of respect for my more sensitive readers, please be advised that this book contains the following: Cursing, Blood/Gore, Death, Violence, and mentions of topics such as Sexual Assault, Rape, and Physical Abuse that some may find unsuitable/disturbing.

*I dedicate this novel to my wonderful husband, Marcus. It's because of his support that I was able to create this story. He encouraged me every step of the way. I love you so much sweetie.*

# Other Stories By A.J. Torres

# CONTENTS

Marazul Ocean

Utemmet

Marineros

Floce Pro River

Ringiovanire
Lake

Bulo Forest

Salvia's
Path

Dissolvenza Valley

Lungo River

Virtu River

Luminosa Valley

Lumen
Magnum

Rosso River

Aldila Ocean

Dispessore
Forest

Gulf

# World of Eldara

# OUR BOND

FIRE DANCED AND SWAYED, a dot of light in an otherwise endless canvas of black. The flames were the only thing keeping the darkness and nightmares at bay. The light flickered and waved unsteadily as the void crept ever closer. The gloom loomed inward as if it were sentient, compelled by a gluttonous need to snuff out the resting world. A chill glided across the plains and attacked the little light.

Salvia's breath hitched in her throat.

On any other night, she could at least find comfort in the moon's luminous glow and the stars which peppered the sky, but nature seemed determined to mirror the turmoil raging inside her chest. A dense cloud cover had arrived with the setting sun and choked out all celestial light. Her little fire was her one lifeline.

Her hands went scrambling through dirt and grass, searching for the stick she laid close in case the flames needed sparking back to life. The fire was dwindling, and as it receded the nightmares grew bold and approached. Frantic screams echoed all around. Embers floated wistfully through the copper-tinged air. Blood pooled on the ground. Death was everywhere. Fires engulfed everything. Homes. Boats. The pier. Nothing was safe.

Salvia released a trembling breath. Her brown eyes stung. Her breathing grew ragged and heart raced. Flames engulfed her vision, and then suddenly, there was her fiance, Lorenzo Aguado, running toward her. Just as he reached her, a spear erupted from his chest and slammed into her with a wet crunch.

*Breathe.* A deep, cacophonous, and reverberating voice entered her mind, causing a shiver to run between her shoulder blades. *Salvia, you have to breathe.*

Salvia hadn't even realized she had stopped. Struggling through the fear, she pleaded with her body to respond. Slowly, she sucked in a breath and exhaled. Again and again. She felt a little better knowing she wasn't alone. The memory of the fall of her village, Marineros, was still fresh in her mind. It had barely been a week since that terrible night.

Salvia VerdaderaFe, the girl who survived.

Her first major tragedy happened when she had just entered womanhood. A terrible plague ravaged her village and took her parents. Many others died as well, but the village pulled through. Years later, the second major tragedy of her life happened. Raiders fell upon her town, pillaging, murdering, and burning everything in sight. The young woman was the only survivor.

The smell of iron and burning flesh lingered in her nostrils. Salvia could even still feel the warmth of Lorenzo's blood on her copper skin. Bile rose up her throat, and a queasy ache formed in the pit of her stomach.

*Slide your hand to the right. It isn't far.* The voice in her head told her. She followed without question.

Dirt rolled loosely under her palm as the bladed grass brushed her skin. The sensation would have tickled if panic wasn't spiraling in her heart. Something hard slid against her little finger, and a spark of hope blossomed to life. She wrapped her hand around the small, round, wooden object. It was her makeshift poker, and just beside it she found the bundle of sticks she had collected before daylight had vanished. She grabbed a few handfuls of twigs and dry brush, then tossed it all into the fading orange glow of the pit.

Sparks flew erratically as the flames spread across the newly added debris. Salvia poked at the branches to strengthen and spread the weak flames. As the warmth grew with renewed vigor, the kiss of the flames sent a prickle across her skin. She released a sigh of relief. Sitting back on her folded legs, her body straightened and her hands fell limp at her sides. Her terrible memories were finally falling silent again, returning to the recesses of her mind. The crackling of the flames quieted. Both warmth and cold evaded her senses. All sensation faded. She felt nothing; not the aching of loss, not the strain of travel on her muscles, not the dryness choking her throat, not even the scent of pine and cedar from the sparse surrounding trees.

She just felt—nothing.

Her poker slid from her hand and landed with a soft thud. Salvia pulled her legs out from under her and slid her knees into her chest, wrapping her arms around them and hugging herself tight. She sat like that for a long while. Her body tensed at the sound of a light grumble emanating from her stomach. She was hungry. It seemed odd to her that that would be the one feeling to persevere where all others had faded to obscurity. At that moment she wondered if hunger was the most powerful driving force in life. After all, more than anything else, everything needed to eat. Hoping to calm her hunger, she placed a hand on her belly and rubbed it in an attempt to quell its muttering, but her hunger only grew more severe.

Turning her head to the side, Salvia found her satchel beside her and reached inside the opening, removing a small parcel wrapped with thin rice paper.

She dropped her knees into a criss-cross position and placed the parcel on her lap. Loosening the white string around it, Salvia unwrapped the paper. Looking down at the contents inside she let out a soft, disappointed groan. Four thick cuts of salted pork were all she had left.

That wasn't good.

There wasn't much left and there was no way to be certain how much longer her journey south would take. She had no map and no idea where the next town could be. With another fierce roar from her stomach, she ripped away a small piece of the pork, barely the size of a coin, and stuffed it in her mouth. Salvia would have to savor what she could and ration what was left until she made it to wherever the Temple of Pride was meant to be.

A face then slowly emerged from the light of the fire. It was ferocious, with horns and fangs, looking almost skeletal. Its eyes were glowing. They stared intently at her. Salvia met the being's gaze, unflinching and unamused, then took another bite of the meat.

"*Hey! You're gonna share aren't ya?*" Ultor, her demon companion from Infernos, asked while forming his fanged mouth into what seemed to be a playful smirk.

The very first time Salvia had met him, the same moment she had heard his voice trickle into her mind, fear froze her as still as stone. It was the night her village fell. Lorenzo was lying dead, his corpse on top of her as fire roared all around them.

Ultor approached and knelt beside her, brushing a few loose strands of umber hair away from her face with a thin, pointed claw. He had grabbed hold of the shaft of the spear and pulled it free of her and her betrothed. The only sound she could make at the time was a sharp gasp.

She found herself panting, a hand clutching her chest as the fire of the pit in front of her danced against the cold night air. The face in the flames seemed nearly incapable of making an expression, but she somehow always knew what the minor movements in the face were conveying. She could interpret the worry in her demon's gaze. Taking a deep breath, she straightened her body and swallowed.

"I thought demons didn't eat human food." Salvia answered, eliciting a chortle from Ultor.

"*Well, that depends on your definition of* human *food.*" He paused on the last two words. The demon then released a deep, throaty laugh as he glanced at the pork. Watching her quietly for a moment, his expression seemed disappointed, likely since she hadn't reacted to his jest. Her posture relaxed somewhat but she remained quiet. With a sigh, he broke the silence. "*You know what? Never mind, your portions are too small for someone like me anyway.*" The demon stated with a hearty bellow. His image faded as quickly as it had arisen.

Salvia stared intently at what was left of the portion of pork in her lap. She ignored the grumbling of her stomach with all the power of will she could muster, knowing full well she couldn't indulge as much as her body was urging her to do.

A loose, dry strand of braided hair slid into view, lightly obscuring her vision. Using only her left pinky finger she pushed it away from her face. She began to twirl it about her index finger and watched the embers as they rose into the quiet stillness of the night, a melancholy hanging over her.

Her hand drifted absentmindedly to her collar bone, then fell to a spot on the very center of her chest. Salvia's fingers slid in a slow, circular motion across the fabric of her traveling dress, searching for the item she knew she'd find hanging there. A slight burning sensation birthed to life within her ribcage, deepening the frown marring her face. She held back a discomforted groan.

*Hey, stop that! If you keep feeling like this . . . it'll only hurt my feelings.* The demon chuckled warmly. There was an unusual comfort in his words, and while she appreciated his concern there was little anything or anyone could do to extricate her from her turmoil. All she could do was clutch onto the object beneath the cloth, squeezing Lorenzo's final gift.

A pang of guilt pierced her heart. Although they had been engaged at a young age, an arrangement made by their parents, and had known him for a long while, she was never able to truly love. Not as a spouse is supposed to.

Why was that? The practice of arranged marriages was common and many assured her that love would follow as it had for them, but that hadn't been her experience. Was she broken?

She cared for the young fisherman, and they did many things together. She baked him her famous quesitos. He taught her how to sail and to fish. They shared in each other's company and learned the intricacies of each other's thoughts, hopes, and dreams. But no matter what, her feelings toward him never blossomed beyond friendship. She had never felt that spark of something more. Salvia was sure Lorenzo knew of her feelings, or lack of, though she never vocalized it. Perhaps that was why on the night of El Festival de la Rosa de Oro,[1] a popular festival in her home country of Cabreo celebrating love and enduring life's many obstacles, he

---

1      Spanish for *The Golden Rose Festival*

set up a picnic and gave Salvia his final gift. He told her that it didn't matter how she felt for him, that he was and could remain patient. That spark had found him, for her no less. He loved her and believed one day she would feel the same for him. No matter how long it took. He would wait. Unfortunately, that day would never come. The fall of her village came soon after that night.

Releasing a shaky breath, she broke the quiet and asked, "Ultor, is there something wrong with me?"

The demon snorted, as if Salvia had just asked him the silliest question. *Of course not, my young friend. Being an immortal, I've come to learn many things. See many lives in various ways. There's nothing wrong with you. Nothing broken. You are just you. You are young, Salvia, and still have plenty of time to discover who you are meant to become.*

"Hmm," looking forlornly at the fire before her, she chose a different question to ask him, "por qué me elegiste?"[2] Her last words were in the Cabreoan language, the language of her country.

Shortly after meeting Ultor, she agreed to be his host and to take him south to a temple held in the heart of the mortal realm. There, they would enact something the demons and angels had called the Finis. Before embarking on her journey, her king and his sons helped return her slain people to their great god Calamar in the sea.

Through her connection to Ultor, she understood and could speak Anglicus, the language of the people of Marlela, where within they would find their destination south of Cabreo. So much of her understanding of the world had changed in that short time. It was almost too much to accept. Gods. Demons.

---

2     Spanish for *Why choose me*

Angels. Limbo. All of it was real and yet, much of what was preached across the known world was not entirely right, nor wrong. The reality was somewhere in between, a tangled mess of truths and untruths.

She then realized Ultor had stayed silent. He hadn't even emerged from the fire. That was until she felt a presence appear behind her. She sucked in a startled breath and glanced back. Someone, or something, was emerging from her shadow. The figure opened its deep violet webbed wings wide, revealing somewhat leathery wrinkled patagiums stretching between rough, stone and skeletal fingers. A chill spread over her skin like a blanket of ice, gooseflesh forming all over. The being pressed himself against her back. Long, thin arms wrapped around her. What seemed to be skin was as hard and as rough as stone. Ultor's arms shined in an icy violet hue against the dancing fire before them. His wings closed in around her, stopping just shy of enveloping her completely as to allow the fire's warmth to caress her skin.

Salvia sat frozen in place. Had she not understood the gesture to be comforting, as close to a hug as one could receive from a being of his unique composition, she would've been terrified. Fortunately, she did know him. Her heart warmed at the display. Raising a hand to his forearm, she found he truly was as cold as ice. Despite being a demon of Infernos, a realm only ever described by mortals as being a land of death and fire, full of molten pits of unending, unfathomable torment, his touch hadn't a single modicum of warmth. Clearly there was more to the demon's realm than any among the living could possibly comprehend.

*"Do you really want the truth or the sweet comfort of a lie?"* Ultor finally answered.

The corners of her lips twitched into a smirk, then responded, her words melodious yet somber in her Cabreoan accent. "You know our pact."

*"Of course I do, but I want to hear you say it."*

Salvia stared into the fire a little longer and took a deep breath. "We shall never lie, and we shall never hate. Our blades will strike true into the hearts of those who have sinned. We will help all who would ask but only should they be deserving. You are my guardian and I your vessel. Now purge our sins."

They recited the vow in unison, their words weaving into a tapestry of beauty and harmony. Their roles were reversed, but the purity and intent behind the vow would shape the bedrock of new beginnings and, possibly, so powerful as to bring everlasting change to the realm of mortals. For good or for ill, that was yet to be determined.

Both remained silent for a moment after, each trying to outlast the other in holding their stern, quiet gaze. In the end it was Ultor who broke first. They lightly began to chuckle, and soon their chuckles turned to laughter as warmth filled their hearts.

She looked down at the salted pork and ripped off a somewhat large piece, then raised it to him. "Here, pruébalo."[3]

Salvia tilted her head, noticing Ultor's hesitation. After a long moment he raised his clawed hand and pierced the sliver of meat between his index finger and thumb. His hands were large and fingers long and thin. She quickly ripped away a tiny piece for herself and watched Ultor, wondering just what he would do.

In their time together she hadn't once seen him eat. Did demons even eat as mortals do, or did he get all the nourishment he needed from Infernos?

The demon eyed the flesh between his claws, turning it this way and that.

---

3     Spanish for *Try it*

Tilting his skeletal face to one side, his expression seemed a mixture of inquisition and caution. He pulled the salted pork up to where a nose should've been and drew in a long breath. His insides flared with light, then faded as he exhaled. Lowering it to his fanged mouth, he took a mousy bite and went still. His eyes stared into oblivion as Salvia counted the moments drifting by. One. Two. Three. The demon's attention then refocused, and his gaze turned down to her.

She couldn't help but snort, both amused and a little concerned. A smile slid across her face as she met his look. "If you don't want it then I'll eat it myself." She stated as flatly as she could.

"*Ha! Go right ahead. I don't think I could if I wanted to, to be honest. I always wanted to try it, to eat as you humans do. A memory lost to me of my life before. Your kind always looks as though they really enjoy it. Unfortunately, it would seem a sensation forever lost to me. For us, mortals are our food. Humans, dwarves, faes, elves, and so many others. The souls of sinners, and nothing more.*"

"Aaaah, I see."

"*Yes, and to answer your question from a moment ago. There was something within you, something that—*" Ultor suddenly paused, a sneer shading his angular, spiked face.

Salvia cocked her head at him with a raised brow. "Ultor?"

"*We are no longer alone.*" A growl reverberated from his chest, taking her aback.

Ultor slowly stood before her, a full seven feet at his tallest, and turned. She ducked as his long spiked tail soared over her head. His wings spread far before her, shielding her view. Salvia pursed her lips and laid her salted pork on the ground, bending low to peek beneath the webbed wings. She squinted and waited for her vision to adjust to the darkness, her heart jumped in her chest. Several knights in azure garb beneath armor of silver and white were approaching atop horses of varying hues.

There were six in all, and based on the emblem emblazoned on their banners, they were Templar Equitums from the capitol city of Lumen Magnum. These were knights of the infamous Cirine faith. Salvia nearly opened her mouth to inform Ultor of who they were but fell silent as the top of the demon's sharp tail pressed firmly against her lips.

*Shhh, Salvia, I can hear your thoughts, remember? Just be still, this will only be a moment.* The sound of his voice rang in her mind.

She closed her eyes for just a moment, feeling the faint dizziness which came with the telepathic link. Ultor said she would acclimate to it over time and even though it hadn't even been a week since their pact was enacted, she was ready for the dizziness to be a thing of the past. Opening her eyes and blinking the haze away, Salvia inspected the templars as best she could.

The banners were azure with shining gold borders, bearing the silver symbol of an intricate cross surrounded by four feathered wings. They halted their horses' gallop about fifteen paces away from the demon. At the head of the group was a knight donned in large, rounded shoulder pauldrons. His helm was decorated with four long white feathers poking high above his head. He raised his hand to the faceplate, slid it back, and showed his face.

Salvia's breath hitched in her throat. He was a young man that looked to be about her age of eighteen, if not a tad older. His skin was fair. A scar was visible across his thin lips, stretching from just under his right nostril across to the left side of his jaw. For some reason, she couldn't help but wonder how he had received such a ghastly wound.

The dark azure of the young man's pupils glared at her demon friend intensely. Salvia's heart slowly began to race as the knight reached to his side and drew a white sword from its scabbard. The man quickly pointed it at Ultor. "You, demon! How dare you show yourself in our holy country! By the holy light of the Great One above I shall slay you here and now. You will never again tempt an innocent soul."

A long stretch of quiet followed. Seconds felt like minutes. Eventually it was Ultor who broke the silence with a harsh cackle. His cackle grew into a deep bellow of laughter, sending a terrible chill up Salvia's spine. She shrank away from him a little and stared up at his thin back.

Ultor's arms rose at his sides, displaying the large, jagged armor plates that covered much of his body. Shining black blades suddenly protruded from the ends of the armor on his forearms just above his wrists, stretching further than any sword Salvia had ever beheld. He slowly spread his arms and webbed wings. He had become a wall of death.

Salvia had no idea he had such a weapon concealed within him. Taking a deep breath in the hopes it would help calm her panic, she scanned the knights' faces. Judging by their expressions, her fear didn't compare to the dread her demon had summoned into their hearts. Her small campfire suddenly erupted behind her, growing into a raging flame that towered over her.

"*Sin.*" Ultor whispered hoarsely, pulling her attention back to him. "*I sense a sinner among you.*"

The horses began to whinny, their front hooves skittering in place and trying to back away while the riders fought to keep the creatures in place. Ultor's spiked tail slowly flailed left and right like a lion ready to pounce. He leaned forward with a deep growl in his chest, looking ravenous with hunger.

"*Salvia, which one?*" Ultor asked, startling her.

It was time.

Her body was trembling. In order for Ultor to act, she had to be the one to divine the sinners for him. Were he to strike at an innocent, he would suffer divine punishment, so he offered her a means to do as needed. She stood up and revealed herself from behind Ultor, startling the head knight, and raised her left hand toward them, palm facing the sky.

Taking another deep breath, she gently closed her eyes and felt the warmth spark to life on her hand. It grew hotter and hotter, feeling like a small weight on her palm. Opening her eyes, she found a ring of fire hovering over her hand no larger than the size of her head. She raised it until her arm was level with her gaze and peered through the haze of heat and flames. She searched the distorted image within the fire and there, one of the knights began to glow brightly in a sickly yellow tinge. Recalling what Ultor had taught her the first time she tested the ability, she recognized the putrid hue to be the color of greed. She looked to the others, waiting, expecting more to light up as well but was taken aback by what she saw—nothing. Only one of the bunch was a sinner.

Ultor noticed her pause and glanced at her. "*What's wrong?*"

She gently shook her head. "Nada.[4] I suspected the one who raised his sword to you and perhaps a few others to be guilty, but it's just the one on the far right."

"*Is that so? Very well then.*"

He crouched close to the ground, his large, spiked horns pointing toward

---

4    Spanish for *It's nothing*

the knight whose soul was marked by sin. Without a moment's hesitation Ultor rushed forward, causing Salvia to jolt in place. He moved so fast he became a blur and struck his left arm blade through the sinner's chest before anyone had a chance to react. The horses reared with fright, causing the still terrified knights to tumble from their saddles to the ground below.

Raising the sinner high into the air, his body glowed brightly in tones of red and orange that danced over his being, like fire. He hung still, lifeless, but the glow separated and took on a human form of its own and writhed, kicking and screaming in agony. Salvia's jaw locked, her body turning icy cold with the realization of her demon companion's power.

Ultor opened his fanged mouth wide and took in a deep breath. He began to devour the glow as it wriggled and desperately fought to escape. The knights all stared wide eyed and frozen with fear at the horrific sight taking place before them. It was like nothing Salvia had ever seen and judging from the knights' reactions, they too were unprepared for this fight.

As she stared wide-eyed at Ultor, sweat beaded on her brow, and her pulse raced. She thought she had understood, thought she had prepared herself for what was to come. To see what he called The Devouring. Salvia didn't expect it to be like this. She knew this fate was the sinner's own doing. Justice was being dealt for whatever atrocities the knight had committed. She should've been glad to see him sent to Infernos for punishment, but all she felt in that moment was pity. The horrific wail of his scream was otherworldly, bone chilling, and a thing of nightmares. She could almost feel the agony he must've been going through.

Her eyes traveled to the body that had now slid to the base of Ultor's blade. Crimson blood spilled down his forearm and dripped to the grass, muddying the dirt. Flashes of her burning village rushed into her mind again, her people running, screaming for their lives. Many fled to the docks, trying to reach the boats in the hopes that they could escape into the vast blue ocean that had always welcomed them. Others tried to fight, wielding oars, shovels, pitchforks, anything they could find. Unfortunately, her people were fishermen and farmers, not warriors. When she closed her eyes, she could still see their chests skewered by swords, their blood painting their village. Women screamed over the laughter of evil men as they were carried away. Not even the children had been spared. Many were tossed, screaming into burning homes. Those lucky enough to live were taken, likely doomed to a fate of slavery, or worse.

"NO!" One of the Templars screamed out, jolting Salvia back from her memories.

As the soldiers regained their composure they quickly drew their swords. Salvia dismissed her fire ring, dropping to the ground, and slammed the same hand hard to the dirt. Breathing in deeply once more and closing her eyes, she called for the binding magic Ultor gave her to protect herself should she ever be in need. Warmth brimmed to life beneath her hand and spread outward. A wave of heat brushed against her face. The spell was ready. All she had to do was focus on the soldiers, will the magic to hold them in place long enough for her and Ultor to flee—

"Kill the witch!" The voice of the head knight ordered, startling Salvia from her concentration.

She'd never heard the word witch before. As she opened her eyes, her heart skipped a beat. It felt as if time was slowed. She watched helplessly as a bolt soared toward her. Salvia fell backward, but there was no time, there was no way she could dodge the projectile in time. Panic set in. She was going to die.

On instinct she crossed her arms over her chest, closed her eyes, and prayed to the Almighty One and the sea god Calamar, praying to anyone who was listening to not let this be her end. She hadn't expected anyone to actually be listening and waited for the bolt to find its mark. Suddenly a rush of wind slammed into her from above. She heard a powerful flap of wings followed by a loud clang, as if a hammer had struck an anvil.

Adrenaline pounded through her veins as she opened her eyes. She was taken aback at what she found. Soft white feathers covered her view. Her mouth fell open. Salvia leaned forward, reaching out to the wall of feathers with a hand, and just as a tip of her fingers brushed against the soft, ethereal plumes, a golden glowing hand grasped onto her.

"Dost not."

A soothing voice filled her ears, sounding more splendid than any bird's song carried on a gentle breeze, more calming than the laps of waves at daybreak, and more relaxing than a soft bed after a long day's work. She turned to its source. Spreading his wings just enough to reveal his form to her, an angel of Hevellum met her gaze, face-to-face. His features were sharp and chiseled.

Her face lit up with disbelief, staring into his aqua green eyes. She quickly crossed her arms into an X over her chest and bowed her head low to show her respect for such a beautiful being. He bowed his head in return, his ebony hair sliding over his armored shoulders and partially covering his glowing golden-brown skin. The being then stood to inspect Ultor who was still devouring the sinner and seemed to be savoring every bite.

As the last vestige of the sinner's glow vanished into the demon's maw, Ultor tossed the corpse to the side where it landed with a terrible squishy thud. The noise made Salvia's insides churn. Ultor then turned his attention toward the bowman who had fired her bolt at Salvia. He swatted the other soldiers out of his way, as if they were nothing more than a simple inconvenience. The woman with the crossbow visibly startled.

To Salvia's surprise she didn't retreat, instead aiming her spare weapon with a bolt already loaded, and loosed it. Ultor didn't even flinch as he snatched it from the air mere inches from his skeletal face. Unamused, he dropped the bolt to the ground, then grabbed the crossbowman and raised her high into the air, looking poised to snap her neck.

"Ultor stop!" The angel screamed out. A burst of light cracked across the sky, punctuating his command with authority. The tone of the plea caught Salvia by surprise. There was no condemnation in his call. Urgent as it was, there were clear traces of concern in his voice.

"*This human dared to loose her bolt at Salvia! This one needs to be punished.*" Ultor snarled. Whatever bravery the woman moments ago had was now gone, replaced by understandable fear. Her hands quivered.

Salvia jolted, fearing what punishment might befall her companion should he devour an innocent. "Ultor, por favor,[5] stop!" She pleaded. "The woman only acted out of fear of what you did. She knew not her actions! I promise you, there are no more sinners here."

Ultor continued to glare at the knight within his grasp, seething as he slightly tightened his grip around her body. The woman groaned in pain as the air escaped her. She clawed at his rough skin with her free hand to no avail. He brought his face

---

5     Spanish for *Please*

closer to the knight, reveling in her fearful, wide-eyed stare. Ultor sniffed her once, twice, three times, as if hoping for a trace of something that wasn't there.

"*BAH!*" He scoffed, sounding disappointed. "*Fine.*" Dropping the woman, he walked over to join the lightly armored angel and Salvia, helping her off the ground.

Salvia glanced at the Templars who stared in disbelief at what lay before them. The leader slowly stood, his hand-and-a-half longsword still tightly gripped in his trembling hand. Ultor and the angel turned to the knights, causing many of the soldiers to flinch, but none dared attack after what had nearly befallen the bowman moments before. Suddenly, one of the knight's horses cantered over to them. It was the one that belonged to the now dead soldier.

Just as the creature reached Salvia, she slowly raised her hand and cupped the horse's chin. She pressed her forehead against the stallion and gently scratched along his jawline.

Ultor then turned to the angel with an annoyed sneer. "*What is this, Abimelech? I heard the call for Finis, but the sinner's I've found so far are few at best.*"

So the angelic warrior's name was Abimelech, Salvia thought, brushing the horse's gray fur and trying to act as though she were not eavesdropping on their conversation.

"Thou misunderstand, *demon.*" Abimelech replied with an annoyed scowl of his own. "The call was not to end the mortal world of Eldara, but to end a single city."

The demon's profound brow winced in surprise, curiosity rising. "*Oh, a city? Please explain.*"

Salvia noticed the head soldier flinch. He was gawking at Abimelech, likely trying to understand what he was seeing.

Swallowing, she decided it would be good to finish the spell she had started before one of the knights had nearly ended her life with a bolt. It would be unwise to interrupt the angel and demon's discussion. Besides, binding the templars would likely be the best way to keep them safe from further antagonizing Ultor. Removing her hands from the horse, she slowly turned to the fire to not raise any alarm and sat herself down on folded legs. Planting a hand on the ground, she resummoned the binding circle and froze the soldiers where they were.

"The city has warped the views of the Almighty One above." Abimelech started to explain. "They segregate and discriminate against all who art different, and murder those who dost not follow their self-proclaimed *true* faith."

A small, pleased smile then grew on Ultor's fanged mouth. *"Don't keep me in suspense Archangel, what's the city's name?"*

Abimelech rolled his eyes in disgust and continued. "The capitol city of Marlela, Lumen Magnum. The selfsame place where the seven Temples of Sin and Virtue reside."

# OUR DESTINATION

**A**FTER THE TEMPLAR EQUITUMS had been bound in place, Abimelech quickly introduced himself to Salvia. He was an Archangel of Hevellum, which was of little surprise to her. He was as magnificent as Ultor was horrific. What she hadn't expected though was that he was, quite literally, her Guardian Angel. He had watched over her since birth, whispering suggestions into her thoughts and subtly guiding the path of her life.

This brought on a subconscious worry in the back of her mind that she had never actually been in control of her destiny. The thought would've, given enough time, festered into an unshakeable anxiety that could've caused her to question her every action. Before the question had even formed into coherent words, almost as if he too glimpsed the seed of doubt taking hold, he confessed that he had only ever interceded a handful of times, owing to her kind and caring soul. It was her natural predilection to help those around her with a warm smile and gentle hand. She should've felt relieved, but somehow the knowledge that he had been there for her and yet hadn't been able to stave off the horrors that befell her village, offered little comfort. Her every emotion, every sense had been dulled since that night. Her every sense, that was, save for fear. Fear was becoming her ever-present companion lingering in the periphery of her mind.

Salvia was sure that Abimelech noticed her stoicism. With everything he had told her, surely she should've reacted in any number of ways, but she didn't. She just quietly listened as she reached for Lorenzo's gift hanging from her neck. Her hand was inexplicably drawn to it, needing to know it was still there, that she hadn't lost it.

The angel then knelt before her and cupped her cheek. His touch was warm and her skin tingled where he had made contact. He tilted her head upward until she found herself looking into his aqua eyes, eyes that seemed so sad and shimmered like gemstones in the firelight. Abimelech flashed her a small smile and began to inspect her.

Positioning her head gently left and then right, up and then down, she assumed he was checking her for signs of injury. Though she felt fine, she kept silent and allowed his inspection. In the quiet moments she sometimes heard sharp, hushed whispers coming from where the silver warriors stood, but Salvia paid them little mind. No doubt they would be dealt with soon enough. Divine loss of memory, or something. It wasn't unheard of. In fact, the idea was relatively common in tales from her childhood and now that she had a demon of Infernos and an angel of Hevellum standing before her, it seemed likely to be real.

"Well, I see nothing abnormal since thine awakening." Abimelech said, brushing her umber hair from her view as he intertwined a few strands between his fingers, most likely examining how dry and straw-like it had become.

In the last town she had come across, Salvia hoped to bathe and sleep in a proper bed, but the people were far from welcoming. In the short time she was there it was clear she was being watched. The people did little to hide the seething hate in their looks. They had already judged her the moment she stepped foot into the town. What it was that had given them their motivation for such open contempt was unknown but the rationale didn't matter. It could've been the color of her skin or her manner of dress, or perhaps a general mistrust of outsiders. The fact was that there was little she could do to change their perception given the short time she had planned to be there. So she grabbed what little food the local butcher was willing to sell to her and quickly left. Ultor objected, promising that he would keep her safe, but she felt it was best to avoid conflict as much as possible. Though she didn't care for how the Marlelains were looking at her, she didn't wish for them to come to harm. Besides, she felt safer out in the woods. At least there it was unlikely that anyone would trouble her.

"Salvia?"

She startled and looked at Abimelech. He was staring at her, and his hands gently grasped her shoulders.

"May I see the wound on thy chest?"

Salvia remained silent and simply nodded. Raising her hands to the dresses collars, she pulled down on the purple and white fabric, revealing two scars which overlapped each other between her breasts. A pentagram scar which looked like a brand left by hot irons, her link to Ultor, covered an oddly sewn scar. It was the scar she received from the point of a spear. That scar had been healed by divine, or rather, demonic magic. Maybe both. She wasn't honestly sure. All that was left of it was a long, thin line where the flesh had reconnected.

Hanging just above the pair of scars was Lorenzo's final gift, a small gold rose hanging by a golden chain. Six red pearls accompanied the pendant, three on either side. Salvia couldn't imagine how much it had cost to have it custom made, but it warmed her heart every time she looked upon it.

Her eyes stung as she wondered if perhaps she should've kept the bracelet she made him. Did she do the right thing by leaving it with him in his final resting place? It was a gold chain with a red ribbon interlaced between the links. It was a simple thing, but he hadn't seen it that way. Lorenzo's face lit up the day she gave it to him. His deep brown, nearly black eyes twinkled with joy. It was a gift to him. For him. She hoped he was able to take it with him in the afterlife, whichever one he found himself to be in.

"Salvia," Abimelech brushed his knuckles softly across her cheek, garnering Salvia's teary-eyed stare, "Lorenzo is safe. In Hevellum, I mean." The words were soft, compassionate. A smile rested on his face. His black hair wafted softly in the breeze, brushing against his glowing golden-brown skin.

The words slowly set in, her mouth twitching with realization. "You-You mean—"

"The flow commenced, and he has passed through." The angel answered. "Thine gift, he holds it to his heart, as thou to thine."

Salvia released a trembling breath, and a tear rolled down her cheek. The uncertainty of what fate had awaited him hit her harder than she had realized. She didn't believe he would go below, to Ultor's realm, he was far too kind for that, but now she had confirmation, she had her answer.

"Gracias."[1] She croaked in Cabreoan, her heart a mixture of happiness that Lorenzo had safely passed on, but also sadness that he was truly gone from Eldara.

Abimelech nodded and returned his attention to her scars. "Now, it is strange that thy mark appeared over the wound. Would that not be problematic?" He asked, the question not for her, but for Ultor.

*"I have no control over where the mark appears."* Ultor answered with a shrug. *"I was told my mark would appear closest to where the final blow had been struck. I've had no issue coming and going as needed, so don't worry."*

Abimelech nodded in understanding and returned to the scar. Grabbing the fabric of Salvia's dresses from her hands, he lifted it and fixed the collars to cover her once more. "When the task is complete, the Mark of Infernos will dissipate, but the other," his eyes intimately met Salvia's which caused her heart to skip, "will remain. Dost thou understand?"

She then realized she had been sitting there slack-jawed and shut her mouth. Salvia hadn't given a great deal of thought to the scars on her chest. Whether they were permanent or not, it felt insignificant to everything else that had happened and would happen still.

Her mind was elsewhere.

Glancing to the fire swirling brightly beside her, she forced herself to nod. If the scars were something she would have to live with, so be it. Let them be a reminder, or more accurately, a reason to activate the Finis. For Hevellum. For Infernos. For herself and the memory of those who were lost.

Salvia jolted as Abimelech brushed a thumb over her dry, cracked lips. Her skin prickled, buzzing with warmth as it had when he touched her cheek. Energy

1   Spanish for *Thank you*

then constricted the muscles in her jaw as it raced from her lips into the muscles surrounding her mouth and dissipated into the rest of her body. The sensation wasn't altogether unpleasant, but the jolt had caught her by surprise. It lingered as she turned her head away, and she felt somewhat renewed. Not exactly well rested but neither was she as haggard as she had been in the still moments before the knights had arrived. If the surge of vitality had been intentional, he didn't show it on his face.

"Thou art dehydrated. Ultor!" Abimelech scolded Ultor.

"*Hey, don't look at me.*" Ultor raised his hands in defense, his gaze remaining locked on the warriors. "*In the last town we passed, the people unsettled Salvia so much that she didn't want to linger there longer than needed.*"

"Ye need to do better." Abimelech said as he stood up and walked around Salvia to speak with Ultor, face-to-face. The height difference between the two caught her by surprise. Abimelech stood no larger than an average human, only slightly taller than her, whereas Ultor towered above every living soul present. "Thou have nary a map, not even enough provisions to journey to Lumen Magnum. AND ye were just attacked. Salvia could have died!" Abimelech chastised.

Ultor's arms were crossed over his chest. He didn't turn to meet Abimelech, keeping his watch on the knights and what looked like an amused smirk on his face. The demon then let out a soft chortle.

"Ultor, art thou listening?" Abimelech asked with furrowed brows.

"*I'm always listening, just not always to those who are speaking. That human is foolish and filled with misguided courage. He thinks you to be a mirage of sorts. A trick of my doing.*" He chuckled to himself, clearly ignoring the rising anger on Abimelech's increasingly reddening face.

"I dost not much care what these foolish humans think. Thou must be more careful with Salvia's wellbeing. If she dies—"

"*I lose my vessel and the call will be for naught. Honestly, I know—*"

"I swear to the Almighty One above ye demons art infuriating to no end!"

"*Uh huh, anyway why didn't you show after she became my vessel? Kind of irresponsible behavior for one such as yourself.*"

Abimelech let out a frustrated groan. A light giggle escaped Salvia's lips. In that moment, the two's arguing brought her back to a time before all the hurts she had suffered. The barriers of her heart and mind subsided. Her old self had emerged, fleeting as the sensation was. She quickly covered her mouth. The two had seemingly never met before this moment, but here they stood, bickering like old friends, just like Lorenzo had with his friends in life.

"Clearly thou art ready to change subjects." Abimelech's voice dripped with exasperation. "Not all of the vessels had yet been chosen. I was forced to wait as thou foolishly took Salvia through a land she has never been to!" Ultor interrupted with an eruption of laughter, which only furthered Abimelech's fuming. "I will not allow thee to endanger the young woman. I hast guarded her since she was but an infant."

"*Yeah, you've done a great job of that so far—*"

Salvia jolted and shot Ultor a stern look. "Ultor, por favor,[2] behave yourself. That was unkind."

She couldn't imagine what it was like for Abimelech to watch the chaos unfold around her in Marineros. True, she didn't know him well, but it seemed to her that if it were possible for him to have prevented the atrocities of that day, he

---

2    Spanish for *Please*

wouldn't have hesitated. There must've been limitations on his ability to affect the mortal world, just as there were on Ultor. Her Archangel's trembling eyes spoke volumes. What Ultor had started to say had clearly hurt Abimelech, she was sure of it.

"Anyway, the last few Papa Regems hast slowly but surely warped the message of the Almighty One above, shepherding the people in a direction of war and enslavement. Elves and dwarves art hunted down. Humans from far off regions of differing faiths art murdered as soon as they enter port. In order to save Eldara from destruction, and with the permission of the Almighty One, we must rid the world of Lumen Magnum and its oppressive sinners. The Seraphim believe this may stave off the coming calamity they bring upon themselves."

"*Do you truly believe ridding one city of sinners can save their world?*" Ultor asked as he finally looked down to meet Abimelech.

The angel stared up in silence. His aqua gaze glanced down, roving left and right deep in contemplation. The moment was long and quiet between the two. Ultor stared at Abimelech carefully, as if unsure of the angel's conviction in their undertaking.

With a deep breath, Abimelech finally met Ultor's glowing violet eyes and answered. "Ay, I dost believe it will work. Ignorant as they may be, I believe the good of the many outweighs the bad in the few. Without the seeds of corruption, they shall blossom anew."

A smirk creased Ultor's face once again. He winked then bowed to the angel before him. "*Then it shall be done.*"

Salvia sat quietly, leaving the two be. She turned her head to the burning pentagram on the ground singeing the grass. The templar's bindings held. Looking back, as though feeling the cold azure stare of their leader upon her, he glared at her furiously. He was distrustful. His stare made her heart quicken nervously. She hoped that after this, she wouldn't see him again.

Turning back to the fire and situating herself comfortably on the ground, she grabbed a piece of salted pork and was about to take a bite when her fingers brushed against something soft to her left. She startled and found the soldier's blue banner lying on the ground next to her. The horse Ultor had called for her was grazing beside them. With that acknowledgement she surmised the banner must've slid off the creature on its approach.

Salvia picked it up, feeling its silky surface as she folded the fabric from end to end. As she did, a symbol peaked through the smattering of dirt that clung to the cloth. It was the symbol of the Cirine order. Brushing away some dirt, she inspected the intricacies of the design.

An elegant, pointed cross sat at the center of its crest. The beams of the cross were of differing lengths each resembling the blade of a sword, the bottom beam being the longest followed by a mid-length beam at its top and a short beam on either side, protruding just above its center. Four thorns jutted from a circular medallion resting at the center of the cross, each thorn nestled at the intersection of the beams. Angelic wings surrounded the cross, two above the middle beams and two below.

She recalled several of the wandering Sacerdotis and Abbatis Commendets who had journeyed to her village within the borders of Cabreo, north of Marlela. Some of them had been kind, helpful even. They visited spreading word of the Cirine faith, letting all know they would be welcomed into the warmth, the holy light of the Great One above. All would be saved if only they confessed their past sins.

Other members of the faith came as well, but were not as pleasant, instead choosing to shame and bully the people into joining. As if telling her people they would be dragged to the depths of Infernos for believing in the gods of their parents, pagan and heathen gods as they called them, would actually sway the people. Salvia remembered glaring at them and her blood boiling in anger for the hateful words they spouted. Her fingers holding the pork tightened just thinking about it.

It seemed the order had two sides to it and its members. Oftentimes they would even have disagreements amongst members of their own order. How could she trust them if they couldn't even trust themselves?

Salvia didn't care to listen to the rantings and ravings of that sort of Sacerdotis or Abbatis Commendet. She preferred the kind ones, found their thoughts and beliefs interesting. Many of them admitted to not having knowledge of her people's gods and even welcomed the education she could provide. She explained that for Cabreoan's there was no distinction between angel and demon. They were simply entities of the divine, each distinct and the reason of their actions unknowable. What would be, would be. Those of whom she explained this to, found it fascinating. Still, they encouraged those within her village who were willing, to try the Cirine faith, to embrace a new perspective on belief since some of her people had received nothing but heartbreak from their current idol, but that was to be expected. They hadn't come here to convert, but to convert others. It was the purpose of their pilgrimage after all.

She considered converting to the Cirine faith for a time. She told her late fiancé Lorenzo about doing so, but he worried their ocean God, Calamar, would drown them if she abandoned her faith. Salvia quickly became disillusioned with faith entirely after the attack on her village. With the death of her fiancé, family, and friends, she wondered, feared, that it was her fault. Was it truly Calamar retaliating in anger simply for her interest in the foreign faith? Or was it the Almighty One being impatient? Who was to say? At that point she wasn't sure if anyone had the answers.

When Ultor came to her, he explained who ruled them all. Her God Calamar, the angels of Hevellum, the demons of Infernos, and the mortals of Eldara. They were all ruled by one being, the great light Themself, the Almighty One. The choices made in life were the actions of oneself, not the divine. Abimelech had further explained that he could only offer suggestions, nudges in the right direction, but he couldn't make her do anything. Which meant, when bad things happened, they happened by a person's actions, not guided by some divine plan. The world was given to mortals, to live as freely as they wished, but if the path they tread led toward the world's destruction, was it only then that the divine would intervene?

Salvia's head started pulsing lightly with pain. It was far too much information to take in all in such a short time.

She was surprised to learn how the faiths were tied together, no one belief true on its own. Each was but a shard of the greater truth. Each branch of faith became distorted over time, changed to fit the needs of the people. The Cirine faith was worse than most, perversely changed in subtle ways over time. It existed now as only a reflection of the true faith, recognizable in its origin but corrupted by those with power and influence.

It was possible the blade-like beams of the cross were meant to be a literal depiction of what the Cirine faith was about. Join their faith, or be cut down. Many of the traveling Sacerdotis had said as much. Why must people spout such things? Perhaps a change was needed to help open everyone to the truth.

"Salvia," Abimelech called, pulling her attention to him, "that banner openly disrespects the Almighty One above. Can thou please toss it into the fire?" A hint of spite bit beneath the soft, melodious sound of his voice, sending a shiver down her spine.

His outrage was written across his face. Salvia didn't think a symbol alone could hold so much power. In Cabreo there wasn't one symbol to represent one's faith in Calamar. They had various symbols to represent him. Each was fashioned with a similar, recognizable base, but every idol was unique in subtle ways. A splash of paint here, an etched sigil there. The item only had significance to the person who made it.

Glancing down at Abimelech's chest, she spotted a symbol on his chest plate. It had a much smaller cross than the templar's. All the beams were equal in length and were slightly arched at the ends with a plain circle resting at its center. A ring lay beneath the cross just slightly shy of its tips, interjecting between the beams with four diamonds placed between them. Surrounding the ring and cross were twelve rays of light, three at each corner.

She wondered if the symbol was meant to show the light of Hevellum shining on all beings equally. Based on everything Ultor and Abimelech had told her thus far, that seemed to be the most likely conclusion and while she could've sought confirmation, at the time it was easier to follow through with her task by having faith that her assumption was correct.

Without question, Salvia nodded and complied, tossing the banner into the fire. Sparks flew wildly as the flames quickly consumed the silk banner.

"How dare you!"

Salvia jumped at the sudden outburst and looked back to the Templar Equitums. Their leader's face brimmed with fury.

"You claim to be an angel of Hevellum, yet you allow this witch to burn—"

"THAT IS ENOUGH!" Abimelech commanded with fiery fury. Many of the soldiers seemed visibly concerned by the angel's outrage but if that sentiment was shared by the commander, he didn't show it. Then, in a quieted tone, Abimelech continued. "I will not be lectured by fools such as ye."

Abimelech's voice demanded silence. The rage in his expression scared Salvia, but she knew he wasn't a threat to her. She stood up and carefully approached the Archangel from behind.

"Thou hast blindly allowed people to guide thee to war, bringing death and misery to the innocent under the pretense of faith! Well, not anymore—"

Salvia couldn't take it anymore. Hearing the fury and sadness in his tone caused a profound sense of dread at her very core. His very words caused her skin to prickle and muscles to tense. The air grew as thick as molasses in her lungs. She felt the weight of the sky on her shoulders. Urgency suddenly stirred her into action. She rushed to Abimelech, pushing through his wings and wrapping her arms around his torso. His soft white feathers tickled. Salvia embraced him as tightly as she could, hoping to bring calm to his rage.

It was clear Abimelech was thrown off by her gesture. He went quiet.

None dared to speak, not even Ultor or the commander of the knights. It was as if everyone had felt what she felt, the weight of divinity raining down on everyone within earshot, pouring forth from his every word. Ultor was mighty in his own right but to anger an angel seemed an entirely different matter. Eventually, she felt a warm palm press against the back of her hands. His silver armor bit coldly under her palms. He finally took a deep breath and as the air exited his body, the sensation plaguing her body subsided.

"*Archangel,*" Ultor called, "*by any chance have you brought something for Salvia? Perhaps a means to buy food for her journey to Lumen Magnum? As you can see, she barely has any left. I sense there is a town not more than a day's ride or so from here. What she has may not last until then. If not, we can take whatever these so-called soldiers have on them. That should last her until we reach our destination.*"

Abimelech sighed. "Unfortunately, nay, I did not." He raised his other hand to Salvia's, gently removing them from his chest. His expression softened after no doubt seeing the worry in her brown eyes, but she hoped he didn't notice. She mustered as much warmth and care as she possibly could in her smile.

His lips then slid into a small smirk of his own, and he thanked her. Raising a hand to her head, he ran his fingers gently through her hair as a parent would their child. "But I hast another method. Salvia, please hold out thy hands."

She tilted her head curiously at him but did as he asked and raised her cupped hands before him. He casually reached behind his back while raising his other hand to hover just above hers. Then, in one swift motion, he swung a hidden dagger past his palm.

Salvia winced at the sudden motion and looked at Abimelech's palm. A small gash on his skin slid open and a gold liquid spilled forth.

She gasped, flinching to grab the Archangel's hand to stem the bleeding, but Ultor placed a heavy hand on her shoulder, keeping her in place. "*Be still, Salvia. It's alright.*"

Her stomach churned into a tight knot at the sight of the wound, but she did as she was asked. The angel then curled his fingers into fists, squeezing his hand. A drop of his golden blood fell to her palms and landed with more heft than she had expected. As more droplets fell, she was taken aback as the blood slowly wriggled about, forming into multiple small, yet unknown shapes. The liquid began to harden, each drop forming into small, thin golden discs. So many formed that they began spilling out of her hands. Salvia stared on in awe of Abimelech's gift, his blood now solid gold coins in the palms of her hands.

Abimelech sheathed his dagger and opened the palm of his right hand once more. The wound was fully healed. He then gently cupped her hands within his. "Take these to buy all that thou may need on thy journey to the city of these sinners. Thou must be careful from now on. Dost thou understand?"

Salvia looked up at Abimelech, then down to the coins in her hands, in awe of the gift. He had bled for her. He was an angel, a being of great significance second only to the Almighty One, and he had offered his blood freely for her sake. Had she any feelings of apprehension left about her given mission, they were gone. She would see this through for all who had sacrificed leading to this moment. She returned her gaze to him again and nodded in thanks.

Abimelech smiled happily, cupping her face in his hands, and leaned forward to kiss her forehead gently. "I wish thou safe travels."

Ultor raised Salvia's open satchel. She slid the coins into the mouth of the bag and dropped them in. Quickly kneeling to pick up the coins on the ground, Salvia placed them into the bag as well. Grabbing the satchel from Ultor, she closed it and turned to face Abimelech with a gracious bow. She stood straight with a small, thankful smile and returned to sit by the fire.

Salvia then glanced up to Ultor, to ask how they should proceed. As she started to form the question she paused, tilting her head at the smirk growing on his skeletal face.

"*Abimelech, enact Vovete on the Captain and the Crossbow woman. Their skills will be useful.*" Ultor said, his furrowed gaze locked on the soldiers who were visibly unsettled by his expression.

"Excuse me?" Abimelech asked with a raised brow.

"*I may not be able to materialize quickly enough to defend Salvia every time she gets herself into danger. Also, a prolonged battle could prove problematic for just me alone. Our bond should strengthen over time, but as it is now, I haven't much strength left.*"

Salvia had no idea the bond caused such a strain on Ultor. She was about to stand again but felt a sudden weight on her head. Looking up, Ultor's large hand was over her, seemingly knowing how she felt. "*Stop that,*" he said with charm in his voice. "*I didn't mean to imply that you're a burden. Despite my features, I care for you, even if you are annoyingly too trusting.*" He chuckled warmly, causing her to laugh gently with him. Ultor then looked at Abimelech with a stern gaze, waiting for a response.

The Archangel stared at the demon a moment longer, then sighed heavily. "Alright, I will enact Vovete on the two. The other soldiers will have their memories altered of this encounter, and I will order them to return to whence they came."

Salvia felt a pang in her chest. She glanced at the soldiers, at the two Ultor mentioned would be traveling with her. Would they really keep her safe, even by force?

Their looks were glaring. They had judged her the moment they laid eyes on her. Hated her before she had taken a single action against them. And now they would be bound to her. Anxiety slowly rose within her. Being around such people made her nervous. They weren't to be trusted, and most often, couldn't be reasoned with. However, Ultor and Abimelech knew what they were doing. She trusted them. So, Salvia would trust in faith.

# OUR BEGINNING

A FULL DAY HAD PASSED since Salvia's encounter with the troupe of Templar Equitums, meeting her Archangel, Abimelech, and thanks to Ultor's persistence, she had now gained two obviously spiteful companions. The angel had enacted Vovete. The spell was only accessible to the angels of Hevellum. While under its influence, the knights would be compelled to follow the will of the caster. They couldn't break the spell. Couldn't fight its compulsion. Once it was cast, the only way to be free of the magic was to complete the task that had been set upon them.

Captain Baldric Fede Cieca and his First Lieutenant Zinnia Colpo Penetrante, were now fated to travel with Salvia, their task to keep her safe from anyone or anything that would bring her danger. They would travel to Lumen Magnum, and only after she had activated the Finis would they be free once more. They wouldn't be able to harm her, no matter how much they may have wanted to. The other soldiers who had been under Baldric's command had their memories wiped and were sent back to whatever town they came from. Luckily, wherever it was they returned, it wasn't the same town Salvia stopped at for provisions and sleep.

Salvia sat with folded legs before a fire. They had set up camp at the edge of the Dissolvenza Valley, next to the Virtu River with the Luminosa Valley at the opposite side of the stretch of water. An iron pan was suspended atop the fire, and slices of meat sizzled within. She poked at the food with a two-pronged fork to keep the slices from burning, unable to ignore the urge to steal glances at the Templar Equitums who sat behind her, Baldric in particular.

The young man had mostly remained stoic, his expression giving little away but behind his eyes she recognized a glare with such intensity it caused Salvia's stomach to churn. She was sure if he were free to act, he would shove her face straight into the fire. With the setting sun at their backs, Baldric was completely cast in shadow. His deep azure eyes were icy and gleamed with the flickering flames of rage. The sight unsettled her. The man's arms were tightly crossed over his armored chest. His hands were balled into tight fists, resting as still as a statue.

Baldric's First Lieutenant, Zinnia, had her back to Salvia. The woman looked surprisingly young as well, possibly a little older than Salvia. Copper red hair adorned her crown and two small crossbows hung at her waist. A quiver of bolts was neatly strapped on her back. In the short time the three had been traveling, Salvia had caught Zinnia's gaze only a handful of times. In those moments the woman's leaf green eyes burned with disgust. A sneer marred the woman's otherwise pleasant freckled, fair skinned face.

Traveling with the two constantly staring daggers at her had been showing to be a challenge, especially with Salvia feeling too scared to say a word to them. They hadn't even done her the courtesy of sharing a meal and refused any food she had offered them. Whatever rations they had must've been running low. They were likely hungry and yet they would rather starve over interacting with her in any way.

Salvia flinched at the sound of the meat popping as it began to burn. She quickly flipped it over, inspecting it and thankfully, she had acted in time. Pulling three small wooden plates from her satchel, she stabbed the slices with her fork and placed two slivers on each plate.

With a deep breath and a long exhale, Salvia turned to the knights and slid a plate to each of them. "In case your hunger has outgrown your hate." Her accent was thick, but she felt assured her words were understood.

"You traitorous witch, how dare you!" Zinnia suddenly seethed and spun around with burning anger emblazoned across her face. Clearly, Salvia had offended her. "How could you choose a DEMON over your own kind?"

Salvia's brow twitched. Again they had used that term. What even was a witch?

"Qué[1]—" Salvia immediately paused with a heavy sigh. There was no point in speaking to them in her language. They were already mad at her and using a language they likely didn't understand would only make things worse. "I don't know the meaning of this word. Witch, explain."

Zinnia stared at her, speechless. "Don't play coy, witch! A whore of the Master of Infernos should at least own up to their treachery."

*If I didn't find your martial skills useful to keep Salvia safe,* Ultor's voice boomed, piercing her mind and, judging by their expressions, that of the knights' as well, *I would skewer you where you stand.*

---

1     Spanish for *What*

Both Zinnia and Baldric glanced around, the color draining from their faces as the moments passed, searching for Ultor. They wouldn't find him. He remained within the confines of Salvia's shadow, resting nestled in his home of Infernos. Both soldiers looked suddenly woozy and frantically rubbed their faces. Concerned, Salvia jumped to her feet.

She was about to ask if they were alright when she realized this was probably their first time hearing Ultor in their heads. It was a dizzying experience. One that she was growing well accustomed to. His voice felt like a presence, a separate and indomitable force intruding where only one's own self should reside.

Only a hint of the effect of Ultor's telepathy brushed smoothly against her thoughts. It seemed her body had finally acclimated to their bond, just as the demon had promised it would. She waved her hand in the air dismissively. "Ultor, there's no need for that. They're just frightened."

Zinnia quickly shot Salvia a glare and gritted her teeth in a snarl. "Stay out of my head you monster! And you, witch—"

*Right, I'm the monster. HA!* Ultor mocked. *I'm sure you've done much more terrible things in your short life than I, so long ago before I became this, all in the name of your so-called faith. I simply punish the sinful.*

Salvia could feel Ultor shrug his shoulders, ignoring the warriors' ire as one would a toddler making a fuss.

*Salvia, to answer your question, a witch in their country is similar to the term behique in yours. Albeit with a more . . . hateful connotation.*

"Behique?" Salvia tilted her head to the fire, expecting Ultor to show his face as he often did, but he remained hidden. "But behiques are healers who commune with nature and spirits. I'm no—"

"That is no witch!" Zinnia screamed out. "Admit to what you are! You've whored yourself to Lucifer, taking his powers so you can manipulate and burn the world, sowing chaos in his name. We saw proof of what you are. Admit it!"

Salvia raised a skeptical brow to Zinnia, now understanding the hateful meaning Ultor mentioned. "Oh, what proof is that?"

As Zinnia opened her mouth to argue, Baldric planted a hand on her shoulder and pulled her back, a cold look in his eyes. "The fire is our proof. You have magic over it, used it to bind us. That's all the proof we need. You're our enemy." He said so calmly and so assuredly as though things were that simple in his world.

Seconds of uncomfortable quiet passed as Salvia waited for him to elaborate. When it became clear to her that he had said all he meant to say, Salvia clenched the fabric of her violet dress at her sides. Her chest swelled with frustration at their biased view of her. "My fire?" Salvia rolled her eyes. "The magic isn't even mine. Ultor lent me his powers so I could mark sinners and stop anyone who would get in his way. That's it. Nothing more."

"Anyone who would ally themselves with a DEMON is not worthy of being in our holy country." Zinnia spat, her face nearly as red as her hair and the green of her eyes looking like a forest fire.

Salvia narrowed her gaze into slits, growing increasingly irritated. Crossing her arms loosely over her chest, she tried to suppress her outrage at their accusations, wondering why it was that these two soldiers were so sure of her and Ultor's malevolence. "Why do the two of you believe demons to be so evil?"

"I doubt a foreigner like you knows the story or could ever understand *our* people's plight." Zinnia answered.

Baldric just stayed silent.

Salvia couldn't help but let her vision drift down to the scar stretching across his lips. She tried her best to be polite, instead focusing intently on the dark blue pools of his eyes. The three of them stared at each other in silence, an air of frustration and confusion hanging over them. Salvia had asked her question, and one way or the other, she would get her answer, even if she had to wait all night.

Eventually, it was Baldric that spoke first. He sighed heavily with annoyance. "In the beginning, the Great One created light and in that light was a garden—"

"The Garden of Vita." Salvia interjected confidently.

Baldric's brow twitched and Zinnia winced, clearly surprised that Salvia would have any knowledge at all of the ethereal garden. The two had clearly mistaken her for a fool. That much was plain in their reaction. Salvia had listened intently when stories from the Cirine scripts were spread. She understood their teaching and history well enough. Then there was the true version which she had learned from Ultor. Perhaps, these two needed to open their eyes and see past their learned prejudices, even if she had to force enlightenment upon them.

"Bueno?"[2] Salvia planted her hands on her hips challengingly. "Don't stop on my account. A foreigner such as I couldn't *possibly* know the rest of the story." Her voice dripped with sarcasm.

Baldric forced a deep breath, undoubtedly annoyed by her tone. "Anyway, in the garden there was all sorts of life: plants, birds, beasts, and eventually even men. The first humans ever created, Vir and Femina, came into existence. They had a happy life with everything they could ever need provided for them. All life within the garden had one simple rule that must never be broken. Ever. Do not eat the fruit of the Tree of Sientia."

---

2     Spanish for *Well*

Baldric raised a hand to his neck, stretching his head left and then right. "Then one day Femina met the angel Lucifer. She was immediately smitten by his beauty. They met from time to time in secret and over the course of their meetings she fell for him. Enthralled by the great deceiver and convinced that they could only be together if Vir fell out of the Great One's good graces, Lucifer gave her one of the forbidden fruits. That night at Lucifer's behest, she convinced Vir to eat the fruit. The Great One confronted Vir for his transgression and was promptly banished from the garden, becoming mortal in the process. Femina remained silent, allowing him to be cast out without protest. Once the deed was done, she sought out Lucifer to give him the news. When he appeared, she confessed what she had done and that they could be together at last. At that moment, the Great One appeared and sentenced her to the same punishment as Vir. Lucifer basked in the ruin he had sown. His plan had worked. He destroyed that which the Great One had conceived. He then attempted to strike the Great One down, to take His power for himself." Baldric promptly shrugged his shoulders. "He failed and was also punished, becoming the first demon. We have been paying for the first one's sins ever since, all thanks to that *demon*."

Salvia tilted her head at Baldric. The story was very different from what Ultor had told her. "That's . . . not right."

Taken aback by her insinuation, Baldric bristled and shot her an irate look. "Excuse me? What in Infernos do you mean?"

Salvia took a deep breath, calming her nerves, and recalled what Ultor had told her, that every choice made was one's own doing, no one else's. "Femina wasn't bewitched or enthralled. She *chose* to deceive Vir, just as Vir chose to eat from the Tree of Sientia. There was a simple rule, and they chose to break it. She could have easily gone to Vir or the *Almighty One* and told them of Lucifer's plan, but she didn't. She made her choice. We humans were given free will and are not beholden to temptation. We choose evil just as often as we choose good."

Baldric stared at Salvia with shock at the notion. "The story was voiced and then written as so. How could you say Femina simply *chose* to doom humanity?"

Zinnia, now fuming with anger, had clearly had enough. "How DARE you! You would defend a demon—"

"Lucifer's an angel, not a demon, by the way." Salvia corrected.

Baldric's eyes narrowed into slits, his frustration shining through his glare. "Correction, Lucifer *was* an angel. Clearly his treachery corrupted—"

"*Actually, it's you who is mistaken. Lord Lucifer isn't a demon. He's the fallen angel who presides over all of Infernos because he lost a war he foolishly started out of love.*" It was Ultor who interrupted this time, sounding more bored than annoyed with the two knights' preaching.

Salvia turned her head to the fire next to her, the demon's skeletal face appearing at the flame's center, looking as menacing as always.

"Stay out of this demon!" Baldric growled. "Demons have *always* tempted humans to do evil! They skulk about in our world, making people commit the most heinous of acts—"

"Abre los ojos!"[3] Salvia interjected with determination. "Demons can't even enter our mortal realm without the express aid *and* permission of the angels of Hevellum!"

Baldric and Zinnia stood several feet before her in utter silence and disbelief. Their eyes trembled. Even Baldric looked to be having trouble returning to his air

---

3    Spanish for *Open your eyes*

of stoicism.

"That . . . can't be." Zinnia mumbled to herself.

Ultor began to chuckle with amusement. "*It's true. We can't enter this world or any other without the aid of Hevellum, not that we would want to even if we could do so freely.*"

Salvia turned her eyes to his image in the fire, a brow raised.

"*It's the atmosphere, the air, it's too . . . new. There's no antiquity to it. And Eldara's pull, how can you stand it? It's so . . . infantile.*" He paused, noticing the looks of confusion on their faces. "*I digress, all we can do on our own is punish the sinners who enter our domain, nothing more.*"

"But . . . But our faith—" Zinnia began to argue before Ultor cut her off.

"*Only preach what they want you to believe. Your so-called order altered your faith in order to herd your people like sheep at your master's hands. No freewill. No freethinking. You must say, do, and be what you're taught, everything and everyone else is wrong. It's . . . quite sad to be honest.*" Ultor's eyes seemed to flare as if daring the soldiers to challenge what he said.

Baldric was silent, his dark azure eyes searching the ground, as if his thoughts were no longer present. Perhaps he was reexamining everything told to him in Lumen Magnum, at least that's what Salvia hoped.

Zinnia, on the other hand, shook her head at the notion. "You're both wrong!" She exclaimed. "The Cirine faith has saved many lives."

"I don't doubt that the Cirine faith has saved lives here and there." Salvia responded, forcing herself to adopt a calm tone. If she were going to erect a bridge between her and her new companions, antagonizing them further was not the way to go about it. "Your beliefs were built on something pure, but due to its perversion over the last few centuries, it has hurt just as many, if not more." She breathed deeply, calming her frustrations over what Ultor and Abimelech had told her of the recent goings on behind the stone walls of the capitol. "I know the Papa Regems have been hunting, even enslaving dwarves and elves. Then there's the murder and slaughter of those from far off lands who mistakenly enter Marlela's shores. People no different than you, just born elsewhere. How many lives must your faith save to justify the amount it ends?"

*"That's not even mentioning your supposed men of the cloth who molest children and rape Soror Fideis. Your faith isn't even protecting its own people."* Ultor added.

Baldric's shoulders seemed to stiffen at Ultor's words. The winds were calm as the sun continued to set slowly on the land. The stars sparkled into existence in the darkening parts of the sky. He stood as still as a statue, not saying a word. Zinnia looked away from Salvia, as if she may have seen things and was too ashamed to admit to them.

"For . . ." Zinnia began to speak but swallowed before continuing. "For years, womankind have been mistreated by our fathers, brothers, and husbands all under the justification of repentance for the choices of Femina. My father beat my mother when he wasn't satisfied and then me when I didn't embrace the role designated to me. Eventually, he tired of me and sent me away to be married to a Duke in Lumen Magnum. I naively thought this to be a blessing." Zinnia's eyes shined in the firelight, blinking back tears. "But he beat me just the same, either when he was angry or just for sport. I've had many miscarriages. Soon after my last he forced me to stand before the Cardinalis of the Cirine faith for my failures in bearing a child. I was worried I would be sentenced to death, but then suddenly," a gracious smile snuck its way onto her face, unsettling Salvia, "the current Papa

Regem forgave our kind—"

"As long as women offered themselves into their service." Salvia interrupted softly, grasping Lorenzo's gift under her dress. "Was that not what you were going to say?"

Zinnia took a deep breath, furious at the insinuation. "No! I was unable to birth a child. The Papa Regem showed me kindness for how I followed his Holiness, proving the strength of my faith."

A strange gleam grew in Zinnia's eyes. It startled Salvia. How could she possibly believe it was her fault she couldn't bear a child? Did she really believe she deserved punishment for that? She didn't deserve forgiveness for such a thing. Salvia didn't believe that the Papa Regem's actions were some saintly thing. He showed compassion. He did what any decent person should've done. But if Zinnia truly believed what she said, what words could sway her from that belief?

"It's because of him I escaped the bonds of my husband. Don't presume to know me just because—"

Baldric raised a hand to Zinnia, silencing her. "The only reason plight befalls humankind is because we have sinned. We are deserving of punishment."

Salvia stared at him in disbelief. Could the faith have really fallen so far as to preach such a thing to its people? Why make mortals believe that?

Baldric raised a brow at her, perplexed by her reaction. "I suppose I should clarify with an example. When I was four years of age, my home was set upon by thieves. I watched helplessly as the thieves stabbed and murdered my mother and father. Soon after an Abbatis Commendet of the Cirine order found me and gave me a home, a purpose in life. He spared me the details of their sins, assuring me it was the Great One's will and set me on my current path."

Salvia let out a light gasp, shocked and saddened for him. No child should witness such brutality, especially one as young as he was, but despite that, how had he survived the attack? She had to know and couldn't stop herself from asking. "That's horrible. I'm so sorry such a thing happened to you. To witness such an atrocity . . . but how did you come to survive the attack if you were there to witness it?"

Baldric's fingers twitched at the question, and he winced. Taking a sudden sharp breath, he took a step back and seemed as though he was recalling that terrible moment.

*Salvia!* Ultor's voice caused her to jump. It rang through her mind. She looked at him in the fire and he shook his head. *Still your tongue for now.*

*But—*

*You've triggered a memory. A dangerous one. A path lies before him, and it's up to him to choose which he will walk.* Ultor said, glancing past her to the soldiers.

Baldric's body was now trembling, eyes wide and his stoicism gone. Zinnia watched her Captain with worry.

Ultor then chuckled in a low menacing tone, pulling everyone's attention to him. "*Honestly, I didn't think we would be measuring cocks here. If that's the case, Salvia has the two of you beaten. She is the only one here who has died after all.*"

Salvia's stomach felt as if burning hot lead had been forced down her throat. She stared at him, confused. Her heart thumped loudly in her ears. It took her a few seconds to realize she was the only one who could hear it. The memories of that night came flooding back. Blood. Laughter. The darkness of night. It played out over and over again in her mind, each time ending the same.

She and Lorenzo were sitting by the beach beneath corozos palms and guava trees. Candlelight hung above and around them. They were speaking of promises that would never come to pass. Screams suddenly echoed across the shores and fire raged through the town. Lorenzo demanded she stay put until he came back with his family, and then ran into the chaos. She stayed put, at least, she tried to for a time. The screaming was only growing louder, closer, worse with every heartbeat, so she ran after Lorenzo, hoping she could help in some way.

Salvia entered the mayhem as fires raged on every home and shop. Cinders rained down all around her. People ran left and right. Many of them were familiar, and many weren't. Blades caught in the firelight. She shouted for Lorenzo, and her legs trembled with fear. In her mind she told herself to run to the boats and to flee, but she didn't. She wouldn't, not without him. Despite her lack of romantic feelings for him, she still cared deeply for Lorenzo. There was no way she would abandon a dear friend just as he would never abandon her.

As he finally appeared from a nearby street, standing between burning homes, the two locked eyes and the tears streaking down his cheeks made panic rise in her throat. Something terrible had happened, she just knew it. She ran to him just as he did to her. They hadn't seen the bandit drawing closer. He had been shrouded in the thick clouds of smoke. Approaching from behind Lorenzo with his spear raised, the bandit launched it at her betrothed. The blade pierced right through his chest and even before she could scream, the blade hit her as well.

The two lay there in the dirt, Salvia just barely conscious beneath Lorenzo's still body. Blood pooled around her. The darkness drew closer. Overtaking everything. It was a void. A cold quiet nothing. She remembered Ultor coming to her as the fires raged around them but had no knowledge of how long she laid there.

"Ultor," she said with a tight whisper, "creo qué[4] you mean almost."

*"I know what happened to you is hard to accept, Salvia, but no, I did not misspeak,"* Ultor replied calmly. *"For a very brief moment, you died. To allow my kind's entrance into your mortal world of Eldara, the angels of Hevellum must completely cease their delivery of souls from your world to the afterlife. They couldn't commence until each of my kind had found a suitable vessel to tether them to this world, one compatible with our distinct energies. During this time, passing souls are trapped in a void we call Limbo, reliving the last day of their lives. Regrettably, you were one such soul, forced to relieve your death over and over until our preparation was complete. Once bonded, your life was restored."*

Salvia stared at him in horror. Her hands trembled lightly at her sides. If Ultor's words were true, how many times had she relived her death?

"Wait, what do you mean she died?" Baldric asked, his tone skeptical but eyes shaking.

Ultor turned his glowing gaze to the Captain, his brows furrowing with annoyance. *"I mean what I said, boy. Bandits came down from the mountains shielding her town, pillaging, raping, doing whatever they pleased. Her fiancé died trying to protect her, but sadly the spear pierced right through him, skewering them both."*

Just then, a challenging smirk snuck its way onto Ultor's face. *"You claim people are only punished and killed because of their sins, but what sin could justify such a fate upon an entire town? What of Salvia and her fiancé? Was it because they believed in, as your Sacerdotises call it, a false god? Trust me when I say Calamar is no such thing. He may have a temper, but he isn't a false god by any means. His role is*

4    Spanish for *I think*

*to watch over the seas and the creatures within. Was it because Salvia was unfaithful? She was most certainly not. Was her fiancé evil? Again, he was no such thing, just a young man trying to earn an honest living for his future wife, and yet you would DARE—"*

"That's enough, Ultor." Salvia interrupted with a defeated, soft tone. "I doubt they care what befell me and my people."

Returning to her plate, the food no longer held any interest for her. Her appetite was gone. She remembered the spear, how it dug into her, but she had no idea she had died.

Silence once again befell the group. The only sound was the gentle breeze and fire crackling wildly beneath the pan. Ultor's image was gone.

Screams. Fire. Then darkness.

A few tears fell down Salvia's cheeks. She wiped her face with the back of her hand and sniffled, forcing herself to take a bite. She had already cooked the slices of meat. Might as well eat them. A lump formed in her tightening throat, making it hard to swallow.

Of everyone she knew, everyone in her town, she was given a second chance at life. What could she possibly do with that knowledge? How was she supposed to proceed? Her family died long ago. She had always felt alone in her farm home, but at least she had Lorenzo and their friends, and now even they were gone. What was she to do?

The sound of footsteps and crushed grass startled Salvia from her grief. She was surprised to find it was Baldric that approached, not that she had expected it to be Zinnia. The two looked at each other. Her breath hitched when she found sorrow in his eyes, despite his otherwise stoic expression.

He bent down, picked up his and Zinnia's plates, and walked away without saying a word. Returning to his First Lieutenant, he handed her a plate. Baldric's back was turned to Salvia, but she heard him take a bite. Zinnia looked at her plate with uncertainty, but eventually she too started to eat. Perhaps, there was hope for the three of them after all.

# OUR FAITH

TWO DAYS HAD PASSED. Two days of traveling in utter silence. The one positive to have come from their last conversation was that the two knights no longer seemed to look upon her with outright scorn whenever their eyes met Salvia's. There was still resentment there, but it seemed to be somewhat lessened.

They had been riding nonstop through the Luminosa Valley and Salvia couldn't take one more moment sitting in her horse's saddle.

It was midday. A warm breeze blew through the hilled lands. Strands of her umber hair brushed against her copper skin and caught in the sweat sliding down her forehead and back. She fidgeted uncomfortably in the hard saddle. Glancing up to the sky, her eyes unfocused and she stared blankly into the canvas of blue. The sun beaming down on her hunched form.

To her surprise, a few tears fell down her cheeks.

Startled, Salvia quickly wiped them away, hoping no one had seen them, but more flowed on still. She couldn't control them any longer. Once again, her mind circled back to what Ultor had said. Salvia had died. She needed to accept that, but how could she? There was a chance she could've continued on to the afterlife with Lorenzo, but she didn't. Salvia chose reawakening, to aid the angels and demons, to rid her mortal world of the evil people who abused, tortured, and murdered for self gain. Noble as that seemed at the time, she almost wished she had instead continued into the next world. It would've been easier. But this was the just path. Salvia thought of the untold many who could still possibly be saved from the horrors that had been inflicted upon her. She had made the right choice. Still, one question swirled in the recesses of her mind, why her?

There were hundreds, maybe thousands of souls in Limbo that Ultor could've approached, but he came to her. Why? What was it about her that made him feel he could trust her? Did that not matter? They only needed her to transport him from one place to another to carry out the Finis. Anyone could've done that. Or maybe there was something else?

Salvia sniffled and took a quick breath, then exhaled. Letting her head fall back, eyes tightly shut, she tried to build a mental dam to halt the flow of questions that threatened to drown her.

Fire. Screams. Endless darkness.

Her body shuddered as memories of that night tried to resurface. Pulse racing and muscles stiffening, she fought the terror back. Salvia fought for control of herself. Then, as if it hadn't happened in the past, as if she was now in that horrible moment, a dull, piercing ache plunged into her chest. She let out a sharp breath, terrified that somehow she had died once more.

It was a memory, she told herself. A terrible, terrible memory. Raising a hand to her chest, she felt the tangle of mended flesh, the scars beneath the fabric of her dress. It was fine. She was fine. Everything was going to be alright, Salvia just needed to focus on the task at hand. What to do with her life afterwards would be a concern for her future self.

A blood curdling scream suddenly echoed through the valley, dragging Salvia away from her thoughts. A few shouts followed, and she realized whatever was happening, it was happening close by.

She quickly pulled the reins of her horse, bringing the creature to an abrupt stop, and frantically searched for the origin of the scream. She looked and looked, but her sight was obscured by the surrounding hills. Turning to Baldric and Zinnia, she saw both had turned toward the southeast, their faces still and expressions flat. Baldric then nudged his horse and continued riding, seemingly ignoring the cries for help.

Salvia's eyes widened with disbelief. "You're not even going to see what's going on? Someone's in trouble!"

"We should avoid needlessly endangering ourselves. If the Great One is with them, they will be safe—"

"You call yourself a knight?" She shook her head with a clenched jaw. "No tienes honra!"[1] Salvia firmly spurred on her horse, commanding it to a gallop, and started up the large hill beside her.

She may not know the full purpose of her being brought back to life, but Salvia wasn't going to squander the second chance by ignoring those in need. She wouldn't.

---

1    Spanish for *You have no honor*

*Salvia!* Ultor exclaimed in her mind. *No matter what you see, DON'T proceed until those two are beside you. Do you understand?* He asked urgently, more a command than a question, but Salvia's mind was moving too fast with the possibilities of what she would find to process her companion's words. People were in danger, and that was all that mattered at that moment.

Reaching the top of the hill, her breath was heavy with dread, expecting the worst. She looked over the valley and a short distance away, there was a small farm being raided. A family was under attack. There were ten men in all, far outnumbering the family. The farmer, sickle in hand, tried his best to fend the attackers off, swinging away at the bandits encroaching closer and closer. Within seconds they had him surrounded. With his attention on the man in front of him, he didn't notice the bandit from behind and before Salvia could even open her mouth to scream a warning, the raider stabbed a blade deep into the farmer's side.

Salvia's breath hitched in her throat as she watched, silently, as blood flowed freely down the man's side. His body then slumped to the ground and there it remained still. A pregnant woman, no doubt the farmer's wife, held a child tightly in her arms. The little girl let out a piercing, horrified cry.

Flashes of what became of Marineros invaded Salvia's mind once again. Her chest felt like it was caving in. Salvia's body shuddered as the murderous bandits drew in on the woman and child. They ripped the little girl from her mother's arms, using chunks of her black hair as hand holds. The woman shrieked, sending icy tendrils of pain through Salvia's blood. Two of them dragged the poor woman into her home and the rest kicked the little girl to the ground, beating her with terrible grins on their faces all the while.

"No!" Salvia yelled out, finally wrestling control of herself back from the fear which continuously tried to bind her. Ignoring the stinging in her eyes and with furrowed brows, Salvia raised her left hand and called forth Ultor's ring of fire. Her jaw was set and teeth were grinding. She wasn't going to let another massacre happen, no matter how small or large, not again, especially when she had the power to stop it.

As the heat emanated from her raised hand, something caught in her vision. It was moving fast. Was it an arrow? The question barely came into her mind as the item whizzed by the head of her horse. It passed just over her shoulder. Whatever it was, it spooked the horse so badly that the creature bucked and reared up, throwing Salvia off balance. Her grip gave way as she felt the saddle slide out from beneath her.

A shriek escaped her throat. Closing her eyes tightly and bracing for the pain that was sure to come with the landing on the hard ground below, something unexpected happened. Something had wrapped around her waist, and she felt herself pulled into a tight embrace. Her heart pounded hard against her ribcage. Rough hands cupped her cheek. When she opened her eyes, she found Ultor over her, shielding her with his massive, webbed wings. She hadn't even realized how heavy her breath was, body shaking, and heart racing inside of her chest. Salvia was terrified, but not of Ultor, of almost dying. Again.

Folding her legs beneath her, she sat forward, clutching her chest and felt the tapping of Lorenzo's rose hanging from her neck on the back of her hand. Ultor gently rubbed her back. His touch was oddly comforting and helped her regain control of her breath. The fear hadn't left her, but neither did it hold her in place.

With a deep breath, she softly said, "Thank you, Ultor."

He only responded with a nod as she wiped the sweat from her brow to clear her vision, then glared out between the gaps of her companion's wings. "Ultor, your wings, please."

With a swift motion, his webbed wings opened wide, revealing the farmhouse and the bandits below. They were now looking up at her. No, not her, Ultor. They were momentarily stunned. They didn't even attack when Baldric and Zinnia arrived beside her on their horses. Raising her left hand in the air once more, heat emanated from her palm, then erupted in a large ring of flames, illuminating the sinners before her in colors of red, orange, yellow, and violet. "Ultor, do you see their sins?"

"*I do, but I want to see what they can do first.*"

Salvia whipped her head around to Ultor, his hungry, yet proud grin on display, but his glowing violet gaze was on Baldric and Zinnia, watching with intent. "But the mother inside—"

"*Trust that no more senseless deaths will be dealt by the hands of those men. I will see to it personally, if need be.*" Ultor interrupted.

She was curious as to why he would allow the templars to fight on their own, however, she did trust her companion and decided to keep quiet.

Baldric unsheathed his hand-and-a-half sword and ordered Zinnia to loose her bolts on the bandits. Dutifully, she complied with a swiftness that many would've taken years to master. Zinnia raised her two short crossbows and took aim. The bandits' movements became erratic, moving likely to avoid becoming easy targets.

Salvia, seeing her chance to help, planted her hands flat on the ground, and summoned the binding pentagram. Heat exploded from beneath her palms and fire raged through the grass, drawing a star, followed by a ring. She quickly looked up, and her gaze fell on two of the bandits by the farmhouse. They stopped dead in their tracks.

For a moment, in the panicked stillness of the air, Salvia glanced to her right and found Zinnia looking at her with furrowed brows. No doubt she was unsettled by the magic at Salvia's command, but there also seemed to be something else. What it was, Salvia couldn't place it.

The sound of Baldric's horse galloping into the fray snapped her attention back to the fight at hand, Zinnia as well. The crossbowman hastily took aim at the panicking men held in place and set her bolts free. The steel pierced their necks and the men dropped. Likely hearing the commotion, the two bandits who disappeared inside the house came out just in time to see Baldric riding into battle.

All of the remaining bandits unsheathed their shortswords and rushed to meet Baldric. He hopped down from atop his horse and raised his sword high in the air, blocking two strikes with ease. Quickly reaching behind his back with his left hand, he drew a hidden dagger and struck in a semicircular arch, slicing the stomachs of the two bandits clean through.

They screamed in horror as their blood spilled forth, staining their ragged clothes. Both doubled over in pain, one dead as his body hit the dirt and the other desperately trying to stop the bleeding, clutching his open wound to no avail with both hands. Baldric spun gracefully to the bleeding man's left and swung his white blade down fast, freeing his head from his body. With another fierce twirl of his sword, Baldric sent a spray of blood splattering to the ground.

Salvia shuddered. He killed so easily, as if it was second nature. Perhaps it was something he had accepted as an occupational hazard. Whatever the case, her stomach churned uneasily at how unfazed he seemed to be.

*Is he unfazed, or is he just good at hiding it?* Ultor asked in her mind, making her heart jump. Neither looked away from the silver-haired warrior.

Did Ultor know something she didn't?

Glancing quickly at each bandit, it seemed to her by their taut jaws and trembling hands, fear was moving its way through them. Now, there were six. Those remaining mustered what courage they had left, and five of the men readied their blades, lunging at Baldric as the sole archer took aim at Zinnia.

Baldric remained calm of breath as he engaged the men. If he were afraid at all, his expression didn't show it. Zinnia hastily began placing a bolt into each of the grooves of her crossbows. As she did, a twang from a bowstring sounded, causing Salvia to jump. She had just enough presence of mind to focus on maintaining the pentagram magic. Turning with fear, her eyes caught the sole archer and bound him, freezing him in place. But it was too late. The arrow was already flying toward Zinnia.

She quickly looked to her companion, about to warn the woman of the arrow, but Zinnia had already slid down to the left side of her horse, latching on with her legs. She took aim and fired. The bolt struck the man in the center of his chest. The light withdrew from his eyes and his body went completely still. He looked like a puppet hanging from invisible strings. Releasing the bind over the bandit, the lifeless body fell with a heavy thud.

Salvia couldn't help but let out a sigh of relief.

The ringing of steel on steel drew Salvia's attention back to Baldric. He was parrying and dodging an array of strikes from the remaining five bandits. She found it remarkable that he had managed to do so well against so many opponents. His breath was heavy and sweat streamed down his face. He seemed tired but otherwise was uninjured. Spinning about the enemy, he dodged an attack on his right then pierced the thigh of the attacker with his dagger. The man screamed out in pain, but the cry was cut short as Baldric cleaved through the man's throat. Blood flowed out of the wound like an exploding dam. The enemy gurgled, clutching his neck and gasped for air. As if to place a period on the end of the man's life, Baldric kneed him in the stomach and stepped back to let him fall to the ground.

Suddenly one of the bandits grabbed hold of Baldric's bluish gray cape and pulled. Salvia gasped and wanted to do something, anything to help but in all the commotion there was no way she could bind a single one of them. Everyone was moving too quickly. The bandit forced Baldric back. A startled expression washed over the warrior's face and yet, Baldric managed to use the momentum to spin on the bandit. A blade just barely missed his cheek. Unable to recover his balance, he held his white sword in front of him as he fell and aimed it for the enemy's stomach, jamming it deep within the bandit's gut as Baldric fell on top of him.

Baldric grunted heavily as he scrambled to his feet. Exhaustion hung over him. As he stood, the remaining bandits looked on in fear. He glanced down and grabbed the gore covered tunic of the slain bandit's corpse and wiped the blood from his sword. His turn to the remaining three froze two of them in place. The third bandit, however, stood a few paces before the others, a dagger held to the child's throat.

Salvia and Zinnia both startled. Baldric's expression then turned to a fury that Salvia had yet seen on the man's face. "Release the child." Baldric growled. "You've lost!"

"Huh! If ya say so, Templar shit!" The bandit held the child in his left arm and pressed the dagger into her throat, lightly piercing her skin. The poor girl winced in pain as a trickle of blood flowed down her neck. She whimpered with tightly closed eyes.

A mighty gust of wind then nearly knocked Salvia to the ground. Above her Ultor had taken to the sky. She watched as he soared silently overhead. The bandits were none the wiser of the demon's movement. Thanks to his stillness during the melee, it seemed that everyone had forgotten about him. Despite his massive presence, he managed to land just behind the two bandits at the rear of the trio.

Both Zinnia and Salvia shared a knowing glance. The color had drained from both their faces, understanding full well what they were about to witness once again. Baldric, to his credit, didn't even flinch when Ultor landed. He kept the gaze of the bandit on himself.

An eerie grin creased the enemy's lips as he stared unblinkingly at Baldric, hugging the young girl ever closer to his person. "Ya'll not be savin' anyone today—"

Ultor summoned his ebony blades from atop his arms and struck. A pair of curt, ear-piercing shrieks rang out which froze the man holding the child in mid-sentence.

The bandit quickly looked to his left, to his comrade, and his eyes turned to pools of pure dread as he spotted Ultor. Slowly turning to his right, likely still coming to terms with his new predicament, he looked to his other subordinate and if he were seeking a glimmer of hope, he didn't find it. Ultor had skewered both men. His blades protruded from each of the men's stomachs and shined with blood. As he retracted his blades, the dead enemies' intestines spilled to the ground and the bodies fell with a wet thump. A putrid, coppery odor filled the air. The lone bandit quaked fiercely as a puddle of urine soaked his boots.

Ultor, who beamed with joy at toying with his prey, bent down close to the man's head and released a breath heavy enough to tousle the soon to be dead sinner's loose strands of hair.

Salvia, knowing all too well the fighting was over, stood from the ground. Her legs were weak beneath her. The carnage laid bare before her made her fight back a retch. Salvia's mind tried to pull her back to her home, but she shook the memory away as fast as it came, trying to focus on the present.

The bandit, no doubt realizing the horror of what stood behind him, swallowed, and slowly lifted his head. Ultor stared down in a violet judgmental glow and met the sinner's gaze. The demon burned with a deep hunger that quieted the waking world. The man's soul was the payment, and Ultor was the ferryman.

In a swift motion Ultor grabbed the arm of the man holding the child, pulling the dagger clear of the girl's throat. The arm holding her loosened, and she slipped from the man's embrace, falling limply to the ground. Ultor proceeded to lift the bandit high into the air. A strange, pleased smile widened on Ultor's terrifying face as he opened his fanged maw wide and breathed in deeply.

The corpses of the bandits around them were instantly engulfed in a bright orange glow, growing brighter and brighter by the second until erupting in an ethereal fire. Their bodies seemingly brimmed with life anew, writhing in horror as the fiery visages rose, their souls ripping free, leaving their corpses to fall motionless again. Their souls grasped desperately to their marred bodies, screaming in sounds most unnatural. They were then devoured, one by one, disappearing down Ultor's gullet.

The bandit trapped in Ultor's grasp stared on in horror. Ultor was saving him for last. Zinnia turned away, unable to watch but Salvia couldn't. This was what befell all sinners and she was the demon's conduit. A small part of her felt she was obligated to witness it. Ultor's hands then wrapped around the man's body. Slowly squeezing him, tighter and tighter, savoring every pop of bone that broke under the demon's might.

Salvia quickly latched onto her churning stomach, feeling bile climbing up her esophagus and slammed a hand over her mouth. This—This right here was a demon of Infernos. A creature who reveled in the torture of those who were cruel in life. Forcing the wicked to feel excruciating pain until . . . Until what? How much suffering did one have to go through to atone for their crimes? Was it even really possible to atone? Despite the questions popping up she didn't really want them answered. Knowing more of what awaited the damned wouldn't bring her any comfort.

Blood began to spurt from the bandit's coughing mouth. His eyes bulged from their sockets. Head falling back, his body went as limp as a bonefish.

Salvia let out a sigh of relief when it finally ended. Her gaze then fell upon the body of the girl. She was just lying there, motionless on the ground.

With a sharp breath, she hopped forward and carefully slid down the hill. She ran to the child and dropped to her knees. Turning the girl over, Salvia was taken aback by the emptiness of her hazel green eyes. They were open, but vacant, staring upward. She could've passed for dead were it not for the soft rise and fall of her chest with each shallow breath.

Salvia's satchel hung from her shoulder. Reaching inside she pulled out a gray cloth, folded it, and placed it gently over the small cut on the girl's neck. The gash was minor, but Salvia saw to it as though it were deep. As she held the cloth to the wound, she scanned the girl for more wounds.

Many bruises dotted her body and face. Her disheveled, ebony hair was covered in dirt, skin as pale as freshly fallen snow, and her tiny, frail frame lay weak and motionless. Salvia assumed the girl to be about five or six years of age. Her blood began to boil with anger, turning to red hot fire in her veins.

Footsteps closed in on where she sat. Lifting her head, she found Baldric. He had stopped only a couple feet away. His armor was nearly fully painted in blood and his short silver hair was now a mess. Worry lowered his brow.

With eyes trembling and slowly giving in to her tears, she recalled his words from only a few days past. "Tell me, Baldric, what possible sin could this girl or her family have committed to receive such a punishment?" Salvia's words were bitter and coated with venom. She didn't care if she offended him. Nothing could've justified what happened here.

He jolted in place as he lowered his vision to the girl in Salvia's arms. His mouth hung open, speechless. If in this moment he felt regret for his words, then good, Salvia thought. She hoped he did. Whatever pain he might've felt from her gibe was insignificant to the reality of the young girl in her arms.

They both turned toward the sound of a sharp gasp as it came from the farmhouse door. There, they found Zinnia. Her hands were clasped over her mouth. Red surrounded her wide, horrified eyes. Tears left trails down her freckled cheeks. She suddenly fell to the ground, removing her hands from her distraught face. "They killed the mother, unborn child and all!"

# OUR PATH

S ALVIA SAT ON FOLDED LEGS before a large wooden basin. A small fire crackled beneath the bath, slowly warming the water within. She swirled a finger through the water to check its temperature. It was still fairly cool. Glancing behind her, she looked at the little girl whose name was still a mystery and watched her for a long moment. The little thing sat there silently, unmoving. She was wrapped in a dark green blanket and stared vacantly at the floor.

A soft, sorrowful sigh escaped Salvia's lips. The sun hung low in the sky, just peeking over the horizon and bathing the land in a pink and yellow glow. Salvia had been left alone to tend to the child while Zinnia and Baldric saw to the disposal of the dead outside. It was for the best. Salvia still couldn't help but think about what befell her hometown when she looked at the bodies.

Glancing back at the water, and then to the child again, she took a deep breath and nodded. Salvia bent low to the ground, trying to bring herself level with the girl, hoping to catch her gaze but despite her best efforts, the little one didn't lift her hazel green eyes.

"I'm going to go get some more water for your bath, alright? I promise, I won't be long. You're safe here." Salvia kept her accented voice low and gentle as she spoke. She then carefully raised a hand to tuck some of the girl's loose ebony strands behind her ear. She had expected the girl to flinch from her touch as she had when they brought her upstairs but to her surprise, the girl remained still. This was progress, even if only slight, and that was something to be thankful for. A small smile inched its way onto Salvia's face.

She then stood up, grabbing the wooden bucket lying on the floor by the bath, and made her way out the room and down the stairs. The well wasn't far, just outside the house, but as she reached the first floor of the meager home she stopped. Baldric was sitting before a boiling pot at the center of the room. There wasn't much down there in the way of furnishings. There was a kitchen stocked with many hanging vegetables and herbs, a fireplace with a couch for two, and a dining table with several scattered chairs around it.

Baldric's back was to her. All of his armor was removed, placed neatly on the floor beside him. He seemed to be rubbing something vigorously on his lap. Salvia watched him work, unsure of what motivated her to do so. Something about him seemed to interest her but she wasn't sure why. He soon stopped and placed what looked to be one of his bracers on the floor. His hand trembled only briefly and then grabbed hold of his chest plate and planted it on his knees. Plunging a somewhat pink cloth into a bucket of dingy red water several times, he began to clean the already immaculate armor's surface.

Salvia felt a pang of worry pierce her chest, wondering what was driving

Baldric to continue the task. Was there something soothing about going through the motions of the mundane task? Did he simply need to be doing something with his hands instead of just sitting and waiting for their journey to resume?

Just as she was about to take a step toward him to see if there was perhaps something she could do to offer him comfort, a sob broke from him. The soft sound caused her body to go taut. His knuckles went bone white as he wrenched the cloth between his hands. Dropping his head low, his shoulders shook and breathing went heavy. He sounded as if he was waging an unseen war within his mind. Just as it seemed he might be losing the fight, he suddenly shook his head and simply returned to cleaning his armor, albeit more vigorously than before.

The battle with the bandits, it did something to him, that much was clear. Ultor's words about Baldric during the battle washed over her. Was this reaction because he was forced to kill, or was it because she had challenged his beliefs, or was there something more?

A flutter burst to life in her chest. Her breath hitched and it felt like something lodged itself in her throat. As panic started to build, Salvia rushed out of the home, carefully stepping over the large dark stain in the doorway, and then slammed her back against the wooden wall of the building. She took a moment to calm herself. Whatever was going on in his head, it wasn't her business. He was in this mess because of her, sure, but a family had been in danger and she couldn't sit idly by to let their fate be sewn. Even so, despite coming to their rescue, they had only been able to save a girl who would now and forever be traumatized, but she was alive. Saving a life was worth whatever price Baldric was paying now but she still felt the guilt of causing him pain.

Salvia released a sigh and let her head fall back. Should she really feel sorry for him? He was a knight. Saving people should be his responsibility. Turning a blind eye and relying solely on the Almighty One was a mistaken belief. All that was needed for evil to thrive was inaction of those with the power to prevent it. If he realized that now, even if it was an uncomfortable lesson, he could save more lives in the future. Or so she hoped.

The sound of shuffling dirt pulled her from her thoughts. She turned her head to find Zinnia a short distance away. Salvia winced as she realized what Zinnia was doing. The crossbowman was standing knee deep in what looked like a grave, shovel in hand and hurling dirt over her shoulder. Glancing to the right, Salvia found the bodies of the farmer and his wife lying close by.

Zinnia was digging a grave for the couple.

*Salvia,* Ultor's voice rang in Salvia's mind, causing her to jump. As she hopped off the wall he continued, *the child has been alone for long enough. Go fetch that water, alright?*

*But—*

*No but. I'm helping Zinnia with the bodies, as you are helping the child with her grief. Baldric needs time to himself. It seems his bloodied, dejected appearance even unsettled his First Lieutenant here.* Ultor went silent after that.

Curling her lips between her teeth, Salvia decided there was nothing else to say and did what was asked of her. It was up to her to take care of the little girl. She rushed to the left side of the house, found the well, and tied a rope to the bucket's handle. Once fastened, she lowered it into the water and filled it to the brim. She pulled with all her might, grunting as she hefted the bucket out of the well and freed it from the rope.

As she carefully made her way back to the door of the house, she stole a glance to Zinnia who was now busy at work digging a second grave. It looked like hard work. Sweat dripped down the woman's forehead, and her breath was labored. Salvia's heart urged her to offer help. A task such as that wasn't one to be taken alone. The toll was equally heavy on body and soul. But Ultor said he was helping. Zinnia wasn't alone. Whatever animosity Zinnia held for the demon, even she should've been able to see the kindness in that simple act.

She quietly made her way through the house to the base of the steps, careful not to interrupt Baldric. He needed his time alone, and though she understood that, she couldn't fight the urge to glance his way. After all, it was she who forced this upon him. He was still sitting where she had found him before, armor all polished and neatly stacked. His scabbard leaned against his leg, and he looked busy at work polishing the blade of his sword. Baldric's arm was moving so fast, she was sure he would accidentally cut himself. To her surprise, he suddenly stopped. Another sob broke the silence of the room.

The weapon fell to the floor with a loud clang, making her body go rigid. His posture crumpled, and his face fell into his hands. Whatever walls he had erected were now gone. He was weeping. Actually weeping. Salvia couldn't believe it.

Tears stung the corners of her eyes as well. It wasn't her place to console him, but she felt compelled to do something. She wanted to ask him what was wrong and if there was any—

*Leave him be!*

Salvia slammed her back against the inside wall of the stairs. Hiding. *But Ultor, he's—*

*I know. Trust me, Salvia, I know. You have to understand, these two have been taught one thing their entire life. Our presence, our words, our mission, is forcing them to question their every belief and the people they swore to follow. Who is right? Who is wrong? Why have things gone the way they did? Was there really anything they could've done? Was it right to ignore the family? Should they have even bothered coming to the rescue?* Ultor laughed softly in her mind. *They need time to think. This is likely the first time they've been left to do so on their own. Your presence, my dear friend, would only confuse them. Do not intrude.*

A knot churned in Salvia's stomach. She bit her bottom lip and considered Ultor's advice. She didn't want to leave Baldric in the state he was in. She had never been able to ignore someone in pain. Her head fell back against the wall with a soft thud, eyes focused on the ceiling above. Doing nothing was one of the hardest things she had ever forced herself to do.

*Remember, you are helping. There is a little girl upstairs who needs you more than they do.* Ultor prodded gently.

She let out a sigh. "You're right, but please—"

*I will let you know if anything transpires. Don't worry. Now go. Settle your mind. Tend to the girl.* As Ultor once again retreated from her mind, Salvia lingered just long enough to hear Baldric's sobbing ebb away.

With a deep breath Salvia continued on, climbing up the stairs and careful not to spill the water in the bucket. As she reached the second floor and entered the bedroom. Several candles dotted the room, bathing everything in a soft warm glow. The space was quite sizable, large enough to fit an adult bed and a child's bed at its foot. There was a wardrobe opposite the beds, and the bath basin was located at the corner beneath a window. The little girl was still sitting exactly where Salvia had left her.

Her heart sank for the child, but with a quick shake of her head, she put on a small smile and poured the water into the bath. She quickly stirred her hand through the water to check its temperature, and her smile turned genuine. It was perfect. Turning and bending down, Salvia placed her hands on the little girl's thighs and spoke softly, "The water is all ready for your bath."

The girl remained quiet, motionless. Salvia then sat in front of the child, raising her hands to the girl's shoulders. "Listen, we need to get you cleaned up. So I'm going to undress you, alright?"

After what felt like a long moment, the girl released her grip on the blanket. She didn't say a word, but she didn't need to. That small gesture was enough. Bit by bit, the girl would get through this. Carefully Salvia pulled back the blanket and helped the girl out of her soiled clothes. Salvia startled as the child's bare skin came into view. She hadn't expected the amount of black and purple splotches that now covered her otherwise fair complexion.

Her insides squirmed uncomfortably. This girl was only a child and from the looks of things was lucky to be alive. With another deep breath, Salvia slid the clothes to the floor and enveloped the child in a protective embrace. She hugged the girl tightly, hoping the little thing knew she meant her no harm. They sat there for several seconds and eventually Salvia picked her up and lowered the child into the bath. The water was only high enough to reach the girl's waist but was sufficient for the task at hand.

The girl suddenly shivered, causing Salvia to lean back, giving her a little more space in case that was what she needed. Then, the girl lowered her hands into the water, folded her palms into a cup, and slowly poured the liquid over her chest.

She was going to be alright. The thought filled Salvia with renewed energy. Smiling, Salvia cupped the water as well and poured it over the girl's back.

*Salvia, Abimelech is here.* Ultor's words drifted calmly in her mind.

Hearing the Archangel's name made Salvia jump slightly. *Do I need to come out?* She asked.

*Nah. He'll say one of two things, either we're taking too long, or we'll make it by a hair's breadth.* Ultor cackled, making Salvia roll her eyes with a smirk.

*It wouldn't be good if we were late, Ultor.*

*No, it wouldn't, but I'm not at all worried, and neither should you be.* The demon replied. *Keep the child company. I'll let you know what he wants.*

*Alright then, tell Abimelech I said hola.*[1]

He chortled warmly. *I will.* Ultor's presence then retreated from her mind, the act causing a shiver to run between her shoulders.

Salvia's attention returned to the girl. Her hands were clasped under her thighs and her chin rested on the tops of her knees. Grabbing a washcloth hanging on the tub's edge, Salvia leaned close. "I'm going to dab at your skin, alright?"

The girl didn't answer, so Salvia soaked the cloth in water and simply waited. She wouldn't push the child. That wouldn't help. She knew from her own experience that things needed to move at the girl's pace. It wasn't long before the child let go of her hands and let them fall to her sides. Salvia nodded in approval and gently lifted the girl's arm, careful not to press against the bruises. Once her body had been cleaned, it was time to wash her hair. Gently lifting the girl's chin with a finger, she brushed the child's ebony hair away from her face and shoulders, letting it fall long down her back where the tips lightly floated in the water. Salvia then noticed a small pitcher that had been tucked behind the tub. Grabbing the handle, she lowered it into the water, letting it fill, and poured the warm contents

---

1      Spanish for *Hello*

over the girl's hair.

She ran her fingers through the girl's thick locks, freeing the knots and removing the larger clumps of soil. Finding a few vials full of oils and soap where the pitcher had been, Salvia popped open each and used them, one by one, until the only signs that remained of what had transpired that day were the bruises, and those would soon be mostly covered once she was dressed. She hummed a few of the songs she had been fond of as a child growing up in Cabreo as she worked.

Once finished, Salvia rinsed away what was left of the soap and moved behind the child. "Let's get you up and dressed." She knelt and slid her hands under the girl's armpits, then counted to three and lifted her gently out of the tub. There were no signs of a towel nearby, so Salvia made use of the thick blanket the child was using earlier. She wrapped it around the girl to keep her warm and did her best to dry her hair.

Glancing up to the wardrobe, Salvia wondered if she would find the girl's clothes in there. It seemed the most likely place to find what she was seeking, and with a shrug, she stood up and walked to the wardrobe. Inside she found very little. A couple trousers and tunics, and a couple of dresses. There were a few folded items at the bottom though and they looked small. These were likely the girl's belongings. Salvia picked out a plain white garment and smiled when she found it was, in fact, a night dress.

She rushed back to the girl and removed the wet blanket, dropping it to the floor and quickly slipping the nightdress over the girl's head, guiding her arms through the sleeves.

As she had done before, Salvia scooped the girl up in her arms and held her close. She walked over to the large bed and paused, just now noticing a shape on the smaller of the two beds. It was a handmade doll made of cotton, dyed in earthen tones with a simple painted face.

"Oh, qué linda."[2] Salvia exclaimed happily.

Sitting the child dead center against the headboard of the larger bed, pillows tucked behind her back and a cotton blanket slid over her tiny legs, Salvia picked up the doll. It was soft. The black hair was made of wool and the doll was dressed as if it were a princess. Salvia had never met a princess before, only princes, but this was just what a princess would look like. She was sure of it.

Clutching it to her chest, she returned to the child and sat beside her, holding out the doll. "Look what I found in your bed. Did your mother make this for you?"

The firelight of the candles on both sides of the bed swayed left and right. The girl remained quiet, causing a pang of worry to grow in Salvia's heart. She then slid the doll into the girl's lap. Just as she did, the child picked it up. Salvia pulled her hands away, waiting to see what the girl would do with it, but she only held it on her lap.

Salvia felt a little disheartened, hoping the girl might've responded or hugged the doll close, but there was no rushing this. She, more than anyone, understood what might be going on in the child's head. The difference though, was that this was a child. Salvia had been fortunate to have already grown by the time she had to deal with such senseless loss. Experiencing something so traumatic, so young, had to be worse. What could Salvia do except be patient, as the royals of Cabreo and their entourage had done for her after hearing about Marineros. She found that was the kindest thing they could've done for her. They helped her send off the dead to the sea. Her heart twisted with guilt for leaving them without a word. She

---

2      Spanish for *Oh how pretty*

hoped they were alright.

Shaking away the thoughts of those she left behind, Salvia raised a hand and gently caressed the girl's head. She then leaned forward and fluffed the feather pillows behind the girl, then slid the blanket further over her legs. Running her fingers through the girl's hair once more, she asked, "Would you like me to braid your hair? It really helps to keep from accidentally pulling while you sleep."

Salvia's smile wavered when the girl didn't answer. She was sad for the child and was trying her best, but she was running out of ideas for what to do. But she promised herself that she would try to be strong, and she had no intention of failing. Bringing the smile back, a new thought popped into her head. When was the last time the girl had eaten? "You must be hungry. I'll go—"

Just as Salvia had shifted to stand from the bed, the little girl reached out with a trembling hand and grabbed Salvia's right index and middle fingers, squeezing them tightly. It brought a light gasp from her lips. She looked back down to the child and that was the first time their eyes had truly met. Her chest felt like it was caving in as she watched the girl's hazel green eyes well with tears. The little girl sniffled once, twice, then a deep frown formed and out finally poured all of the raw heartache. Tears streamed down her cheeks. She hugged her doll close. The child then surprised her further when she released Salvia's fingers and reached for her.

Salvia's heart nearly jumped out of her chest. She enveloped the girl in an embrace, hugging her as tightly as she could. As much as she wished to tell the child everything would be alright, that she was safe and nothing would ever harm her again, she couldn't bring herself to lie. Instead, silence permeated the room as the girl sobbed freely into Salvia's chest.

The sudden thud of footsteps approaching caused Salvia to tense. When she opened her eyes, she found Baldric standing in the doorway. She blinked at him, surprised, then glanced down and saw the two bowls in his hands. "Oh, you cooked? If you were hungry, I could've made you something?"

Salvia raised her eyes back to his and her breath hitched in her throat. The area around his eyes was red and raw. It shouldn't have been a surprise. She had seen him, heard him crying downstairs, but the sight made it all the more real. Was he going to be alright? He hadn't yet met her gaze, instead staring at the floor. An urge to comfort him swept through her but would he welcome that? They hadn't exactly been on friendly terms until now. Deciding to heed Ultor's advice, she fought the feeling back with difficulty.

Baldric cleared his throat. "No, it's the least I can do. Besides," he added as his eyes met hers, his expression a veil of stoicism, "I thought it best that you tend to the girl, especially . . . as you've been through something similar recently."

It was true that she had been through something similar, but Salvia was no expert in trauma. Sure, she had used her experience and it seemed the girl was making progress, but everyone deals with pain in their own way. At least that's what the Cabreoan King had told her, and his wisdom had thus far been proven correct.

Baldric swallowed. The moment had stretched into an uncomfortable quiet, and she wasn't sure how to respond. He then took a step forward, followed by another, and another. He crossed the room quickly and started to hold out one of the bowls but paused, looking down at the girl still clinging tightly to Salvia.

"Oh, one moment, Baldric." She said, just then realizing it was the first time she had said his name. Baldric, Zinnia, and her had been traveling for several days and the closest thing any of them had exchanged even resembling a title was when

Zinnia had referred to her as a witch. She knew she was partly to blame. Sure, they had treated her with open contempt, but it wasn't like she had put forth any effort either. Their time together was to be short lived and until now, she had been focusing on her mission as a means to escape the looming memories of her death. The little girl's presence had forced her to open her heart to the future.

Clearing her throat, she slid her hands to the girl's shoulders and gently distanced herself from the embrace. "Come, it's time to eat." She said, wiping the tears away from the child's face.

She then flashed Baldric a gracious smile and accepted one of the bowls from him. It was warm to the touch and steam floated up into the air. He had made soup. The broth was white, probably made with cream, and floating in the liquid were potatoes, meat, and a variety of vegetables bobbing in and out of view. It looked and smelled delicious. She was suddenly starving, mouth watering. With everything that had transpired, she had been too busy to realize it until now.

Fighting the urge to scarf down the meal herself, she prioritized the girl. Salvia took the spoon in hand and stirred the broth, mixing the spices that had settled at the bottom of the bowl. She then lifted the spoon to her lips and blew softly over the broth so it wouldn't burn the girl's mouth. The little one looked to have returned to her regressive state, motionlessly staring down at the doll in her lap.

Salvia's heart ached for the child, but she needed to eat.

"Esto no está bien."[3] She whispered softly to herself.

"What's wrong? Is she alright?" Baldric asked, the worry in his tone catching her off guard.

She looked up at him but didn't really know what to say. An entire day had

---

3     Spanish for *This is not good*

nearly gone. Salvia couldn't force her to eat but neither could the child be allowed to starve. When Salvia had been in her position, it had taken two full days before her rageful stomach finally forced her to eat. At the time Salvia hadn't been pressed for time as they were now. They couldn't stay here and would have to bring the girl with them to Lumen Magnum, but then what? How dangerous would the city be? She couldn't be there when they enacted the Finis. They would need to find a safe place for the girl before passing through the city's gates.

The light thumping of footsteps coming up the stairs pulled her from her worries. Both she and Baldric looked toward the door just as Zinnia came into view and leaned against the frame with crossed arms over her chest. "You know, if we happen across another family on our way to Lumen Magnum, maybe they will take the girl in. If we can explain what happened I'm sure someone will care for the girl. She must've helped her parents tend to the animals and the garden outside. Despite her young age, someone might see her use as a farmhand."

"True, but . . ." Salvia started, looking at the girl. "What if they aren't patient with her?"

Baldric and Zinnia went silent, most likely also realizing that predicament. Given the trauma the girl suffered, it was unlikely she could be looked after as one would a normal child. In the days after Salvia's ordeal, some of the people with the royal envoy proved they didn't know how to treat her. Some acted as though she were as fragile as a glass chalice. Others proved far less empathetic, acting as though she were a burden, an injured animal needing to be put down. The girl would need someone compassionate to take her in but that seemed to be a quality as rare as gold. Not to mention there weren't many who had the means to take in another mouth.

*Why don't we just bring the girl to an orphanage in Lumen Magnum?* Ultor's question ran through Salvia's mind. The room was quiet and judging from the expressions on both knights' faces, they too had heard the suggestion.

Baldric's eyes widened as if unsure how to take that suggestion. Zinnia, on the other hand, slammed a fist against the wall beside her and exclaimed with a snarl, "Why would you suggest such a thing? If what you say is true, the city—"

*Lower your voice. You're scaring the child!* Ultor commanded with a growl of his own.

Salvia had expected Zinnia to grow even angrier at the chastisement, but to her surprise, the woman quickly clasped her hands over her mouth and glanced with concern to the child. It seemed that beneath her prickly demeanor there was a kindness in her after all. Salvia found that thought to be somewhat comforting. Perhaps there was hope for the knight yet.

Salvia quickly whipped her gaze back to the little girl, her face now buried in the doll and a tremble running through her body. Setting the bowl of soup on the nightstand beside her, Salvia gently rubbed her palm in circles on the child's back, assuring her that everything was fine and that there was no need to worry.

Ultor groaned loudly in their minds with clear annoyance. *The Devouring will only affect the sinners. The truly faithful, hopeful, and innocent will be transported out of the city for their safety as the event begins. Normally they would be transported to Hevellum, but since the Finis will be confined within the city walls, they will be just fine, instead remaining here on Eldara. However, the same cannot be said for their homes. Those may be destroyed in the process.*

The girl eventually, but slowly, looked up at Salvia. Her hazel green irises moved left and right searchingly. She was scared. Salvia smiled calmly and gently rubbed her head. Taking the girl to Lumen Magnum probably wouldn't be a bad thing, and if they really could find an orphanage to take her in, then there truly wouldn't be anything more to worry about.

Salvia made up her mind. They would take the girl with them to the city, and if Baldric or Zinnia had an issue with it, well then they would just have to deal with it. There was no other option.

The roar of a hungry stomach filled the room. Salvia placed her hand over her belly and felt the vibration run the length of her palm as the noise sounded again. "Oh." Salvia said as she looked up to find Baldric blinking at her, stunned. "Um, sorry. I must be hungrier than I thought." She added and chuckled lightly with embarrassment.

A soft giggle followed and to everyone's surprise it was the girl. Her hands were over her mouth and her cheeks blushed brightly pink. As if in response to Salvia's body's demand for sustenance, a light grumble squeaked from the girl's belly, and she hugged her doll even tighter. The little one pointed to her stomach and Salvia understood. She was asking for food and that made hope bloom in Salvia's chest.

As she was about to reach for the bowl on the nightstand, a weighted warmth pressed against the top of her hand. Salvia gasped and when she looked up, she was taken aback to see it was Baldric who had placed his hand on hers. He was smiling. Before that moment she wasn't sure he was even capable of that. He then pulled her off the bed, handed her a bowl, and quickly took her place beside the child.

"That bowl is meant for you." Baldric said while taking the other bowl from the nightstand.

Although his lips were marred by a scar, Salvia found this new side of

Baldric—quite pleasant. She continued to stare at him in disbelief as he stirred the soup. He blew on the thick white broth and glanced at Salvia. Her cheeks suddenly burned with a rising heat as she realized she was staring at him.

"You should eat and rest for the night, Salvia," he said. "We still have a full day's journey before reaching Lumen Magnum."

He lifted the spoon and brought it to the girl's lips. She stared at it for a long moment, looking mostly unsure, but reluctantly opened her mouth. Baldric carefully placed the head of the spoon to her lips, tilting it ever so slightly, and fed the girl with a tenderness Salvia wouldn't have guessed he was capable of. As he removed the spoon, the girl's eyes opened wide with surprise. A smile broke on the child's face as she happily chewed the food, nodding her head for more.

Salvia released a soft breath, and a small smile broke on her face. She watched for a moment longer as the girl enjoyed her meal. The man before her, the same man who had such a stern and stoic air about him for several days just—seemed to shed the facade, even if for only this moment. He talked about how he made the soup as the child stared up at him in amazement. She then raised her doll to the soup, as if wanting it to try some as well, and Baldric laughed. As he did, Salvia's heart began to flutter.

Was this why she had been given a second chance? Was Salvia meant to help people like Baldric and the child? Whatever the case, she was now more determined than ever to activate the Finis. If the people ruling that city were abusing their faith, keeping people like Baldric and Zinnia on terribly tight leashes, then a change had to come, even if by force.

# OUR CROWNS

THE FULL DAY'S RIDE from the farm had been fairly uneventful. Baldric and Zinnia remained quiet for most of the journey. Salvia sang and told stories to the young girl who sat nestled in her lap on their horse. Their night's rest had been brief, arriving at the outskirts of Lumen Magnum only a few hours before sunrise and making camp on a hill overlooking the city's massive walls. As the sun slowly crawled into the sky the group readied themselves for the day ahead.

Before the gated entrance of the wall was a small town. The homes and stalls looked to be earthen made, composed mostly of clay and wood which was in stark contrast to the stone and iron of the city beyond the walls. Carts filled with fruits, vegetables, trade materials, and farm animals likely destined for the butcher, traveled the road to and from the capitol, passing the lackadaisical guards stationed around the city gate.

Ultor's voice entered Salvia's mind. *The Templar Equitums go about their duty, acting as though nothing could possibly penetrate or disrupt their so-called great city. This may actually be easier than I thought.*

She nodded in agreement, taking in the *great* city before her.

The stone wall that surrounded Lumen Magnum embraced the Capitol in a semicircle. Large ballistae dotted the top of the wall from end to end, each pointed downward toward the town below. The wall stretched to either end of the Cerchio Gulf, a great body of water at the city's back. Though unable to see the harbor for the buildings, large cargo ships could be seen sailing in and out of view. One building towered over all others, the Concilium Vaticanum. It was constructed to, as Ultor put it, represent the ever-watchful eye of the grand church.

The geometric building was decorated with archways and large balconies overlooking the city. Stained glass dome-shaped ceilings shined brightly in the early afternoon sunlight. Elegant white stone statues of angels perched on every corner, each brandishing sword or spear pointed downward toward the citizens below. It was as beautiful as it was oppressive. Salvia couldn't help but feel a sense of dread as she gazed at each of the statues. She thought them more akin to jailors than saviors.

The sharp, gold Cirine cross was prominently displayed atop the center of every domed ceiling. The way each caught the sunlight was nearly blinding even at such a distance. Azure banners, embroidered with the Cirine insignia, hung from many of the building's towers and swayed lightly in the breeze.

The air surrounding the city felt thick, heavy, and more than a little unsavory. It was as if a layer of tar hung over the place, a darkness Salvia couldn't explain. It unsettled her greatly. Her heartbeat started to quicken and her breathing labored.

She jumped as the orphan girl, Rose, clutched to her arm. They had discovered her name thanks to Ultor. He had been playing with her the night before and searched the child's soul through her eyes. Salvia looked down at the child and found her staring back up at her. Rose's brows were heavily curved, as though she could sense Salvia's unease. Forcing a smile, she assured the little girl that everything was alright and returned her focus to the city, her grip tightening on the horse's reins.

*It's alright, Salvia. Just take a deep breath, hold it in for as long as you can, then gently release. Repeat until your heart calms.* Ultor's caring tone drifted through her mind. She then noticed Baldric and Zinnia had been staring at her. They were likely apprehensive about her mission. It was to be expected. They had not chosen this as she had; it was forced upon them.

Salvia knew things would only grow harder for them as they drew closer to their goal, but she had made a vow. There was no going back.

With a deep breath, she counted backwards from ten. Nine. Eight. Seven. Once Salvia reached zero, she exhaled, envisioning all her trepidation leaving her body. To say she was nervous would be an understatement. Raising out her left hand with another deep breath, she summoned forth the ring of fire. Heat emanated from her palm. The view of the city above her hand started to waver, rippling and distorting as the heat built and built. A small spark burst from the palm of her hand and ignited a large ring of fire the size of her head. They had to be prepared for what lay ahead. Had to know the extent sin had enveloped the city. When she gazed through the warped ring of flame, her breath hitched and eyes widened with disbelief.

Baldric whispered something to Zinnia, but Salvia's mind was reeling from what she found in the ring of flame.

"I-I . . . No lo puedo creer.[1] There . . . There are so many sinners. How can this be? It's as if the city is engulfed by them!" Salvia's voice broke with every word.

Group after group, figure after figure, they were covered by an intense glow. The differing hues coated her vision as she panned across the city in a horrific rainbow of sin. Salvia quickly tilted her hand and dismissed the fire in a small whirl. She forced her shoulders to relax as she pondered on how to proceed. Just then, a cage full of elves and dwarves rolled through the gates, catching her attention as the citizens of Lumen Magnum laughed and jeered boastfully at their new prisoners. No, not prisoners, Ultor had called them slaves. At least as prisoners they would mostly be left alone, locked in solitude but otherwise provided for.

Being a slave meant you were treated as lesser. Many were sold into work camps, often used in back breaking labor and fed only enough to see the next sunrise. Others who were even less fortunate were sold into the sex trade. That took an even greater toll on the individual, inflicting pain to both body and mind. There was no end to what a slave could be used for. They were no more than a tool to be used, and if they broke, another could easily take their place.

Cabreo had no such system. Her people never trapped others into indentured servitude, not even in the name of Calamar. To Salvia, people who misused their faith to bring others down were nothing but beasts themselves, finding ways to draw blood and feast on anyone they considered helpless or weak.

Her heart ached for the people cowering and huddling close together in their cages, trying to escape the objects lobbed at them. How could a society behave this way? These so-called holy people, members of the Cirine faith, behaved as though the whole of the world belonged to them alone.

---

1     Spanish for *I can't believe this*

Salvia's blood started to boil in her veins. Her hands tightened upon the reins of her horse, turning her knuckles white. All were citizens of Eldara and none deserved such treatment.

"Why don't . . . Why don't we first drop Rose off at an orphanage." Baldric suggested with a bit of caution in his tone, as if he could feel her anger. "Ultor, do you know of one that will treat Rose well?"

*Yes, it isn't far from the Temple of Pride.* Ultor answered.

"Alright then, what say you, Salvia?"

Salvia remained quiet for a moment, lowering her head to look at Rose sitting before her as the little girl hung her head back to meet Salvia with a warm smile. She couldn't help but return the smile at that little face and caressed the girl's black hair.

Although warmed by Rose's presence, Salvia's thoughts remained on the intimidating, corrupt city before them, knowing they would soon have to part and that the girl's life would no longer be in her care. She feared for Rose, but hoped the child would find happiness once their mission was finished. Perhaps her hardships would remain behind her.

Salvia took another deep breath, calming her racing heart, and answered. "Yes, let's see to Rose's safety first." She gently kicked the sides of her horse and began toward the town, to pass through the gate and, should they be lucky, enter the city without issue.

They made their way past the small buildings of the town at a steady pace. Everything was simply made and looked to be well kept. The common people walked with their heads low as they scurried about, some heading home and others to stalls.

A few eyes turned their way, the people furrowing their brows or narrowing their eyes in suspicion and seeming to pay special attention to Salvia. Others whispered to each other in hushed tones as she passed them by.

Salvia's nerves rose as she lowered her head and raised her shoulders, trying to make herself inconsequential. She hugged Rose close against her chest while her insides squirmed uncomfortably inside her stomach. Baldric and Zinnia looked to be ignoring the stares with a practiced stoicism, sitting at attention in their saddles with eyes ever forward. She blinked in amazement. The two held themselves so confidently while all she wanted to do was shrink away.

Eventually the group caught the eyes of a band of Templar Equitums, five men in total. One of the knights stepped forward. He was dressed in armor similar to Baldric's and his arms were crossed tightly over his chest. Something was clipped to his chest plate. Salvia squinted to adjust her eyes, trying to make out what it was. On closer inspection, it was a yellow cloth with a white, six-pointed star that hung over his right shoulder.

Was it to show proof of his rank? If that was the case, did Baldric have one too? She glanced back at him to confirm but found him frantically searching for something in his bag. He seemed tense. As they drew closer to the group of knights, Baldric let out a soft groan. His head hung low for a moment. He then quickly shook his head, rolled his shoulders back, and stiffened to attention.

The head soldier with the star over his shoulder stood firmly before them, preventing the group from continuing any further. A smug grimace rested on his face. He stared curiously at Salvia. His gaze made her uncomfortably fidget in her saddle. "And what brings you here, *foreigner*?" The man asked with a sneer. His smug smirk grew into an eerie grin, causing her skin to crawl.

Baldric stepped forward, blocking Salvia's view of the head soldier. He looked down at the knight from atop his horse. He exuded command, his very presence demanding submission. "The young woman and her sister were part of a trade transport meant for Lumen Magnum. Sadly, the caravan was attacked. These two were the only ones who survived. I'm taking them to a convent to recuperate. Hopefully their family will come looking for them, in due time," he stated with a shrug of his shoulder, as if not at all bothered by the fictitious tale he told.

"And who might you be, pretty boy?" The head knight asked as he and his men chuckled in condescension. Puffing up his chest, it was clear he was posturing.

Salvia could feel an air of annoyance radiating from Baldric. This was like watching a chicken taunt a lion. He didn't stand a chance in front of true strength of character.

"I'm Captain Baldric Fede Cieca of the White Angel Division, under Cardinali Deacon Limus, and you are?" He glared down at the soldier and his men.

The band of knights froze as Baldric spoke his name in full. If they had tails, they would've been surely tucked. Salvia then wondered how notorious her companion was in Lumen Magnum. His name clearly held weight, that much was certain.

The head knight's knees trembled, and he swallowed. "Ca-Captain Baldric! Your reputation precedes you, Sir. I-I'm Sergeant Emerick of the Silver Angel Division." Emerick glanced at Salvia and, in a hushed breath, whispered, "Dammit, just what we need, more *rames*."

Salvia raised a brow at the man, unsure of what the word meant. Clearly it wasn't anything good as the moment it left his lips, both Baldric and Zinnia bristled at Emerick.

"What was that!?" Baldric yelled, less a question than it was a dare for him to repeat the statement. Emerick jumped, and the men under his command took a step back. Salvia guessed that if there would be a punishment, only their leader would take the fall. None of his men looked to have spine enough to stand with him.

She gently shook her head in confusion, wanting to understand. "I don't—"

*It's a racial slur for your kind, Salvia,* Ultor quickly interrupted, *a term referring to your copper skin. For now, keep silent. Let Baldric and Zinnia handle this fool barring our path.*

Salvia's eyes trembled lightly, nervous at what might happen next. She hesitantly decided it would be best to follow Ultor's suggestion and remained quiet, holding Rose tightly against her. Should Emerick be foolish enough to challenge Baldric, she would see to Rose's safety.

"WELL! I'm waiting." Baldric demanded.

Emerick took another shallow, nervous gulp, his body rigid and eyes shaky. "Captain, please, it was nothing. I just don't understand why the Papa Regem continues to allow—"

"Now you dare question our holy Papa Regem?" Baldric interjected with an air of confident command. Salvia wasn't sure it was truly in defense of her or the holy figure that controlled the city with an iron fist. Whichever it was, it seemed Emerick had miscalculated and this battle of wills was over. "He's a generous and kind man," Baldric continued, "who opens his arms to all who wish to become one with our Cirine faith."

Zinnia stepped forward only slightly, her face sullen. "Such doubt is cause for death." She added with narrowed eyes. "I wonder how our Papa Regem would feel if he knew one of his Templar Equitums questioned his kindness and generosity." The tone in her voice gave the impression it wasn't an idle threat.

Emerick jolted in place, eyes now fully wide with fear. He quickly bowed his head low and apologetically pleaded, "Please, Captain, I meant no disrespect! I was wrong to question the Papa Regem's kindness. Please forgive me."

"Hmph." The noise was the only response Baldric gave. He then snapped the reins of his horse, signaling for it to continue to the gates ahead. Zinnia followed suit, both holding their heads high and expressions flat, like the ordeal had been even less than a trifle to them.

Salvia looked at the two of them for a moment, then back at Emerick who was still bowing as Baldric and Zinnia rode by. His men hung their heads low in shame as well. Why did they hold such blind disgust for her?

She had only heard rumors of their xenophobia, but until now, never experienced it firsthand. It caused anger to build inside her. They looked down on her simply because she was different. Because she was born somewhere else and had different physical traits. Salvia had copper skin, umber hair, and brown eyes, but she was still a person. Just because she didn't share the Marlelains' fair skin didn't make her lesser. Emerick even had dark brown hair and eyes. The other soldiers' hair colors ranged anywhere from red to blonde to black, with eyes of green, blue, and brown.

Why did it matter where she came from or what she looked like? It was a ridiculous notion to spread such prejudices. Everyone bled red and had gone through similar plights and traumas. So why teach others to hate those who are different? Now more than ever before, Salvia felt her conviction at a peak. She would activate the Finis and hoped it would rid the world of Eldara of all its forms of evil.

She snapped the reign of her horse and followed after Baldric and Zinnia, ignoring the people around her, eyes strictly forward.

As the group reached the gate of Lumen Magnum, Salvia noticed a symbol of the Cirine faith carved into one of the massive stone tiles on the floor. Tilting her head to get a better look, she found that surrounding the symbol were two rings. Inbetween them were strange runes she had never seen before.

*What in Lucifer's name! I've never heard of angels teaching humans the ways of holy magic.* Ultor exclaimed into her mind, his tone laced with confusion.

"What does it mean, Ultor?" Salvia asked.

"It's purification magic," Baldric answered for him. "Its origins in regard to our people are locked away within the Concilium Vaticanum, held in the very center of the city. As soon as you step on the symbol, it will glow and inspect you. If you're possessed by a demon, you'll be exercised. You'll be saved."

Confused, she asked, "Has it . . . actually worked?"

His gaze locked on hers. Baldric's dark azure eyes looked soft and unsure. He remained silent and gently kicked the sides of his horse, continuing forward without answering. As soon as the hooves of his mount stepped on the symbol, it illuminated beneath the creature. Zinnia followed after, both unaffected by the magic. Salvia looked down at the still glowing symbol, wondering if it might actually pose a threat to Ultor.

*It's alright, Salvia.* Ultor said softly in her mind, seemingly already knowing what she was thinking. *Continue forward. It'll be fine.* He chuckled, assuring her.

Salvia was nervous, but who else but a demon would know whether or not this holy circle would hurt him? She gently kicked the sides of her horse.

The gentle clomping of his hooves against stone was somehow soothing in its rhythmic repetition. As the horse stepped onto the symbol, she felt the magic surge invasively through her body. It was as though millions of ants were crawling just under her skin. Her insides rumbled uncomfortably. Salvia's body went stiff, as well as Rose's, but as they passed, so too did the light.

Rose viciously massaged her arms. Salvia's body trembled, as if trying to rid itself of the odd discomfort brought on by the magic. She was then overcome by a strange queasiness and for a moment couldn't parse whether it was coming from her or Ultor.

*Ugh!* Ultor groaned, making Salvia jump in her saddle.

"Ultor? I thought you said it would be fine? Are you well?"

*Aye . . . for the most part.* He answered with a strain. *Don't worry. Though Hevellum's holy magic can be quite potent when used on my kind, harmless spells like that can, at most, only make us sick. Now if it had been a more powerful spell, well, I probably would've perished. Spells like that one are used on foolish demons who dare to defy the Almighty One above, to push them back into submission.* He chuckled with a joking tone.

Salvia sighed with a mix of frustration and relief. "Ultor please, don't take chances like that again."

*Hey, don't worry about me. It worked out, didn't it? Although I'm curious to know how it is that these humans have come to learn any of these spells and circles?*

While Ultor pondered the thought, Salvia looked up and caught Baldric's confused gaze on her. He stared at her a moment longer, his expression sliding into his comfortable stoicism, then turned away and continued with Zinnia in tow. He seemed to have the faintest hint of unease on his otherwise expressionless face.

Salvia wasn't sure if maybe it was just her imagination. She wondered if he was alright, but still didn't feel familiar enough to ask such a question.

Dismissing her worry for the time being, she followed the two knights into Lumen Magnum. Taking in the city, there were quite a few square shaped stone buildings. The way their layout had been designed made her feel surrounded, like she was boxed in. Not a single one was kissed by the sun's warm embrace. They were each dwarfed by the sheer magnitude of the wall surrounding the city. On the inside of those walls, surrounded by the shadowed stone, the atmosphere was akin to a prison.

The people all wore stern expressions as they passed each other in the streets, not a single one of them making eye contact or even offering the briefest of smiles to passersby. They went from stall to stall, buying only what was needed with as little interaction as possible before continuing on their way. The children remained close to their parents, their heads down and faces miserable.

Salvia raised her shoulders nervously with a shrug. "Ultor, which way to the orphanage? I don't wish to see more of this city than necessary." Her voice was soft and saddened at the lack of kindness in the people of Lumen Magnum.

The city was dreary, to say the least, and yet unnaturally clean. Not a crack nor dirt covered wall was in sight. Families walked together in complete silence, not engaging each other in the slightest, unless it was pertaining to something needing to be purchased or a task needing completion.

A commotion then caught her attention. A father slapped his son to the ground. The boy couldn't have been more than ten years of age. Tears fell from his eyes, though seemingly not of sorrow or pain, but of anger. His father yelled, berating the boy, accusing him of being an embarrassment.

A few of the surrounding citizens watched, some looking as though they wanted to help, but even if that was their heart's desire, they ultimately did nothing and scurried away. Others smiled in approval, a few even cheering the father on. Many ignored the commotion and went about their business. Salvia wondered if this was a common occurrence which only served to further sour her mood. The boy cowered before his father, flinching at every fist that came his way, but the rage in his bright blue eyes remained. This was clearly not his first beating at the man's hands, but hopefully with the Finis, it would be the last.

Salvia's hands trembled with anger. Blood boiled violently in her veins. She wanted to stop that man. To make him be a proper father who cared for his child. Salvia nearly turned the reins of her horse toward the father to interject, but startled as Ultor's presence entered her mind.

*Don't worry, Salvia,* he said calmly. *The father will receive his punishment in due time. The abuse that man has unleashed on his children has not gone unnoticed. He will get his turn, my dear. For now, just continue down this road to the square and you'll find a small, narrow road to the right.*

Doing nothing proved difficult. It simply wasn't in her nature. But Ultor was right. If she did step in, she could surely stop this singular beating, but by bringing attention to herself in such a way might also endanger their mission. If she failed to enact the Finis, how many more beatings would the child endure? Perhaps one day the father would simply go too far and actually kill the child. How many more would suffer a similar fate? By acting in the here and now and putting everything at risk, they too would be doomed.

She squeezed her hands tightly around the horse's leather reins, hating that doing nothing was the wiser choice. Logically it made sense but that didn't make it feel justified. Didn't make her feel like some part of her was letting the boy down by doing as all the other bystanders did, absolutely nothing. She would continue on, make the evil disappear and help the good prosper. There was no comfort in her determination, and yet she continued on all the same. She headed after Baldric and Zinnia.

Soon they reached a city square. The space was massive, at least seventy yards wide and ninety yards long. Buildings lined the perimeter. Large clusters of people crowded in front of stages on each end of the square. Many of them were yelling numbers and raising their hands, pointing at those unfortunate enough to find themselves up on stage, no longer people but merchandise.

Salvia's eyes opened wide, her stomach churning with disbelief. Elves, dwarves, and humans different from those native to the city, some with darker skin and others with uniquely shaped eyes, likely foreign to these parts, were paraded on display atop the stages. Their clothes were tattered. Iron cuffs and chains bound their wrists and ankles.

The elven people's hair shined in beautiful hues of browns, silvers, greens, and blues, but their braids were loose and messy. Their long ears surpassed the cover of their locks, and though visibly sad, their bright eyes shined like various gemstones in the sunlight.

There were dwarves that had long, thick beards and mustaches. Their hairstyles were decorated with gold, silver, and iron beads. Each of their glaring dark eyes, so full of rage, were directed at the people bidding on them as if they were simply livestock.

The foreign humans were dressed far differently than Salvia had ever seen. Their clothing, likely of their homelands, was torn and dirtied from abuse and harsh travel. Many children, adults, and even elderly waited on the four different stages, powerless to change their fates, while the rest were huddled tightly close by within caged carts at the back of the square. Their faces were worn, bruised, and stained with streaks from crying.

Centered at the back of the square, sitting in a decorated dais of white, azure, and gold, rested an aging man with strong features though a few wrinkles marked the area around his eyes and mouth. He donned white, silk robes which were decorated with many gold chains and sapphire gems. A two-crowned papal tiara rested atop his head. His piercing, sky-colored eyes stared menacingly at something in the center of the square. Salvia followed his gaze and found two people who were bound and on display.

One was a young man with fair skin and black hair. The other was a woman with umber skin and reddish-brown hair, which was braided uniquely in rows atop her head. Their wrists were bound behind their backs, and they knelt on the ground over a large, wooden chopping block, tears flowing down their faces. The people yelled out, calling the young man a traitor while many hurled a barrage of slurs toward the woman, most of which were unfamiliar to Salvia.

"Captain, do you have any idea who that man is sitting next to the Papa Regem?" Zinnia asked, pulling Salvia's attention away from the square.

She turned her head to Zinnia, and her eyes grew with realization. "Wait! That man in white is the Papa Regem?"

*I'm afraid so.* Ultor answered with a hungry growl. *He has twisted the teachings of the Almighty One to coincide with his abhorrent ideas of a perfect society. It sickens me!* The demon bellowed. As Salvia listened to Ultor's string of colorful and quite creative insults that followed, she looked back to the Papa Regem, and then to the man sitting next to him who looked visibly nervous. The guest's throne was a good head or two smaller than the Papa Regem's, likely a not so subtle way of showing dominance over any visitor who might be sat there.

Salvia startled as she recognized the man next to the Holy King. It was her King of Cabreo. "That's el Rey[2] Benigno Dalí Cardona."

Baldric and Zinnia turned to her, Baldric raising a brow. "So, he's King Ray or something?"

Salvia let out a heavy sigh and explained, "No, he's the ruler of Cabreo, *King* Benigno Dalí Cardona. What I don't understand is why he's here. All of Cabreo follows the sea God Calamar, so why . . ."

She studied King Benigno, hoping to find the answer to her question. The last time she saw him and his sons was in Ponce, the city on the other side of the mountains backing Marineros. It was the same day she left without a word, starting her journey with Ultor to Lumen Magnum.

Benigno was wearing an uncomfortable scowl. He was a handsome man with thick, wavy dark brown hair, a trimmed beard and a mustache above his lips. A simple gold crown sat atop his head. His eyes were a deep shade of brown and his skin was as copper, only a tad lighter than Salvia's. He wore a crimson and gold Cabreoan garb which was vastly different from that of Marlelains. The sleeves were puffy from shoulder to elbow and tightened around his forearms. The tunic hugged his body comfortably. White ruffles stuck out from his sleeves and collar. A gold, decorated kraken symbol hung from his neck and a long, fluffy, dark crimson cape draped down from his shoulders. His pristine hands clutched the arms of the mahogany throne as he slowly sank into his chair, his face growing ever sourer.

---

2     Spanish for *the king*

Salvia scanned the rest of the dais, her eyes landing on a man in different garbs than that of the Papa Regem. His blonde hair was peppered with gray. He had piercing bright blue eyes that shined in the sunlight and he wore a robe of red. She recalled the members of the Cirine stating that if she was to ever meet a man in red, it meant his rank was of Cardinali, the highest rank in their order aside from the Papa Regem himself.

The man in red was whispering something into the ear of the Holy King.

A sharp gasp sounded beside Salvia. It had come from Baldric and when she looked at him, her blood froze. Baldric trembled in his saddle. His eyes were so wide they looked as though they engulfed his entire face. He looked . . . scared?

Following his gaze, he too had been looking at the man in red who was now disappearing behind the pair of thrones. Just who was the man to Baldric? Salvia wondered. Who could command such a reaction from him?

Zinnia turned to Baldric as well, her expression filling with worry and eyes glancing down to his fisted grip around the reins of his horse. "Um, Captain?"

Baldric jolted in his saddle, and as he met Zinnia's stare, he relaxed, slipping back into the comfortable role of Captain. "We should continue." He stated flatly.

"Is everything alright?" His Lieutenant asked with a shaky breath.

He immediately turned away to face the square, his stoicism once again walling off any possibility of finding out what was going through his mind. "Yes, everything's fine."

Zinnia's brows furrowed lightly over her eyes. She didn't believe him, and neither did Salvia.

For the briefest moment Baldric had let his true self slip. Facing the square once more, it was clear that something was troubling him deeply, but what?

Whatever he had been feeling since the farm, Salvia was worried it was building in him, and that soon he would find himself at a crossroads. He had opened up ever so slightly, giving Salvia hope for a bright future for the man. Glancing at Zinnia, she on the other hand had grown more silent, but attentive. For her, Salvia worried things might not go so smoothly. Every time their eyes met, Salvia got the feeling she needed to watch her back. She was scared for them both. For now, she would watch them carefully, and hope for the best.

"We stand here today in witness and revulsion for an unspeakable, *unholy* union between this man and this . . . slave."

Salvia startled in her saddle, the Papa Regem's booming voice echoing in the now quiet square.

"For their crimes of unsanctioned fornication and betrayal of their own kind, they are sentenced to death, by BEHEADING!"

The cheer from the crowd was almost as terrible as the Papa Regem's words. They were overjoyed by the decree. All eyes turned to the two people bound and kneeling at the center of the square. An executioner stood by each of the individuals who had just been sentenced. The men raised their massive axes high over each of the prisoners' heads, and Salvia's eyes widened, heart racing as she watched on in horror and shock. The executioners looked to the Papa Regem, waiting.

The Holy King took one last look at the two poor souls, their faces in tears, staring at each other. The man mouthed something to her, but they were too far for Salvia to hear it. She watched his lips and he seemed to say, *I'm sorry*. The woman just sobbed in response, and Salvia hugged Rose close to her chest.

That's right, Rose was here, watching the square with her.

The faintest grin creased the Papa Regem's lips. Salvia gasped and quickly shielded Rose's eyes from seeing the horror that was about to follow. With the wave of the Holy King's hand, the executioners heaved their axes down, burying their blades in the prisoners' necks and promptly separated their heads from their bodies.

# OUR TRUST

AS THE HEADS THUMPED to the ground, blood poured forth and stained the white cobblestones beneath. Their bodies slowly slid off the blocks, lightly twitching as their nerves and muscles fired for the last time.

With the softest of whimpers, Salvia's mouth fell open. These people just murdered two people for simply being together? The two had been in love, Salvia was sure of it. She could see it in their eyes. They were condemned for it. Salvia couldn't stomach to witness anymore of these people's cruelty. She couldn't be in the presence of that so-called Holy King another moment. If she lingered, no amount of willpower or good sense would stop her from confronting him for his actions. But what good would that do? Anyone who could commit such an act wouldn't see the wrongs they had wrought. She couldn't sway a monster with words alone. Salvia would likely die along with her companions. The Finis wouldn't happen, and the innocent would be left to suffer.

Glancing to her right, trying her damndest to ignore the bile clawing its way up her throat and the molten ball of rage burning in her gut, she spotted a small road tucked to the side of the square and began to move. She hoped it was the road Ultor mentioned, the way leading to the orphanage. Tugging on the horse's reins she began down the path, not caring who was in the way. The urge to be anywhere else grew with every passing second, and she didn't even signal for Baldric or Zinnia to follow.

*Salvia what are you doing? You need to calm down!* Ultor pleaded, his words echoing through her mind, but she couldn't hear him. She didn't want to. So long as she escaped the square, distanced herself from that man, that monster—

Something suddenly tugged on her horse's reins, forcing the creature to stop. It neighed with discomfort, and she lurched forward, clutching tightly onto Rose. To her surprise the little girl squirmed to push her away. Had she squeezed Rose too hard?

Salvia's sight blurred, full of tears as her breath heavied. The spectacle in the courtyard unnerved her. She'd witnessed her home burning but even that paled in comparison. It wasn't just that the Papa Regem had killed those people, it was the crowd's reaction, the open cheering for such a senseless death. It just made her sick to her stomach. Something like that could never happen in Cabreo, at least not in Marineros.

She jumped as a hand clapped on her shoulder. It squeezed gently as if offering comfort. Turning her head to the side, she was met by Baldric, looking at her with an apologetic expression. "Come. Let's take Rose somewhere safe. Is that alright?"

Salvia couldn't speak. She opened her mouth and not a single sound came out. Shock had stolen her voice, so she managed a nod. Her tears flowed down flushed cheeks. Settling his horse to stand beside hers, Baldric kept the reins of her horse in hand and the two rode on, side by side, mostly in silence. Ultor provided him with directions and Salvia kept to herself, even leaving Rose be, holding only the saddle and watching as the little girl looked about.

As the path began to narrow, leaving just enough space for the two to pass, her nerves began to ease. Zinnia brought up the rear which offered her a small modicum of comfort. She wouldn't attack while Baldric rode beside her, not that Salvia really felt it would come to that, and should they come under attack, Zinnia made for a fierce ally.

They traveled away from the main path following the back alleyways, and as they did, the pristine utopia faded away. It was a facade hiding the city's true colors.

They passed empty homes and run-down shops, looking somewhat ravaged by time. Signs of struggle were present if one looked close enough. Doors hung slightly ajar on cracked frames, and footprints, likely that of soldiers, led back toward the main road. It was as if the residents had been torn away and their homes forgotten.

Eventually the trio came upon a somewhat small building, resembling a church, but its construction seemed to predate what she had seen of the city thus far. An old woman stood at its entrance, sweeping dirt and dead leaves from the steps. She was a Soror Fidei from the looks of her flowing gown. The outfit was black and white. A white rope belt was tied firmly around her waist and a long, azure chaplet was fastened neatly to it with a silver Cirine cross hanging at the end. A white cap and black veil covered her hair, leaving her lightly wrinkly face on full display. Confidence and resilience emanated from her eyes. A wealth of lived experience and hardship shined through the dark brown pools of her irises. The woman stood tall, no hint of weakness nor frailty shone in her character.

The woman looked up and was visibly taken aback as she spotted them. She glanced at Baldric and Zinnia's armor, and her eyes softened with resignation, as though expecting the worst and knowing she would be powerless to do anything to stop it. If her two companions noticed the old woman's trepidation, they didn't show it as they both climbed down from their saddles.

Baldric approached Salvia, hands reaching for Rose. "Let me pass her to Zinnia, then I'll aid you down."

"Oh, alright." Salvia did as Baldric said, passing him Rose and in turn, he passed the girl to Zinnia.

Salvia was surprised to find a sincere smile on the woman's face. She hadn't until this moment thought she knew how to smile, at least not a true smile, one brought on by warmth and joy. It was surprisingly pleasant and brought Salvia some much needed hope. Perhaps everything would work out. Zinnia then tapped Rose on the nose, making the girl giggle. Salvia grinned at the two.

Baldric reached out to Salvia next, and she peeled her eyes away from Rose. With a deep breath, she swung her legs over to one side, allowing him to grasp her waist, and carefully he lowered her down. The closeness between the two made her breath hitch, and he looked . . . stunned? Baldric quickly let her go, clearing his throat as he took a step back. Zinnia then approached with Rose. Taking the child into her arms, Salvia gave Rose a tight squeeze and walked toward the Soror Fidei. There was a hint of surprise on the old woman's face.

Quickly leaning her broom against the wall next to the doors of the church, she lifted the fabric of her skirt to her ankles and walked down the small steps. As her feet touched the ground, the old woman relaxed and interlocked her fingers together, resting her hands over her waist. She stood firm and awaited Salvia's greeting.

"Well, I don't think I've ever seen a Cabreoan accompanied by two Templar Equitums before, and with no chains in sight no less." The Soror Fidei said flatly, not betraying a single emotion in her tone.

Both Baldric and Zinnia were taken aback. They shared a glance and abruptly looked away with guilt, giving merit to the old woman's implication.

Salvia, noticing her companion's discomfort, stepped forward to the Soror Fidei, hoping greeting her with a sweet smile could lessen the air of tension. "Hola,[1] my name is Salvia VerdaderaFe. On our trip to Lumen Magnum, we witnessed a family attacked by bandits. Captain Baldric Fede Cieca and First Lieutenant Zinnia Colpo Penetrante were very brave in facing them down, but," she paused and looked at Rose with an apologetic expression, to which the little girl tilted her head curiously, "sadly only Rose could be saved. We were hoping she could stay with you. Maybe even find a fresh start?"

"Oh! By the Almighty One." The Soror Fidei murmured with surprise. She looked at the shy girl in Salvia's arms, the little one clinging tightly to Salvia's shoulders and staring back at the old woman with growing worry.

Resting her hands on her chest, the Soror Fidei leaned forward slightly, greeting Rose with a smile. "Hello, Rose. You must've been very brave to survive such an ordeal. Is it true? What Salvia has said?"

Salvia was startled by the old woman's question. Did she not believe the story? Would she not help them? She steeled herself, unsure of the woman's intentions.

---

1      Spanish for *Hello*

The old woman noticed the surprise on Salvia's expression and stated with sternness in her tone, "I'm not in this small alley because it suits me. I'm here solely to protect the children. What reason do I have to trust what you say? I don't know you. I need to hear it from the child."

There was no way the Soror Fidei was as mistrustful or hateful toward Salvia as that knight Emerick had been. She didn't feel the scathing hatred in her words as she had with the man before. However, she recalled the old woman's words. They hadn't been directed at her, but to Baldric and Zinnia. Was it because they were Templar Equitums? Was the Soror Fidei hostile toward members of her own order?

"Your words from before, when we arrived at your doorstep, you clearly expected a confrontation. You have no love for the knights of the Cirine faith, do you?"

The old woman gave her a single nod. "I don't trust *most* in my order."

Salvia squeezed Rose a little tighter. She had been unsettled ever since stepping foot into the city, and the old woman's answer seemed to prove that her senses were justified. "I'm quickly coming to agree with that sentiment." Salvia responded.

The Soror Fidei inspected her carefully, as if looking for any signs of deceit. "I've met many liars in my days here. You're an honest one, I'll give you that much. That's a dangerous quality to have in a place like this." The old woman shifted her attention back to Rose, her face now buried in Salvia's bosom. "Judging by the way Rose clings to you, you've either gone to a lot of trouble just to trick an old nobody such as myself, or you're genuine and in real need of help. Truth is, I'm hiding here. I'm one of the very few who are still vocal against the Papa Regem and his *ideals*. I've witnessed many atrocious acts committed in the name of those ideals. People around here have a tendency to go missing without a trace. Some of those now gone voiced their opposition freely. They even took some whose only crime was being born without adhering to the arbitrary standards set by the *Oh-So-Great* Papa Regem himself. Murdering people whose only distinct difference of appearance was the shade of their hair, and saying it was a sign that their blood was tainted by foreign influence, as if that justifies the act. As if any of us are given a choice of our heritage at birth. They went as far as to disguise themselves so that it couldn't be linked back to the church." The old woman sighed, looking tired as she rubbed her wrinkly forehead.

Salvia heard a sound behind her and glanced back. Baldric stared in shock at the floor, his eyes roaming left and right so quickly, it was as though he was trying desperately to find something, but what? Was it something the Soror Fidei said? Did it jog an old memory awake? Or was he still battling with the realities of his order?

The old woman shrugged, weightlessly slamming her hands to her sides. "Still, there's only so much *I* can do. Until something is done about this place, I'm afraid things will only get worse before they have a chance to get better."

Salvia nodded in understanding. "I'm sorry to hear that, but, um," she looked at Rose again, gently caressing the back of her head with a hand, "there's more you should know of Rose."

"Oh?" The Soror Fidei tilted her head curiously. "What else is there?"

"Well, it was clear that after the ordeal, what she witnessed traumatized her. Since then, we haven't been able to get a word out of her. Rose is slowly opening up to us though."

"Really? Then how did you come to know her name?" The old woman smirked with a raised brow, almost as if she knew something Salvia didn't.

"Oh! Well—You see—"

Salvia hadn't expected that question. The last thing she was sure she should do was to reveal Ultor. Doing so would likely only ensure the woman wouldn't help them. She needed to think of something, and fast.

"We played a guessing game with the girl." Zinnia interjected with a chortle. Her answer was so confident and sincere that Salvia nearly believed it to be true. "We started by asking if she was named after something or someone. From there it was just a process of elimination. All Rose had to do was nod her head, yes or no. Eventually, we got to Rose." She said as she gently patted Rose on the head, a large smile appearing on the girl's rosy-cheeked face.

The Soror Fidei couldn't help but smile at the display of affection, seeing the trust Rose had with Salvia, Baldric, and Zinnia. "My apologies," she responded kindly, "I haven't properly introduced myself. My name is Heather. I will take good care of Rose until you return."

"Gracias,[2] Soror Fidei Heather, but—"

"Thank you," Baldric interrupted, stepping in beside Salvia, his expression completely unreadable, "we'll hold you to that."

Turning to glance at Baldric, Salvia found herself surprised. She hadn't expected him to want to return for Rose. He took notice of her gaze and bowed his head lightly. The faintest hint of a smile crossed his lips.

Blinking at him, she was stunned. After a brief moment Salvia shook her head and composed herself, thinking she might just understand his feelings and nodded.

---

2     Spanish for *Thank you*

He likely felt a kinship with Rose. They had both lost their parents under similar circumstances, and probably felt some sort of responsibility for her wellbeing. Feeling Rose's tiny grip on her shoulders, she refocused her attention. Now wasn't time to speculate about her companions. It was time to say farewell to Rose and get on with the Finis.

Rose looked at her with pouty pursed lips. Her brows curved heavily over the child's face. Salvia raised her up and touched her forehead to the little girl's, gave her the sweetest smile she could muster, and said, "Alright Rose, it's time for us to part—"

"No!" Rose exclaimed. Her voice was squeaky but pleasant.

Everyone jolted in place. It had been the first thing the girl had said since the attack on her family. Salvia stared at her, speechless. The girl's eyes welled up with tears and she pulled herself into Salvia, wrapping her small arms around her neck and embracing her as tightly as she could. Rose refused to let go, and Salvia couldn't bring herself to forcefully separate the girl. She instead looked to Baldric, silently pleading for aid, but he seemed just as dumbfounded as she was.

Heather stepped forward, cautiously, as if any sudden movement might spook the child. She gently placed a hand on Rose's back, caressing the child in soft circular movements. Rose slowly turned her head to see the old woman as tears flowed from her hazel green eyes. The girl's trepidation broke Salvia's heart. She didn't want to leave the girl behind, but she had to.

The Soror Fidei then smiled sweetly, her once stern dark brown eyes now soft and filled with compassion. "It's alright, Rose. Where they're going, it won't be safe for you. When their deed is done, and all is well, they'll come back. Can you trust me to care for you until then? I promise I won't let any harm come to you."

Rose's eyes lingered on the old woman a little longer, clearly debating whether or not to trust her and leave the safety of Salvia's arms, but Heather's intentions must've sunken in because Rose eventually loosened her grip and lifted her arms. Heather picked her up and held her against her chest.

The little girl turned to look at the group and waved a tiny hand in farewell. "Come back," she said, making Salvia's chest tighten.

With trembling lips, she found herself nodding. "O-Of course, Rose."

Baldric and Zinnia bowed their heads and turned back to their horses. As Salvia tried to turn and follow, she found her legs wouldn't move. She was worried for Rose, but why? Rose was in safe hands with Heather, she was sure of it. Then it hit her. No place was truly safe. If the child's parents hadn't been able to protect her, if she hadn't been safe in her own home, how could anyone claim any place to truly be safe? Once again she was reminded of the importance of her mission. If she succeeded, there was a chance no child would have to go through what Rose had endured. True safety would be possible.

Her body suddenly jolted as a hand clapped on her bicep. "Come on, Rose'll be fine," Baldric said gently.

Licking her lips and trying to swallow the lump in her throat, Salvia simply nodded, and raised a hand in farewell. Exhaling, she forced herself to turn around and started toward her horse. She only made it a few steps before hearing Heather clear her throat, and paused.

"Will you be going to one of the forbidden temples?"

The group stopped dead in their tracks. How did Heather know of the temples? Looking at both Baldric and Zinnia, they were just as confused as she was. Salvia turned to the old woman and found her looking at them with a sly smile on her face. Clearly she knew much more than she had let on. Just as a seed of fear started to grow, Heather began to speak.

"It was a while ago. One early morning, just as dawn was breaking through the sky, I heard a strange call. It sounded like a lituus but was very far in the distance." Heather looked up and stared into the vast emptiness of the bright blue sky. "Soon after that, I started having strange dreams. In the last dream, a winged figure shrouded within a blinding light stood before me. They informed me that I would be meeting several people in the days to come and asked me to please help them in any way I could. So, here I am." She shrugged and patted Rose on the back, as if she understood just what it was that the group aimed to achieve.

Salvia stared at Heather with wide, astonished eyes. The angels of Hevellum had come to Heather, asking her to help not just Salvia, but the other hosts as well? Were the others already in the city? What had Heather done for them? Many questions flooded her mind, but as curious as she was, if the other hosts were already here, then she couldn't dawdle. Slowly forcing herself to relax, she nodded in understanding and thanked the Soror Fidei.

Heather bowed a farewell and spun away with Rose to enter the church turned orphanage. Salvia watched as a few kids peeked through the windows, giggling and greeting them while the old woman neared the door. Rose kept her eyes steady on Salvia until the two disappeared behind the doors of the building. Salvia stood there for a short time after.

"Salvia, you ready to go?" Zinnia asked, startling her.

"Qué? Perdón,[3] yes, let's go."

Salvia quickly returned to her horse. Just as she reached out to pat the snout

---

3      Spanish for *What? Excuse me*

of her mount, Baldric grabbed her from behind, forcing her to face him. Her heart leapt into her throat, and she heard Zinnia call to her Captain. While his grip on Salvia's biceps was strong, she didn't feel like she was in any danger. It wasn't because she knew the magic binding them would prevent it nor was it because Ultor would be there in an instant to save her. It was because she felt the tremble in his arms. This wasn't hostility.

His head hung low and his breath was heavy. Baldric's grip tightened and she let slip a small whimper from the pain, but otherwise kept quiet. Clearly something was on his mind, so she was patient and would wait for him to speak.

His head slowly raised and as she saw his face, it was the tears falling from his terrified eyes that shook her the most. She knew he was struggling though he had done his best to hide it. She likely wouldn't have even noticed if he hadn't felt drawn to him for reasons still unknown to her. There was something to him, something she found profoundly interesting about the man that even then she couldn't put into words. When he finally spoke, his voice was low and constricted.

"Listen to me, and listen well, Salvia." He looked her dead in the eyes. "If anything happens to me, if I disappear, promise me . . . promise me you *will* return for Rose. Promise me you *will* come back for her! Please—" His voice cracked and cut off abruptly.

Salvia's eyes were locked with Baldric's. She was so used to the emotionless expression he wore as a shield, but not even a glimpse of that remained. His face was overrun with concern and sorrow and maybe even . . . pain? He slowly drew closer, sucking in a sharp breath. Baldric's arms quickly wrapped around her waist. His hold was iron as he buried his face into her neck. Her heart raced. Every beat was so powerful she thought it might push him away. A shiver ran through her body as his tears fell on her skin.

"Please, I don't want her life to end up like mine." Baldric whispered against her skin.

Salvia had no idea what to say to that. She hadn't expected this. Not at all. Baldric was so . . . vulnerable. She had so many questions, however, one was louder than all the others. Just what had happened in his past to make him like this? What was his life like after his parents were murdered?

Worried for the man in front of her, Salvia realized she had been quiet for far too long. She needed to answer him. Taking a deep breath and struggling to calm her racing heart, she responded with complete sincerity, "I promise, Baldric." Salvia raised her hands to embrace him in return. She wanted to comfort him in some way. "If anything happened to you, I will come back to Rose . . . Is there maybe something you want to talk ab—"

Baldric quickly let her go, startling her, but it wasn't his sudden pulling away that scared her. It was the rage now burning in his deep azure eyes.

"Ultor," Baldric called with a growl, "which way to the Temple of Pride?"

# OUR FEARS

**W**ITH ROSE IN THE CARE of Soror Fidei Heather and guided by the demon Ultor, Salvia, Baldric, and Zinnia set out to find the Temple of Pride. Salvia took the lead with her companions following close behind. The path through the winding alleyways narrowed with every step. Forced to leave the horses behind, Salvia and the Templars had to continue by foot.

Glancing upward, Salvia clutched Lorenzo's rose close. The surrounding buildings towered high above her. Only a small sliver of the slow-moving clouds was visible in the sky above. As the walls grew closer still, funneling them toward an uncertain destiny, Salvia's vision began to blur, and her hands trembled. She had never been fond of close spaces, and this was exceeding her limits. It was just barely enough space to stretch her arms out at her waist; any higher though and she would scratch her skin against the aged stone walls.

Baldric walked a few paces behind Salvia, and Zinnia took up her position in the back. The path seemed to extend farther and farther, the walls stretching and growing ever closer. Her heart thumped hard and pulse raced. Finding her footing became an onerous task.

Everything felt so tight. Why was it so tight?

In Marineros, everything was open and spacious, smelling of the salty sea and the earthy forest. Lumen Magnum's air was stale, mildewy, and thick. It was constricting, as if she was descending deeper and deeper into a cave that she wasn't sure she would ever escape.

Salvia hated every moment of being in this city. Head spinning, she was ready for all of this to be over. Ready to feel the wind in her face and the earth beneath her feet. More than anything she—

"Salvia?"

She jolted, having trouble focusing through the weariness of her mind. Baldric was looking at her with his usual stoicism, but it seemed to be somehow softened as of late. His brows curved over his eyes, and she could tell he was genuinely concerned.

Stretching out his hand, he kindly said, "Come walk with me, maybe having a companion by your side will help hasten your excursion through this alley." His tone felt warm and his words were soothing.

Glancing quickly around her, she realized just how bad of a state she was in. Salvia's breath was heavy as she hugged herself against a wall. She hadn't even noticed the scrapes on the back of her hand, but now as she looked upon the tender reddening skin, the pain came into focus. Trying to ignore the pounding in her chest, Salvia slowly pushed herself off the wall.

Looking at Baldric's hand, she reached out but paused, watching in surprise at just how much her arm shook. Perhaps she should've anticipated the claustrophobic nature of this city. She might've readied herself for it, but it was too late now that she was in the thick of it. Just as Salvia's fingers brushed against Baldric's leathery gloved hand, a jolt of energy shot through her and she suddenly lunged into his side, latching as tightly as she could to his arm as if it were her lifeline.

"I . . . suppose you're not used to being in a city then, huh?" Baldric asked.

Her eyes were tightly closed, and she tried to bury herself deeper into his arm. She had no idea what his expression was like. Stoic. Compassionate. Judgmental. In her current state she must've looked no more capable of protecting herself than Rose had on their days traveling together.

He started with a few small, cautious steps, gently caressing her knuckles with his free hand. Maybe it was meant to help soothe her, she mused.

"M-Marineros was a town." Salvia finally answered, not caring to hide her accent at that moment. "A *very* spacious fishing town. Homes and shops were built a good distance apart. We felt the sea air against our faces. Smelled pine and oak from the surrounding forest. Even dug our feet in earth and sand and we went about our days. I've never experienced anything like this place." She slowly opened her eyes, keeping her gaze low to the cobblestone road before them, daring not to look ahead. "If Ponce was like this, I wouldn't know. I didn't stay long enough to get a good feel for the place. I just left and . . . came here." She let out a long sigh.

Baldric stayed quiet for a time as they walked, even his hand stopped patting though he had left it resting over her hand, which she appreciated. A tremor ran across his fingers. With a sudden deep breath, his chest quickly rose once and he looked up toward the sky. "I've lived in this city my whole life, having never seen its tighter corridors as anything other than a mild inconvenience. Granted, I likely feel this way because I was born into it. This city, Lumen Magnum, feels no less familiar to me than my own sword. I'm sure it's because I was raised here that I never thought anything of it, the feeling of being closed in. I was just as blind to it as . . . I was its darker side." His grip tightened over her hand and a deep scowl formed on his face.

He didn't speak anymore after that. Just stayed quiet the rest of the way while Zinnia followed wordlessly behind them.

The trio walked and walked and eventually found themselves swallowed by a massive shadow of something looming high above. Salvia was afraid to look up. The experience was as if a tidal wave was about to come crashing down upon her. But it couldn't be that. They were in the heart of a massive city. She calmed herself, steeling her nerves and commanded her eyes to open. When she finally looked up, she found the facade of a massive building filling the small openings between the rooftops and walls. She stopped, causing the others to do the same.

"Ah," Baldric said, "the building above us is known as the Concilium Vaticanum. It's home to the Papa Regem, each member of the Cardinali, and a select few other high-ranking members of the Cirine faith."

*Strange they would build their seat of power between the Seven Temples of Sin. I wonder why they would cover them, overshadowing the temples with such a gaudy thing?* Ultor stated with curiosity.

Salvia squinted as she scanned the stone face of the building, finding a multitude of colorful stained-glass windows bathed in sunlight. What could they be depicting? She could barely tell from where she stood. Around the windows, the edges were lined with gold and seemed to sparkle. Even the angelic stone statues wore golden armor, each with the Cirine cross held in one hand and a weapon in the other. Although in the darkness of the building, an array of colors shimmered off the gold surfaces, most likely decorated with gemstones.

It seemed a bit much to her, for a holy place to flaunt its wealth upon their idols.

Baldric then tapped her hand to garner her attention. "Come on, we should keep moving forward."

Looking ahead to the path, to the ever-shrinking alleyway, Salvia felt the familiar trepidation flowing back into her muscles and joints. With a swallow and nod, she hugged herself back into Baldric to continue on. Ultor's voice filled her thoughts, assuring her that their destination wasn't much further. That gave her the push she needed.

Though her heartbeat quickened and she felt the walls closing in, she narrowed her focus. Just one more step. Now another. And another. This wasn't going to work. She felt faint and each breath was shallower than the last. The world tilted. Everything was too close. She wanted—needed a distraction.

Salvia quickly looked around, and as a flash of Baldric filled her vision, there was a flutter in her chest. What was that? She questioned. Her gaze drifted up from his chest to his face. She watched him from the corners of her eyes, trying to keep her face forward so as to not alert him of what she was doing. It then occurred to her that they had never been this close before.

There were small glints of violet in his otherwise dark azure eyes. A silver strand of hair swayed back and forth over his right eye. His expression was stoic; no surprise there, but she'd come to notice the minor hints of emotion that sometimes shined through. Her eyes then drifted to the scar on his lips. It was caused by a blade, Salvia was sure of it. The line was too clean, too straight to have been caused by blunt force or a broken bottle, and looked to have happened a long time ago, but why? Was it perhaps from a training accident?

"Um, Baldric," Salvia started, trying to swallow down the nervous lump forming in her throat, "I've been meaning to ask—and it's not my intention to offend—but . . . how did you receive that scar?"

He glanced down at her, silent as ever, but she spotted a flicker of sorrow betraying his otherwise unflinching gaze.

Averting his eyes, looking back ahead to the path, he asked, "Is this the place?"

*Yes,* Ultor answered, *our destination lies within.*

Salvia and Baldric stopped, and she traced his gaze forward. Her body felt immediately lightened. The space before them was huge. Several paces ahead of them was a cylindrical, white marble building stretching barely half the size of the ones surrounding it. At the top of the structure stood five Seraphim angels carved from marble. The angels were all men, each with eight wings open wide and a unique weapon in hand, their beautifully sculpted and posed forms on full display.

"These are the five Guardians of Hevellum." Baldric stated. Salvia stared in contemplation, glued to the statues. "Michael, Gabriel, Raphael, Uriel, and Azriel. According to previous Papa Regems, having one or more atop your home is said to bring divine protection, safeguarding you and your family from evil." Baldric proceeded forward a couple of steps, his expression turning sad. "My parents had two atop our home." There was a deep sorrow behind his words.

Once more, the question that had been gnawing at the back of Salvia's mind came into focus, demanding to be spoken aloud, but she didn't dare give in to the temptation. She wanted to ask him just what had happened. What were the circumstances behind his parents' deaths and what happened to him afterwards? She wanted to know more about him and wanted to understand the source of his pain. How could she begin to understand him if she didn't know what caused him to erect such a barrier around his every emotion?

His past was off limits. That much was clear by his every mannerism. And of all the people he might be comfortable enough to confide in, she felt that due to the nature of their relationship, the Vovete spell binding them into servitorship, she was at the bottom of the list.

Returning her attention to the statues above the temple, she realized there was something very wrong. For starters, each and every one of them was depicted incorrectly. "This, um . . ." She paused, trying to think of the correct words in the soldiers' language. "This is a blatant disrespect to all the true Seraphim of Hevellum." She didn't even try to hide the disappointment in her tone.

Baldric glanced back at her, and in that moment, she worried he would argue with her, but his face was unflinching. His mouth opened and only a simple question came forth. "What do you mean?" He asked in a staunch, monotone voice.

Salvia released a breath she didn't know she was holding. Pointing up at the statues, sure her irritation was growing more and more transparent on her face, she continued. "Well, two of the Seraphim are missing for starters. Also, of the ones present, not all of them are actually men. Three are women. Gabriel, Uriel, and Azriel." Her eyes gazed between them, inspecting each detail on the statues. She quickly grew sure of one thing. "Well, I doubt the Seraphim actually showed themselves to your ancestors. I think these were done to appeal to your leaders rather than for accuracy."

"Blasphemy!" Zinnia exclaimed, making Salvia jump and turn to her, seeing the outrage and confusion across her face. "Hold your tongue! How could you possibly know the other angels are female? It's not as if you've actually met them."

With a deep breath, Salvia calmed herself. She was growing concerned for the red-haired soldier and knew that meeting her elevated tone would lead to more anger. Despite everything that Salvia and Ultor had shared with the knights, Zinnia still held to the lies she had been raised in. Those falsehoods shaped so much of her life. To acknowledge she had spent so many years under the control of others, her every belief and action built upon a rotten foundation, it was no wonder she was struggling. Holding the woman's gaze, Salvia chose her next words carefully.

"First, I said women, not females. In Cabreo they have different meanings. If you only look at things in terms of black and white, you'll miss the beauty in the gray. Secondly, I have met them. It was brief, but they came to me the night after I became Ultor's vessel. They warned me to tread carefully on my journey and to not give trust lightly. It was," she glanced to the floor, unsettled, "honestly, quite the foreboding experience, and not just a little overwhelming." Salvia met Zinnia's gaze once more. "But I took their words to heart."

Zinnia stood stiff, trembling before Salvia, as if she had no idea how to respond to that. Her eyes wandered aimlessly, like she was trying to find answers that were just out of reach. She looked to be at war with herself and there was no sign of which belief she would choose to be true. With Baldric, it seemed the seeds of doubt had already been present before their fateful meeting, but clearly there were no such doubts in Zinnia. She was a true believer of her faith.

When she finally spoke, her words were clipped and voice was deeply distraught. "Wh-Who do you think you are to burst into my life, to disrupt and question every—"

*Yes, very strange indeed.* Ultor interrupted, irking Salvia which felt intentional. *After Vir and Femina were banished from the Garden of Vita, banished to a life in Eldara among all its dangers, the Almighty One feared that man would give in to hate and sin. With the aid of the Great Creatures of Creation, each of the seven Seraphim, and even the Demon Lords, created the Seven Temples of Sin and Virtue on the heart line of the world, at the very center of this realm. If man ever became intent on destroying this world, Hevellum and Infernos would be ready to spirit away the good and the innocent, the faithful, to Paradisum. Meanwhile, the sinners, the evil, and the vile would be sent to Infernos to endure eternal punishment. The Great Creatures of Creation would then remake the world anew. Eldara isn't ours to toy with, to destroy. It falls upon us to care for it, to nurture it, to keep it strong.*

"You say you will spirit away the good to Paradisum, yet a day or so ago on Rose's farm you said they would simply be teleported out of the city. Which is it?" Baldric asked, his tone as indifferent as if he had just asked about the weather or some other inconsequential thing.

Ultor chuckled, sounding impressed. *You are correct. I did not misspeak if that's what you're worried about. The Finis is an end, but as I said before, it can be controlled. We could end the world if we wished and all who are good would be sent to Hevellum, but that is not our goal today. We are only ending this city, to stop its corruption from spreading. Lumen Magnum believes itself greater than Hevellum. Your leaders chose this fate. The good will be spirited away, true, but only to the outskirts of the city walls. For their safety, of course.*

Baldric remained quiet. He looked up at the structure before him, to the statues and peak of the spire. Salvia wondered what could be going on in his head, but he was as unreadable as always. His gaze eventually slid back down to the base of the building, and he seemed taken aback. "Wait, there's no door. How are we supposed to enter?"

Zinnia stepped beside Salvia but still kept some distance between them, and each inspected the face of the temple. All three searched for any signs of an entrance but all they found was a small silver plate. It was lodged a few feet above the ground and was firmly fastened to the wall. A semisphere of metal, just larger than the palm of a grown man's hand, bulged out from the plate's center. On the surface of the sphere was a pentagram etched within two rings. A singular triangle rested between each point of the star, each unique in appearance.

Looking at it carefully, a whisper suddenly entered Salvia's mind. It didn't belong to Ultor, or any person she'd met before, but it started to grow, repeating over and over. Louder and sharper, the whispers scraped at her mind like nails on the inside of her skull. Her hands clenched tightly into fists, turning her knuckles white. Her face tightly contorted. There was a weightless darkness enveloping her, holding Salvia in place. Trembling, she struggled to breathe. To speak. Air, she needed air.

"Salvia!"

She jumped in place and suddenly she could breathe. Air filled her lungs as she opened her eyes. Looking up, Baldric was staring at her with wide, concerned eyes, reaching out to see if she was alright. The voices had ceased, but now there was something swimming at the edges of her thoughts, like something she had known for a very long time, and yet was completely unfamiliar.

Feeling the tension draining from her muscles, she turned to the temple, to the pentagram etched into the silver sphere, and walked to it. Baldric called to her, and though she heard the worry in his voice, she couldn't stop. Some unseen force compelled her forward. She wanted—needed to open the way.

Standing before the sphere, she placed her left hand on the symbol. Words of an unknown origin poured from her mouth just as easily as water from a toppled cup. "Cum haec Foedus, ego autem quod vestra Sicut Enim Vas. Autem patentibus quod ita ut Superbia."[1]

The symbol glowed brightly as she spoke. Violet light radiated from beneath Salvia's palm. The building and the ground beneath her began to quake. Two small streaks of light shot up from the base of the wall like shooting stars, no wider apart than the alley just behind her, one on either side of the glowing symbol. The lights moved in sync, both traveling up the wall and stopping several feet above her head. The lights then abruptly turned toward each other and met in the center.

They formed a shape.

It was a door.

Slowly, the section of wall within the newly formed frame slid down and revealed their way inside. The doorway slipped beneath the small marble step, disappearing and becoming one with the frame.

"Salvia how . . . how did you—"

Salvia glanced back. Both Baldric and Zinnia stood stunned, wide eyed and open mouthed. She inspected the newly formed opening for several long moments, then turned to them, shaking her head and shrugging her shoulders. "I don't know, but," grabbing both her dark violet over dress and white chemise just below her neckline, she slid the fabric down, allowing both soldiers to see the area just over her heart. Lorenzo's golden rose necklace hung there, shining in the pale

---

1      Latin for *With this Pact, I will be your Vessel. Now open the way to Pride.*

sunlight, and just under the rose, was a pair of scars. One was from her death, the mark of the spear that started her on this journey. The other scar was identical to the symbol that appeared on the door. "This scar, the pentagram, appeared on my skin just after my pact with Ultor was sealed. I think it's because of my pact that I was allowed to open the door. A whisper came into my mind. It was . . . hard to make out and painful. The words I spoke were of the language of Hevellum and Infernos. I remember it from my early days of . . . reawakening." Salvia straightened her dresses, sheathing the symbol again beneath the fabric.

The mention of her own death left a coppery bitter taste on her tongue. She had no memory of her death, of the moment her heart stopped beating and her final thoughts faded into oblivion. Maybe that was the point. It was quick. Over and done with. Of course she wouldn't know she died. She was trapped in a loop that felt like a nightmare. She quickly shook her head, trying to bury the thought, to be rid of it. Salvia needed to move past that knowledge if she were to continue on.

Turning her head slightly, she looked over her shoulder, down the dark stairwell leading into the temple. The passage seemed to go deep, leading far beneath the city. Salvia then looked back to Baldric and Zinnia. A calm, serene smile stretched across her face. "Gracias por todo lo que has hecho por mi.[2] You two are free to go. Please, take care of yourselves, alright?"

With that, Salvia quickly spun and entered the temple. She had only briefly seen their startled reactions as she descended down the stairway and vanished into the darkness. She needed to do this alone.

Ultor's chuckle echoed within her mind. *You're very kind Salvia, but they*

---

2     Spanish for *Thank you for everything you've done for me*

*can't be free until our task is complete.* He said warmly.

"I know," she answered. She recalled the spell Abimelech cast on them, remembering clearly his words, but she was worried, terrified, that her companions were close to a breaking point. "They still hold doubt over what must be done. I don't want them to be forced into taking actions they may regret. Baldric might be coming around, but I fear Zinnia would hold onto resentment if she continued on."

He laughed knowingly. *I figured as much. You don't have to explain yourself to me.*

# OUR PAST

S ALVIA CONTINUED DEEPER down the winding stairway, descending further into the ancient temple. Darkness surrounded her on all sides save for the dim flicker of the small flame floating just above the palm of her left hand, one of the many perks of her binding with Ultor.

The flames danced in the air, bathing her and the cobblestone brickwork in its soft orange glow. Her right hand glided across the bricks, using the wall to keep her balance. She was surprised at the smoothness of each stone, having expected something rougher, more porous akin to the buildings surrounding the entrance above.

For a time the only sound she could hear was the soft thudding of her steps and the pounding of her heart against her ribcage. Again, she found herself in a narrow passage. Sweat formed on her brow and the skin on the nape of her neck prickled. She was thankful for the darkness. It allowed her to imagine the space as being larger than it probably was. Unable to see more than a few feet ahead, her vision couldn't play tricks on her as it had in the alley, couldn't move and stretch as it had then, which had caused the muscles in her legs to turn to jelly.

A new sound then echoed through the tunnel. It was faint but growing rapidly. The clanking of metal was closing in and fear started bubbling to life in her breast. Was it friend, or foe? Was it one of her companions and if so, had they chosen to live the lie they were born into or had they accepted the truth? Whoever it was and whatever their intentions may be, they would be here soon. Salvia quickly spun around, readying herself to face them.

"Salvia!"

She recognized that voice. So it was Baldric who had come, and to her relief, she heard the concern and panic in his tone. Only seconds passed before he emerged from the darkness and while she hoped that he had come to help, that same panic could've just as easily been born from a need to hold onto his current beliefs.

There was only one way to be certain.

Baldric stopped before Salvia, mere feet away and out of breath. "S-Salvia—" He said, struggling to control his breath. A hand rested on his thigh and the other on the wall. How far had he run to catch up with her? How far had she descended? Salvia had lost all sense of time down there. Seconds felt like hours. She wasn't sure if it was the claustrophobia, the all-encompassing darkness, or her building fear of finally completing the Finis and having to confront the reality of what to do with her second chance at life.

"Please, don't go any farther."

Dread rose within her. Had he truly come in here to stop her? She took a careful step back and readied to run. "Baldric," she said softly, "this has to be done."

Baldric's eyes narrowed for a moment as confusion crossed his face. He then exhaled and shook his head. "No, please listen. That isn't—"

A loud gong sounded in the distance, echoing from the entrance above so loud they both clasped their hands over their ears. Baldric immediately looked up through the darkness and several more chimes went off, the sound vibrating the very walls around them.

"What is going on up there?" Salvia asked, growing nervous with every passing moment.

Baldric shook his head. "I don't know, but if that many bells are ringing, it can't be a good—"

The tunnel suddenly shook around them. The boom of an explosion above caused the ground to quake heavily, startling them both. Dust rained down from the ceiling as what could only have been described as a roar shook the city above. Salvia's eyes shot wide, and her body trembled. When she looked at Baldric he too looked just as afraid.

*It seems some of the others are exercising less tact in getting into position.* Ultor's voice rang through their minds. *Our time is growing thin. Baldric, what was it you came—*

Salvia's breath hitched in her throat as concern welled inside her. Without hesitation, she rushed down the steps with renewed vigor. She wasn't going to fail. Not herself. Not Lorenzo. Not Rose. Not Ultor. And not Abimelech.

Baldric was screaming something behind her, but with all the chaos echoing from above, she couldn't make out his words. Only a few managed to break through the clatter.

"Please . . . I . . . below . . ."

She wished she could've heard him out, but the other hosts were heading to their temples as well, and she didn't want to waste any more time. Whatever it was he needed to say, it would have to wait.

Salvia ran as quickly as her legs would carry her, following the stairs down into the seemingly endless depths of the temple. She ran and ran, and the sounds of the surface faded into obscurity. With each step, she felt her body begging her to rest. Her lungs burned and pulse raced, but she pushed forward, her sense of duty giving her the strength to carry on.

She immediately stopped, reaching the end of the staircase and seeing an opening just a few paces ahead. She was out of breath and exhausted. Baldric had fallen behind, likely because he didn't have a light source as she had. She placed her hands on her knees and breathed deeply. Why had Baldric seemed so desperate to catch up to her? If he had meant to stop her, he could've, but he didn't. There had to be something she was missing. As she attempted to stand herself erect, and her labored breath quieted, she became aware of several faint sounds coming from the shadowed chamber before her. A shiver ran down her spine as Baldric's voice carried true.

"Salvia, please wait! I think a trap waits for you below!"

Fire suddenly ignited within the room, burning brightly on iron sconces. In the very center of the now massive dome chamber stood a small group of Templar Equitums, forming a figurative wall with arrows nocked and aimed directly at her.

Salvia's eyes grew wide with alarm as her body froze. How could they have entered this place? They couldn't have known the password.

A moment hadn't even passed and yet, the arrows were already in flight. They hurtled toward her. Salvia's body wouldn't move, and even if it did, there was nowhere to hide. Was this really how things would end?

The arrows cut through the air with deadly precision.

She was going to die, but how could that be? She had come so far. Her goal was right there. She couldn't die. Not here, not now. Salvia had to—needed to move.

She then felt a sudden hard tug from behind, the fabric of her dark violet dress closing tightly against her chest and waist. Her vision was a blur as she fell backward at an unnatural speed. Salvia braced, closing her eyes, and expecting to crash against the hard stone stairs at her back. She anticipated the pain but was instead met by a strange, freezing sensation as liquid flowed around and swallowed her whole. It was thick, like she was floating in a pool of molasses, but also as soft as cotton.

There was no pain. That was a good sign. Salvia recalled the sensation of her skin and muscles tearing, bone cracking and giving way to the sharpened metal blade of the spear. She imagined being shot by an arrow to be much the same, and since she felt no traces of that familiar stinging ache, she had to have been alright. That, or the arrow had struck her in the heart and the tugging she felt was of her soul leaving her body. Though fearful to learn the truth, she opened her eyes and found herself surrounded by nothingness, a blackened empty void. The air was thin. The only light in this space was shining from a hole at her feet and through it, she could just barely make out the familiar stones that made up the base of the staircase.

She was upside down, floating in the void. Her body was nestled in the oozing black liquid. Moving proved impossible. She was just barely able to breathe. Shock started to fade away and panic was taking its place. Moments went by, though each felt like an eternity. Salvia wasn't sure if this was a spell or if death had finally found her. Maybe she really was dead. The first time she died she had been stuck in a loop. Perhaps this was what it was like when you actually passed through the barrier, when you were truly gone from the world of the living.

No. That couldn't be. Surely, if she were dead, Abimelech would've been here to ferry her to Hevellum. She desperately wanted to return to her world. To her village. Her family. Her fiancé. All that had been taken so long ago. Her mind lingered on them, on the peaceful life she once had.

Salvia's final moments with them came crashing through her mind, cascading in a tangled web of visions and emotions. The grief nearly consumed her. Tears flowed from her eyes and turned into crystals as they raised toward the light. Watching as they rose, she caught a glimpse of her reflection. She looked as much a helpless victim in this moment as she had that day in her village when her simple life had changed forever.

Watching the crystalline shards slowly twist and sparkle in the light, Salvia was reminded of her first meeting with Abimelech by the fire. Back then her reflection seemed different. She was mistaken. She was no longer the naive girl she'd once been. With renewed vigor, the memory of her task flooded back into her mind. Salvia tried to move her arms through sheer determination and willpower, attempting to reach out to the light, but it was no use. Her body refused to move.

A chilling violet light then flickered into life behind her. Suddenly, she felt a hand gently press against her back. Pushing her forward, the force blurred her sight once again and disorientation clouded her thoughts. Faster and faster she rose into the light, and as it enveloped her body, she felt two more hands wrap around her waist.

As her sight began to focus, she saw Baldric. He was the one who grabbed hold of her and was cradling her in his arms, his eyes wide with confusion. "Salvia! Where in Infernos did you just go?"

She rested there for a moment, looking into his eyes and unsure of how to answer. "I—No sé[1] . . . but I don't dare to return."

Her body trembled. A thin, cold mist rose from her body and clothes, fading with every passing moment. Salvia's heart raced nervously in her chest. Though she was shaken and still trying to process the experience, she knew they couldn't just sit there and sat herself upright.

"What of the Templars?" she asked quickly. "Why are they not releasing their arrows?"

Baldric let go of Salvia and immediately stood, his body somewhat obstructing her view of the domed chamber. He then turned away from her, facing the entrance, and took a few steps into the dim light.

In the center of the chamber was a massive symbol etched into the marble floor, obscured by the ten Templar Equitums who stood atop it. The armored knights suddenly stood in salute and parted. They created a path at their center and as they did, an older man approached. He was dressed in robes of scarlet. A silver Cirine cross hung from his neck. A gold rope belt was tied about his waist and a small scarlet cap rested atop his wavy blonde hair that was peppered with gray. Salvia then recognized the man. He was the Cardinali from the town square who had been speaking into the Papa Regem's ear.

As the old man entered the light, Salvia noticed a change in Baldric. He was somehow even more rigid than he had been on the day they met. But how could

1    Spanish for *I don't Know*

that be? Back then, Baldric had been face-to-face with a demon, a real demon in the flesh. Her companion, who didn't even as much as flinch at the sight of Ultor, was now barely holding his composure. Just who was this old man to elicit such a response?

The older man's piercing blue eyes bore heavy disgust as he looked in their direction. "My my, Baldric? Is that you?" The man asked, an eerie smirk growing on his somewhat wrinkled face.

Salvia looked at Baldric, only able to see the side of his face, hoping for a sign that things would be alright. What she found instead were eyes that grew wide with terror. Her eyes darted back and forth between the two men, and with Badric's signs of distress she knew she needed to be ready, needed to be on her feet to face whatever came next. Salvia cautiously stood while staying safely behind Baldric. She kept quiet and vigilantly watched to see how things would play out.

"You're almost as beautiful as the first time I laid eyes on you." The old man said, his tone calm and silky, delivering each word tenderly as one would to a lover. It sent an uncomfortable chill down Salvia's spine. Baldric's posture went taut, hands clenching and jaw tightening. "Shame you have that scar defiling an otherwise exquisite face. Oh, the things we could've done together." The man shrugged dismissively, a triumphant smirk on his face.

Beads of sweat slid down the side of Baldric's cheek. "H-How are you—Why—"

"Hm?" The old man raised a brow, seeming irked. "Stop stuttering boy." The command was clipped and momentarily harsh, but then smoothed back into the sickening sweet honey drawl. "It's unbecoming of a Templar Equitum. After all the strings I pulled to get you to where you are, you haven't forgotten your loyalty to *me* have you, my dear boy?"

Baldric's breath started to labor, and Salvia teetered on helplessness. What could she do to calm him down? As she started to raise a hand to his shoulder, she jumped at the sound of metal footsteps behind her. She spun around, fearing an ambush. But what Salvia found was so much worse than she expected.

Zinnia stood before her. The woman had navigated the crossroads at their parting and chosen her course. The crossbow was at the ready and was pointed steadfast between Salvia's eyes.

"Zinnia?" Salvia questioned, her voice just above a whisper. The name just poured from her mouth without conscious thought. Her eyes saddening with fear, but not for herself, for Zinnia.

"You-You can't . . ." Zinnia croaked. Her hand trembled and green eyes so wide that it was clear the woman was filled with conflict. She looked to be in shock and panicking. "I can't allow you to do this, Salvia. We . . . We've been taught— our whole life that we are the children chosen by the Great One. We have divine protection and leadership. This world is ours to take, to rule!" Her words came erratic and quick.

The Cardinali laughed, causing Salvia to glance back at the man but she didn't let her eyes linger. She couldn't be distracted by him, not now. She quickly returned her gaze to Zinnia. As the older man's cackling calmed, he continued. "You are correct, girl." His voice dripped with condescension. "*We* have been chosen by the Great One. We are given divinity from on high. We are the holy light in this bleak and sinful world. Whatever this *witch* here has told you has been nothing but lies. Now, do your duty as a holy knight of the Templar Equitum and put this unholy being out of her misery. Only then can we tend to the others defiling our great and holy city."

Salvia and Zinnia stared at each other, neither moving a muscle. Salvia saw the confusion in the crossbowman's eyes, faintly visible through the dim firelight. She could see Zinnia's gaze shifting between her, Baldric, and the Cardinali. Her usual steady aim was now unpredictable.

Sensing the pain welling in her companion, Salvia's heart ached. They weren't friends, not really, but the life Zinnia lived, an armored tool blindly doing her order's dirty work, couldn't—shouldn't have been forced upon her. Salvia hadn't tried to help her before. She didn't feel it was her right to do so, given the circumstances of their journeying together. Perhaps that was an error on her part though. She wished she hadn't let that reasoning bring her to inaction. Maybe it wasn't too late. Relaxing her body, she stood herself erect, and now filled with conviction, opened her mouth to speak but was too late.

"I'm waiting, girl. Don't test my patience." The Cardinali warned through gritted teeth. "Prove your devotion!"

Zinnia flinched, and the conflict that had been there seemed to harden. Her brows hung heavily over her eyes and her expression grew deadly serious.

Tears burned in Salvia's eyes. Zinnia wouldn't pull the trigger, would she? All the things Salvia had been ready to say vanished. What could she possibly say to sway her? She watched in silent horror as Zinnia's index finger drew closer and closer to the trigger. Salvia's breath hitched in her throat. She needed to do something, and fast.

Slowly raising a hand, Salvia kept her voice as soft and calm as she could. "Zinnia, I—"

"End this heathen's life, NOW!" The Cardinali screamed, his voice echoing the chamber and making Salvia jump. Zinnia released a startled breath and her hand flexed to pull the trigger.

Salvia's heart broke. Zinnia had made her choice, embracing the lies of her order. However, the bolt hadn't fired. As Zinnia's index finger twitched in place, the trigger remained unpulled. The warrior looked just as stunned as Salvia felt. Zinnia looked down at the weapon with confusion, trying again and again to press the trigger, but it wouldn't budge.

"Wh-What is this?" Zinnia demanded as she turned her weapon to inspect it.

Baldric then rushed past Salvia and held Zinnia's crossbow aimed to the floor. His expression seemed both angry and understanding. "Don't bother, Zinnia. I've already tried."

Salvia's world spun as she took in the meaning of what he said. Baldric had tried to kill her? When? How?

Zinnia looked at him questioningly. She hadn't known either. Baldric glanced at Salvia, and in his face she knew he could read her every thought in that moment. He stood in place between the two women, sorrow, anger, regret, and many other emotions flashing across his face as he let his hands fall to his sides.

"The night we argued, when we learned of your death and resurrection, you were the first to fall asleep, and Zinnia soon after. I was meant to stand guard, but instead I . . . I took it as my opportunity to end your life. I wanted to free us from this bondage. I unsheathed my dagger, hoping to strike at your heart, to give you a quick end but," he took a deep breath, "you looked so much at peace that I couldn't do it. I couldn't look you in the face and do what, at the time, I thought needed to be done. So, gritting my teeth and finding my resolve, I carefully turned you over onto your stomach. Fortunately, I suppose, you're a heavy sleeper."

Salvia grasped her hands over her chest, watching and listening to Baldric in disbelief. He actually tried to kill her and she didn't even know it, but Ultor would've, wouldn't he? She could hear her demon friend chortle somberly in the recesses of her mind. Of course he had known. But why didn't he tell her?

"I raised my dagger, but try as I might, I couldn't lower it." Baldric shrugged in defeat. "It wasn't my nerves that time. I had found my resolve and still, my arm remained aloft. Your friend Ultor then exposed himself, hovering over us both as he laughed in condescension. He told me of the mark the angel Abimelech placed upon Zinnia and me. Vovete, the pact forcing us to protect you, to keep you safe. No matter what, we can never take action that will bring you harm, no matter how hard we try."

Her breath hitched in her throat. That was right. With all the commotion Salvia had forgotten the spell. She scanned the ground for several long seconds before landing on Zinnia, who now looked even more shaken. It seemed she too had forgotten.

Baldric cleared his throat, garnering their attention. "I've . . ." He started, his voice cracking as he spoke, "come to regret that night, to regret my attempt on your life. My beliefs and mistrust were mistaken." Confidence then returned to his eyes. In them, she thought she could see a raging inferno. He then turned his hardened gaze at the Cardinali, his rage sending a terrible chill through Salvia's being.

The Cardinali raised an irritated brow at Baldric and cocked his head to the side. "What is it, boy? You've something to say?"

Baldric stood quiet for a moment, his head hung low. His jaw was hard set and the very air around him bristled with energy. He looked as though he was about to explode. "You know, I sometimes wonder why terrible things happen to me. I witnessed my parents' murder by the hands of two thieves. I replayed that day in my thoughts over and over, and now I've come to realize something. After they killed my parents, they didn't search our home." His accusing eyes flicked up to the older man. "They didn't even steal anything. They just left. What kind of thief does that?"

The Cardinali stood as still as a statue, arms folded casually behind him, still waiting for Baldric to get to the point, but Salvia was more perceptive than most. She saw the subtle twitch in his brow. He rolled his eyes with a heavy sigh and cleared his throat, flashing them an amused look. Salvia wasn't sure if he seemed uncomfortable or bored, but this was certainly a practiced response. Just as he opened his mouth to speak, Baldric continued.

"I've started to hear things recently. Interesting things." Baldric's voice went deep, verging on a growl as he glared daggers at the old man. "Such as people being dragged from their homes, assaulted, and murdered . . . even when they've done nothing wrong, only because they looked a little different. All on the order of people like *you*, Deacon Limus!"

The Cardinali, Deacon, let out a small, uncaring chuckle, causing Baldric to snarl with outrage. "What of it?" The older man shrugged. His open acknowledgement of what transpired made Salvia's stomach hang heavily with unease. "We uphold the image given to us by the Great One. Only a very few can be allowed to live and even fewer to live in comfort in the Great One's light. These other so-called *humans* and races dare to think they deserve to live alongside people such as *you and me*? It's preposterous." A sinister grin creased Deacon's thin lips with a sneer.

"Tell me why?" Baldric barked, "Why were assassins sent to kill my mother and father? It can't have been for something as trivial as their appearance!"

Examining his nails, as if already bored of this conversation, the Cardinali looked almost pleased with himself. "Are you insinuating *I* had something to do with that? Silly child. It must've been the Great One's will." He shrugged nonchalantly with a flourish of his hands. "Maybe if they accepted my offer to bring you in as an altar server, they wouldn't have met such a fate. Maybe that's what they get for defying our righteous faith." Deacon smiled with an eerie grin. He had done everything but openly admit he was behind their deaths and as he spoke, he seemed to darken into complete shadow.

It would've made Salvia fear the old man had she not felt the anger rising within her too. Zinnia looked completely caught off guard by the man's insinuations, unsure of how to even respond, but Baldric looked akin to a rabid wolf ready to rip open Deacon's throat.

Salvia understood how he felt, but then it occurred to her that he might not be going down a path of justice, but one of revenge. If he gave in to wrath—The thought was cut short by Baldric's frantic screams.

"Don't you lie to me! You—ugly—PIECE OF SHIT!" Baldric roared, and as he did, one of the knights by the Cardinali drew his sword.

Deacon raised a hand in the air, signaling for his templars to stay where they were. A smirk remained plastered on his face as if Baldric's outburst was no more than an amusement to him. The old man's demeanor completely baffled Salvia.

"You had them killed so you could draft me into your service?" Baldric exclaimed, his face red with veins popping on the side of his forehead. "You really are sick! You claim to *care* for children such as I, but I know better. I remember everything. You sought me out most of all, singled me out in your stash of terrified children." Baldric's eyes glossed with tears. A sense of pure dread turned to molten lead in the pit of Salvia's belly. She had wondered what it was that happened to him, and now, putting the pieces of information together, she hoped she was wrong.

"You went on and on about my looks, saying that I had been favored and blessed, that I should be proud to have the *attention* of a man with such *godly* influence. You said the Great One bestowed divine love and protection upon me every-every time . . ." His voice broke, falling quiet as his rage turned to disgust.

Salvia's head was shaking, denying what Baldric was about to say before he could even say it. Zinnia was backing away from him, looking just as mortified as Salvia.

"Hm? What are you going on about now?" Deacon asked, the corner of his smirk turning sickeningly upward. "Fond memories, are they?"

"You collected children—" Baldric took a deep breath and bellowed, "TO FUCK IN YOUR BEDCHAMBER!"

# OUR FINALE

S ALVIA GASPED, her hands flying to her lips. She had never heard of such depravity before, had never considered such wickedness to even be possible. How could someone do that to a child, let alone countless children?

She had known something was off about the Cardinali, but this . . . this was unspeakably evil. He was a monster. She couldn't imagine what it must've been like for Baldric, having to endure such hideousness. Her eyes burned with tears and a lump formed in her throat. What could she possibly say to him? No words, no matter how empathetic or how comforting could possibly soothe his anger.

The rage radiating from him was like a terrible heat. She could feel it pushing her away. Salvia wanted to help him, but she just didn't know how.

Deacon's smirk had dimmed and a bead of sweat slid down the side of his face. "My dear boy, whatever do you mean?" His sickeningly sweet tone had taken on a hint of indignation, and his every word caused Salvia's skin to crawl. "I am a righteous man of the cloth. My love has always and will always be that of a parental nature. I would *never* partake in such deviant acts. To think you interpreted such kindness so despicably, well, it brings into question just what your parents did to earn their fate. Perhaps you vilify me when it was actually them who—"

"Don't you dare!" Baldric interrupted with a snarl, a hand clutching tightly to his sword's scabbard. "You twisted the minds of so many children that they actually competed to gain your favor! They even hated me for being your *chosen* plaything!" His voice croaked. "One-One night, one of the children grew so angry . . . so jealous of the attention you, the *great* Deacon Limus gave me, that he drew a dagger, intent on killing me. I stood there, frozen. Terrified . . . at first," the corner of his lips twitched into an unnerving, triumphant grin, "but then I realized something. I remembered how you always droned on and on about my looks. If the boy scarred me, you wouldn't want me anymore. I would be free of you. I begged him. Pleaded with him to mar my face. I wanted out. I WANTED TO GET OUT!"

"Oh please." Deacon responded with a yawn of boredom and a roll of his eyes. "You've certainly woven quite the tale. Yes, the boy scarred your face, and frankly I found it to be quite grotesque. I was disgusted by the imperfection. You were not the smartest nor the most devout of my flock. Your only real quality was what your face did to brighten a room, and well, you wouldn't keep a torn painting, no matter how beautiful it was before it was damaged, so I sent you off to become a Templar Equitum. You simply weren't of any use to me anymore, not because of this molestation drivel you accuse me of, but because the holy light of the Great One above abandoned you." His face turned to disgust. "That's why our Great One gave you that . . . grotesque scar on your face. It's nice to see it has lessened somewhat over the years, but I still can't stand the sight of such an unholy imperfection."

Salvia's mouth hung open. She couldn't believe the words coming out of this abhorrent man's mouth. How could someone be so callous?

As she glanced at the soldiers around Deacon, none of them so much as looked at each other, or even the Cardinali. They seemed completely unphased. It was as though they truly believed the old man to be righteous? But how could they? Did the words of a fellow soldier mean nothing to them? Did they not recognize the pain and hurt in his voice?

Baldric's face was now to the ground. His silver strands shielded his eye, but his shoulders trembled and his teeth were bare.

Deacon's glaring bright blue eyes bored into Baldric. The air of condescension and superiority exuding from his sly smirk was as pungent as spoiled fish. "What now boy? Have you no more nonsensical accusations? No more fanciful tales of self delusion?"

Baldric was quiet for a moment, but soon released a breath. His snarl was gone as he stood himself erect, his gaze still low. "I see. So, you plan to just keep shifting the blame? You won't even accept the monster you are? FINE!" Baldric immediately unsheathed his sword and dashed toward Deacon. "Then I'll make you pay for what you've done myself!"

Salvia jolted, as did Deacon. He quickly stumbled behind the safety of his Templar Equitums. All of them held their swords at the ready. Baldric's sword clashed with one of theirs, and with a roar, he shoved the soldier back in an attempt to push through as the other soldiers surrounded him.

Salvia's heart leaped into her throat. Everything had happened so fast she hadn't been able to react, instead just standing there watching in horror. She clutched Lorenzo's rose beneath her dress. Baldric wasn't fighting like he had on the farm against the bandits. His sword swings were wild and his twirls, while swift, were careless. He was angry—No, he was beyond that. His rage was lashing out at anything in his way, and that would be his undoing.

"Baldric, please—"

*"Salvia, you must identify the sinners! I can't help him if I don't know who to spare and who to punish!"*

Salvia jumped, realizing Ultor's cacophony voice hadn't been in her mind. She looked over her shoulder in surprise, following her shadow to the stairwell's entrance where there, shrouded in the darkness, stood her demon. Swallowing the fear trying to take hold in her throat, she nodded in understanding and turned to face the battle raging ahead of her.

Raising her left hand level with her chest, she opened it wide and faced her palm up. A burst of flame exploded at the center of her hand forming a ring in midair. As the ring closed, a distorted image appeared within the boundaries of the flame. All but three of their foes glowed brightly in colors of yellows and greens, and even one violet.

"Ultor, do you see them?" Salvia asked, her breath heavy with concern. Her lips tightly pressed together as she watched Baldric, dodging and attacking erratically, but somehow managing to fend off the foes.

Ultor let out a deep, growling, ravenous burst of laughter. *"Oh, I see them my dear!"* The words were filled with a sinister hunger. With a gleam of joy across his face, he emerged from the shadows of the stairwell and made his presence known. Ultor lifted himself to his full, oppressive height behind her and spread his wings with a burst of wind that washed over the chamber. His thunderous roar left a ringing in Salvia's ears.

Deacon and the templars furthest from Baldric's wrath turned and froze. All eyes were locked on Salvia's demon friend, and a palpable sense of dread filled the room. Ultor summoned forth his black blades from his forearms and as he did, nearly every one of them took several steps back. Even the knights fending off Baldric's attacks seemed to notice now.

In a flash, Ultor dashed past Salvia. A soft shriek escaped her lips. In the span of a heartbeat, he had already cut down a few of the knights with ease, their blood painting the floor in a dim crimson.

Salvia's chest felt as if it might cave in on itself. The sight of the carnage brought her right back to the night of Lorenzo's death. Her breath was shallow and came in short bursts. Clutching to her late fiance's rose, she struggled to focus on the present, praying for the strength to get through this. Blood sprayed into a thick crimson mist as limbs flew through the air. The sounds of bones cracking and metal slamming against metal echoed through the room.

Bile clawed at the back of her throat. Salvia couldn't take it, couldn't watch anymore and turned away. To her surprise she found Zinnia standing by the base of the stairs. Her back was hard pressed against the stone wall. The color seemed drained from her face, and her expression was one of pure shock and confusion. She reminded Salvia of a wounded tiger. As frightened and helpless as the crossbowman looked, all it would take was one small misstep and she would attack. Salvia wanted to comfort her but again had no idea how to even begin.

Just then, a roar from Baldric turned her attention back to the battle. She stared at him in horror. His eyes were wild with rage as he fought the fellow members of his order, furiously trying to reach Deacon. She wasn't sure if it was thanks to the other knights' skills with the blade or Baldric's singular focus, but no blood covered his sword. He hadn't killed a single one of them. Still, Salvia was deathly worried for him. The sounds of the battle faded with the beating of her heart, thumping louder and louder as a thought entered her mind.

No, she didn't want to believe it. He couldn't have. It couldn't be. Something within her, a gnawing feeling in the pit of her stomach told her to point the fiery ring at Baldric. With a gulp and hoping beyond reason that he wasn't lost, she slowly panned the ring of fire toward him. The view was unclear, the flames seemingly burning hotter than they ever had before. She wondered if it was this place, this site and its connection with Hevellum and Infernos. She stared through the ring, trying desperately to decipher the rippling image of the battle. So many colors twisted and blurred together in the clash that focusing on any one person was nearly impossible and yet there, in a momentary break as Baldric pulled away from his attackers, she saw it. Her eyes slowly widened with the realization. Her fears had been warranted. Baldric began to emit a faint red glow. She quickly dismissed the flame, terrified that Ultor would notice and be forced to attack him.

As Baldric reentered the fray, he parried a soldier's blade with his sword and drew a dagger, stabbing it deep into the man's shoulder. Quickly grabbing the knight by the neck, Baldric shoved him out of the way, leaving the small blade buried in his shoulder. He rushed through the opening toward Deacon, flying past corpses and injured soldiers as they wailed in pain. It seemed those who were still fit to fight were preoccupied with Ultor. Salvia prayed Baldric wasn't going to do what she thought he would and watched on, unable to do a thing.

He clutched his sword tightly in one hand and stomped toward his target.

Closing the distance, Baldric suddenly dropped his longsword to the floor and grabbed the panicked, terrified Cardinali by the collar of his crimson robes. He unleashed blow after blow on the vile man's face. Baldric didn't even say a word. His rageful eyes glared down at the old man who had tormented him since he was but a boy. It was as if each and every horror from his past, the death of his parents, the rape, the gash on his face, and untold others were kindling to the inferno of hate raining down onto Deacon's face. Even after the sound of bones cracking, Baldric didn't relent. So much blood spattered Baldric's glove that no trace of azure remained. He pummeled the Cardinali until he lay there limp, no longer even trying to shield his face or grasping at Baldric's arms.

Tears flowed down Salvia's face. Baldric had Deacon by the throat. It was a miracle that the man was even still breathing. Blood bubbled from his mouth as he wheezed in pain. Panting, Baldric held his fisted hand in the air and looked to be surveying the damage he had wrought. Salvia couldn't fathom what might've been going on in his head at that very moment, but whatever it was, he needed to stop.

Salvia had to stop him, but how?

Deacon's face was a battered, bruised, and slowly swelling lump of flesh. His nose bent irregularly at odd angles. Bone was visible through a cut on his cheek. One of his eyes was swollen completely shut and was in the process of adopting the shade of a no longer ripe plum. His other eye seemed to have somehow escaped the brunt of the assault. Deacon then opened that one good eye and glared upward. He hadn't lost consciousness.

Baldric stared at him a moment longer and then released the old man, letting the Cardinali's body collapse to the ground. The man groaned and tried to prop himself up with one arm which seemed to take an agonizing effort. Were he anyone else, Salvia might've felt pity, but the only reason she felt glad that he had managed to cling to this side of mortality was that it meant Baldric wasn't yet completely lost.

While keeping his rage-filled eyes locked on Deacon, Baldric slowly knelt to the ground, and wrapped his fingers around the hilt of his sword.

Salvia then realized that he hadn't stopped himself from completing his vengeance. He had merely chosen a different tool to complete his task. Her body started to move before she even knew what she was going to do. She took a hesitant step toward Baldric, followed by another, and another, ignoring the bodies and blood adorning the path to him. She needed to calm herself. If she could do that, then maybe she could help him.

Standing once more, Baldric reached out and grabbed hold of Deacon by the throat, pulling the man to his knees. Baldric's sword arm raised high and pulled back into a perfectly angled harbinger of death. Small beads of sweat slid down the side of Baldric's face. The blade shook lightly. He was hesitating. Something must've been telling him that what he was about to do . . . was wrong. It had to be. There had to be another way for the Cardinali to pay for his sins. Salvia was sure of it, and then she remembered, there was.

Baldric suddenly shook his head, as if trying to quiet the voices arguing against his current course of action. "No! I will have justice for your sins. For everything you've done!" He yelled, his pain dripping from every word.

"Oh—" Deacon coughed hoarsely, "please. I doubt that, boy!" His words gurgled through blood and missing teeth. "I have the holy light of Hevellum on my side. I am—righteous. I am DIVINE!" Grabbing Baldric's wrist over his throat, Deacon's swollen lips formed an enraged snarl, resolve blazing through his one bright blue eye. "You, on the other hand, will be—severely tortured by the demons of Infernos. You—will rot—alongside your HEATHENOUS PARENTS!"

"SHUT UP!" Baldric roared as he squeezed the hilt of his sword, ready to thrust the blade down into its mark.

A surge of determination propelled Salvia forward. "Baldric, please stop!" She shrieked, crashing into his armored back and embracing him from behind.

He startled but didn't move. Deacon remained in his grasp, the blade held locked in place and Salvia hugging him tightly.

The chamber was now eerily quiet, save for the heavy breathing of Baldric and the wheezing of a barely conscious Deacon. Baldric didn't look at Salvia, but he also wasn't pushing her away. After a moment, his body slowly began to relax. Despite the cold metal of his armor, she hoped he could feel the warmth and care she desperately tried to convey.

Salvia understood his anger. Baldric had every right to be furious, to want compensation paid in blood for what had been done to him, but this, murdering the man responsible for his years of misery wouldn't heal those wounds. That much she was sure of. If she ever faced the men that destroyed her village, took her friends and Lorenzo from her, she too might feel the burning hate that was driving his actions. She wouldn't forgive them; how could she? But she still wouldn't take their lives. Doing so wouldn't bring her loved ones back. All she would accomplish would be adding her soul to the list of the damned.

She tightened her embrace, tears flowing down her cheeks like a burst dam. As she opened her mouth, finally deciding on what to say, the words turned to lead in her mouth. A shadow fell over them. As she looked over her shoulder her blood froze. There, within arm's length, stood the soldier that Baldric had left for dead with his dagger buried in the man's shoulder. He was lightly hunched and across his face was clear, murderous intent. He clutched the handle of the dagger and pulled it from his shoulder. Blood poured from the gruesome wound, but Salvia's attention remained fixated on the dagger, rising higher and higher as if in slow motion over his head.

As the blade began to plunge downward, the man suddenly bobbed forward, an invisible energy radiating from a single point and dispersing through his appendages. The dagger fell harmlessly to the floor. Protruding from just above the bridge of the man's nose was the sharp, blood-covered tip of a crossbow bolt. The man's eyes rolled to the back of his head, and he fell to the ground with a heavy, lifeless thud.

It all went by so fast she barely had time to process what had happened. She had so many brushes with death, she thought that by now the shock of the moment would be somewhat lessened. Salvia was taken aback as the full story came into focus. Zinnia stood statuesque in the distance, her crossbow still held at the ready. Her green eyes trembling under furrowed brows. Tears stained her freckled cheeks. The crossbow slipped from her hands and fell to the floor with a clatter.

Salvia was speechless. She released a breath she hadn't realized she was holding. Her heart started to calm, and she simply nodded in acknowledgement, making a mental note that when everything was said and done, she would give the woman a proper thanks. Zinnia returned the nod and began removing each article of armor that tied her to her order from her body.

In the end, it was Zinnia who was there for Salvia. Even though she felt that she had failed Zinnia at every opportunity, Zinnia had pulled through for her in the end. The warrior was still likely far from being alright, but now, Salvia had hope for her.

Returning to Baldric, she hugged him as tightly as she could. Cold teardrops fell against the skin of her hands resting atop his chest. He was crying. Baldric was finally letting out his pain.

"Baldric, I know how much you're hurting, but falling into despair will not help you move past this." Salvia said as calmly as she could with a tight throat. "Giving in to your vengeance will not give you the justice you and your parents deserve. Please, please don't give in to wrath. Don't let rage drive your actions. Don't fall for this man's hateful words. He wants you to be damned so that you share in his fate. Don't give him that."

Baldric didn't respond. His chest slowly rose and fell under her hands. Eventually, he relaxed his grip on Deacon. The old man slowly slipped away and fell to the floor with a groan.

A large, winged shadow slowly loomed overhead. Ultor stood over them and peered over Baldric's shoulder. A pleased smile rested on his skeletal face. As he scanned the Cardinali, he chuckled and nodded once with approval. He then leaned down, wrapping his long, stone-like claws around the old man, and picked his limp body up off the ground with ease.

"*Don't you worry, Baldric.*" Ultor said as he turned his back to them. "*I'll see to this man's punishment for what he did to you, and others alike. His existence will be nothing but suffering even after your time in this world has been spent.*"

Ultor walked to the other side of the chamber and there, Salvia was surprised to find a second entryway. It wasn't like the one she had taken though. It looked as if the wall had collapsed in a shape just larger than a man. That was how Deacon and his men had entered this place, by tunneling their way inside. That struck her as odd.

She then noticed three Templar Equitums tied up by the entrance. Salvia had forgotten about the few who were unmarked by sin. As Ultor approached them, the chains about their wrists and legs suddenly disappeared. He freed them. They stared up at her demon friend with fear and confusion in their eyes. They didn't know whether to attack or run, but Ultor made that an easy choice. He bellowed something she couldn't quite make out, and the soldiers scurried away down the dimly lit tunnel.

Then it was just Ultor and Deacon. Salvia wasn't sure what was about to happen, whether Ultor would suck the man's soul from his body, as she had seen him do so many times now, or kill him outright. Instead, to her surprise, Ultor dropped Deacon to the floor. He then raised a leg high in the air and slammed his clawed foot down onto the Cardinali's legs. The old man gave out a howling scream, causing Salvia to wince. She didn't feel sorry for the man, but the sound of crunching bones was hard to ignore. Even the stones underneath the man seemed to shake at the impact. Somehow Deacon still didn't black out. He actually attempted to crawl toward the crudely made tunnel.

Ultor turned around and caught her looking at him, but all he did was nod, then returned to her. He gave her a signal that all was safe now. There was no way the man could escape with those wounds. He wouldn't even reach the end of the tunnel before the Finis claimed him.

Salvia let out a breath of relief, only to suck it back in when the ceiling started to glow. Ultor and Salvia looked up and saw the true symbol of Hevellum shining brightly on the dome. It was the same symbol she remembered etched on Abimelech's armor. The light of the symbol glowed brighter and brighter until finally, a large form emerged and joined them in the room. The light was nearly blinding before it quickly shattered. When it did, she was met by a familiar winged being. Abimelech floated down to the center of the chamber. He stared at Ultor who returned a nearly contemptible grin. After a moment, the two bowed with respect to one another and began taking their positions.

Baldric had yet to move a single muscle in her embrace, save for the minor trembling in his hands. He then released his sword, dropping it with a loud clang and was suddenly falling to his knees. Salvia shrieked his name as she attempted to catch him, but Baldric was far too heavy for her. Instead, she did her best to carefully guide his fall and landed on folded legs.

Scooting herself to kneel beside him, her heart sank. Baldric was staring blankly at the ground. His eyes looked tired and were encircled by dark rings. He seemed as though in the aftermath of the battle, he was uncertain of how to proceed.

What could she possibly do to help him through this? As she raised a hand to cup his cheek, Ultor called out to her. It was time for the Finis. She knew she needed to go, but she couldn't bring herself to turn away from Baldric.

"*Come, Salvia.*" Ultor said gently. "*This must be done. You can tend to him when the city has been devoured.*"

With a sigh of defeat, she nodded to Ultor. She looked at Baldric once more and leaned over. Brushing the loose strands of silver hair away from his eyes, she leaned forward and kissed the top of his head. "Don't worry, everything will be alright. I promise." Her voice was a soft whisper. Though he was in a state of shock, she hoped her words were able to pierce through the veil of his troubled thoughts.

With a final smile she forced herself to stand and stepped away. She joined

Ultor and Abimelech in the center of the chamber. Zinnia sat by the chamber's main entrance. Her arms were wrapped around her knee and back rested against the wall. Her silver armor and weapons were discarded off to the side, not neatly stacked but tossed aside. Salvia doubted she would ever wear it again and thought that would be for the best.

Her lips curled anxiously between her teeth, feeling terrible for forcing her companions through such hardships. She hoped that once they had healed from their wounds, both physical and within, they might remake their order from the ground up, teaching kindness and compassion. Through them, the people of this land might learn the Almighty One's love for each and every living thing. But whatever they decided, Salvia hoped that above all, they would find peace and happiness.

After everything she, and they, had been through, she wondered if such a thing was even possible. It had to be. She needed to believe that or else why had they suffered so much to get here? She wouldn't let those doubts start to set in and instead sought a distraction.

On the floor, at the center of the chamber, she found a symbol etched into the stone. It was confusing at first. Each line was connected, twisting and turning with seemingly no end in sight. She stared at it for a long moment before it finally started to form a familiar shape. It wasn't a single symbol, but two overlapping one another. It was a combination of both the symbols for Hevellum and Infernos. They were encased within a massive triangle. Three silver spheres lay lodged in the floor, one at each point of the triangle. The spheres were pristine, shining brightly in the torchlight, but they bore no markings and somehow went completely untouched by the carnage of the battle.

Abimelech stood before the sphere at the triangle's base right. Ultor stood at base left. It was clear then where she needed to be and made her way to the head of the symbol. There she looked to the two for guidance, wondering what it was they needed to do next. Abimelech and Ultor both smiled at her then knelt before the small spheres below them and each placed a single hand atop it. Salvia mimicked their action, placing her right hand upon the sphere. She remained quiet, motionless for a few moments, but nothing happened.

Glancing up at Abimelech, she opened her mouth to ask if everything was alright, but just as she did, a spike of pain stopped her. Something had emerged from the sphere and pierced clean through her hand. Salvia gave out a shriek and Abimelech grunted with a grimace. Ultor on the other hand, somehow remained stoically quiet, as if the odd spear didn't hurt him at all.

Looking down at her hand, the strange object opened up like a flower in full bloom and locked her in place. Crimson blood spilled from the wound and unnaturally flowed to either side of the sphere, continuing into the etched crevice on the floor and along the symbol's path.

Salvia's breath hitched as she watched ichor continue to flow from her wound. Oddly enough, the loss of blood didn't have any effect on her. She expected to feel faint, but she was fine. She watched with confusion as the blood flowed through the grooves. Her heart raced as her nerves started getting the better of her. Feeling trapped, she looked to her guardians, but neither had a trace of panic on their faces. Ultor's dark violet, nearly black blood and Abimelech's gold blood did just as hers was.

The foundation around them began to quake. It was soft at first, but quickly turned violent. It felt as though the entire chamber would collapse. Startled, Salvia dropped her other knee to the ground, trying desperately to balance herself. She tried to pull her hand free to no avail.

"It is alright, Salvia." Abimelech stated with a focused stare. There was a tenderness behind his words, which seemed to chase away her fears. "Thou will be freed once the blood ritual has completed. You will be alright. I promise."

With a swallow, Salvia took a deep breath and watched as her blood filled the lines to the brim, drawing ever closer to Ultor's and Abimelech's. Each moment stretched on for an eternity, but eventually their blood streams met. Just as they touched, the symbol illuminated in a vibrant violet hue. The Hevellum symbol on the ceiling began to glow as well in a brilliant yellow, beautiful as the morning sun.

The cones binding their hands closed just as quickly as they had arisen and retracted into the spheres. She was free but there was no time to be thankful because the violet glow at her feet turned an eerie orange. A portal of swirling darkness spread above the blood-infused symbol, and a massive shadowy figure raised from within, sending a terrible chill throughout Salvia's being.

At the same moment, the yellow light from above quickly turned blindingly white. Salvia shielded her eyes but even so, its radiance enveloped her. She attempted to peer through a small crack between her arms, wanting to see her friend Ultor, but all she could make out was his subtle silhouette through the light. Salvia tried calling out to him but was unable to make a sound.

The world quaked fiercely under her feet as the glow continued to brighten, embracing them in its holy white light. She stumbled back, feeling a terrible pressure overtaking her, pushing her to the ground.

Salvia was scared. There was too much going on, and she was unable to even scream for help. Her vision darkened at the edges, and a desperate urge to sleep took her.

"*Salvia,*" Ultor's voice cut through the mayhem, "*you are brave beyond measure. Your kindness is boundless and beautiful. It has been the brightest pleasure to know you. I bid thee farewell, my friend.*"

# OUR WEARINESS

**A**LL WAS QUIET, save for the crackling of torches all around. Salvia's skin prickled at the cool air's touch. Her body was heavy and weak. She could barely move, unable to even open her eyes.

*Salvia?* A soft whisper called to her. It sounded so distant. *Salvia, can you hear me?*

*Ultor? Eres tú?*[1] Salvia replied in her mind.

A warm palm pressed gently on her cheek, slowly turning her head.

Salvia struggled to open her eyes, her vision blurry. Her mind whirled from the pounding pain in her head. It was as if she had been struck by something heavy. Raising a hand to massage her temple, she stopped and held her palm before her eyes. A cloth was wrapped tightly around the wound.

"Salvia?"

---

1    Spanish for *Is it you*

Salvia slowly turned her head and found Zinnia kneeling over her, worry shining in her green eyes. "Zinnia? What . . . What happened?" She asked, her mouth feeling like sandpaper.

Zinnia let out a sigh of relief, shaking her head with a small smile. "I'm not exactly sure. When the light faded, you were just lying here on the ground." She gently took Salvia's right hand and inspected the cloth wrapping. "I'm sorry, but I didn't have the proper supplies to treat the wound, so I had to improvise. I tore a white cloth I found in your satchel. This should do for now, but we need to find you a healer. Whatever pierced your hand left a gruesome opening."

Zinnia released her hand, allowing Salvia to look at it herself. Crimson blood stained much of the white cloth, leaving it a pale red. Raising a finger, she gently caressed the wound and felt a small void in the middle of her hand. A light jolt of pain spread to her wrist and fingertips, causing her to groan.

A sudden, unusual emotion welled within her. It was a strange, aching sadness. She didn't understand. It was as if something was missing, a part of her, but Salvia couldn't pinpoint what.

Shaking the thought away, she took a deep breath and turned to Zinnia, forcing herself not to dwell on it. "Dónde está Baldric?[2] Is he alright?"

Zinnia remained quiet for a long moment. She looked past Salvia, staring at something behind her. Confused, Salvia tried to turn herself over, to see what Zinnia was looking at. As she did, a weight came over her body. Her vision blurred and dizziness made her movements sluggish.

"Take it slow, Salvia." Zinnia said gently, rubbing her back in small circular motions.

---

2     Spanish for *Where is*

With a few deep breaths, she nodded and tried again, moving slowly and carefully. As Salvia attempted to lift herself up off the ground, she glanced up and a small smile of relief broke on her face. There, just a short distance away, was Baldric. Salvia silently thanked the Almighty One, and even Calamar, that her companion still remained in Eldara. He had yet moved from the position she left him in before the ritual, which was more than a little concerning.

With a deep breath, she placed her hands flat on the ground and pushed firmly to raise herself up. A surge of pain ignited from her injured palm and rushed up her right arm. She let out a shriek through gritted teeth and folded in on herself. Zinnia was quick to place her hands on Salvia's shoulders. It was comforting to know Zinnia cared enough to be there for her now, but Salvia couldn't help but be angry with her weakness. She was sure a wound like this wouldn't have stopped Zinnia or Baldric. Lifting her right hand up, she stared daggers at it, watching the red spread across the bandage. She couldn't even stop the trembling.

"Do you need help standing?" Zinnia asked with an outstretched hand.

Salvia looked up and gave her a thankful smile but was taken aback by the look in Zinnia's eyes. She then understood. This kindness was fueled not only by compassion, but by regret for her actions during the fight. If it hadn't been for the binding of the pact forced upon them, Zinnia would've killed her. In that moment of weakness, Zinnia might've doomed everyone.

Carefully placing her hand in the woman's, Salvia nodded in affirmation. There was no way Salvia was going to bring up what happened before the Finis. Emotions were running wild for herself, for Zinnia, and for Baldric. She was sure that neither of them wanted to speak of it, at least, not until they were ready.

A small smile flashed on Zinnia's face as she carefully helped Salvia up from the floor. Her body felt so heavy, as if stones were to her very soul, binding her to the ground. Why did she feel so terrible? Her stomach was queasy. Nauseous. Could this be what blood loss felt like, or was it something else?

Once on her feet it felt like the world was still reeling from the Finis. But if that were the case, Zinnia would be having the same trouble as she was. Salvia took a few heavy breaths, trying to ease the spinning of the world around her. Her heart calmed but her body ached. As her thumb ran across the cloth around her right hand, a thought occurred to her.

She turned to Zinnia with the sweetest smile she could muster. "Zinnia, gracias.[3]"

Zinnia looked at her with mild bewilderment, causing Salvia to giggle warmly. She then focused and tried again in Anglicus[4]. "Thank you, um, for my hand, and for saving me earlier."

"Oh!" Zinnia looked away, her cheeks turning brightly pink. "It was the least I could do."

Salvia gently placed a hand on Zinnia's shoulder for balance, her injured hand resting gently over her stomach. "Vamos,[5] I believe, um, a friend needs our aid." She tilted her head toward Baldric.

Zinnia chuckled in agreement. "Right," she responded, "but try not to push yourself. You look like you might keel over any moment."

Salvia nodded in understanding, taking things one step at a time. As they walked, Salvia focused on her breathing. She then noticed Zinnia looking around with somewhat pinched brows.

---

3       Spanish for *Thank you*
4       This worlds *English*
5       Spanish for *Come*

"That's odd." The woman whispered to herself.

"Hm?" Salvia cocked her head in curiosity. "What is?"

"The bodies." Zinnia stopped. "They're all gone." They both stood in place and surveyed the massive chamber. "I know the Captain and Ultor took out many of the templars, but the place has even been swept clean of blood. It's as if no battle took place down here. It's strange, is all," she said with a shrug. "Though after everything, I don't know why I'm surprised."

Salvia also found it strange. There were no stains. No severed limbs. Nothing. However, as her eyes landed to the other side of the chamber, the entrance the Cardinali and his templars had used was now caved in. Nothing but rubble remained. It sent a shiver down her spine.

"You're right." Salvia agreed with a trembling breath. "Maybe it was, um, the Finis? The event . . . could've taken them, body and soul?"

Zinnia nodded. "I was thinking the same thing. These temples are supposed to be sacred after all. Right?" Zinnia wrapped an arm around Salvia's shoulders, helping her keep her balance as they continued toward Baldric.

Sacred. Salvia hadn't really put much thought into it until now. She recalled how Abimelech and Ultor spoke of the temples, their words seemingly reverent as they had detailed her mission. At the time, she barely knew her angel and demon and assumed they always sounded as such. Of course these temples were sacred, but to sweep the unwanted visitors away was still unexpected. It was now as though not a single trace of them had ever existed in this place.

Finally reaching Baldric, Zinnia and Salvia knelt on either side of him. They inspected him first for injury, careful not to make any sudden movements that might startle him in his consternation. His dark azure eyes were weary with sadness and bloodshot from the tears he had shed. He kept his gaze low, but if it was a conscious choice, they had no way of knowing.

Was he ashamed of what had happened? Salvia wondered.

With a deep breath and a swallow, she carefully raised a hand to his forearm and placed it on his gauntlet. The cold of the metal stung her skin lightly, but she didn't care. Despite the confusion Salvia saw on Baldric's face, she wanted to comfort him in some way.

"Salvia." Zinnia called softly. "Can you help me remove his armor? I don't think he needs it weighing him down anymore."

Salvia looked at Zinnia for a long moment and then Baldric. The armor was a means of protection, true, but now she saw it for what it represented. It was pain. Sadness. Oppression. A reminder of all they had gone through under the Cirine order. Hatred. Subjugation. Enslavement. With luck, all wickedness was gone from the city and the two would never need the armor again.

Salvia turned her gaze to Baldric and with a calm, steady voice, asked, "Baldric, would you like us to remove your armadura—I-I mean armor?"

His silver hair was tousled over his face. Salvia watched him carefully, waiting for any sign of consent. Then, it happened. There was a small twitch of his fingers. He had heard her, and soon he turned a hand upward. The buckles and hinges were laid bare. She tenderly raised her hands and cupped his arm. A small smile of relief creased her face and without another moment's hesitation, set to work. She began unbuckling the gauntlet, careful not to aggravate the injury on her hand while Zinnia worked on the clasps of his pauldrons.

One by one Salvia managed to unbuckle each hinge and carefully slid the gauntlet off, followed by his azure glove. Zinnia removed the pauldrons from his shoulders, placing them on the ground at her side. She then proceeded to the hinges on the left side of his breastplate while Salvia worked on the other gauntlet. Zinnia seemed to be struggling, reaching under his arm to get to the breastplate's buckles, likely not wanting to force Baldric to change positions if he wasn't ready to move.

As Salvia finished with the second gauntlet and glove, she noticed Baldric's gaze on Zinnia, and felt a slight tremble run through his arm in her hands. He then swallowed and shifted his weight to change positions, which startled the two for a moment. Baldric slid his legs out from under him and raised his knees in front of his chest, then rested his arms on them with hands clasped loosely together.

Zinnia sighed, looking relieved, and proceeded to unbuckle his breastplate unabated. Baldric's eyes remained steadfast on the floor between the two women, not once trying to look at either of them.

Salvia had the sudden urge to embrace him, to wrap her arms around his neck and tell him that everything was going to be alright. That he would be safe and nothing would ever hurt him again. But would he even welcome that? Their relationship was still very new. Salvia wasn't even sure if Baldric considered her a friend.

Immediately shaking the thought away, she decided to focus on the task at hand. Looking him over, the only pieces remaining were his greaves. As she reached for his right leg, Baldric suddenly grasped her uninjured hand. A sharp breath escaped her lips and her instinct was to pull herself free, but she fought away the urge. His touch was surprisingly warm. As he turned her hand over, his thumb slid over her palm and up to her fingers, caressing the light scars over her joints. His eyes shined as if he was about to cry.

"I-I fished a lot." She blurted out. It was the first thing that came to mind. As Baldric's expression softened, he met her gaze, causing her stomach to flutter. Salvia's heart beat loudly in her ears. Ignoring the burning in her cheeks, she swallowed, and the words continued pouring out. "Sometimes my friends took me out sailing. We often rode the waves and fished." She chuckled with a light shrug, unsure where she was going with this story, but as images of their faces filled her thoughts, her smile soured. "One of them taught me a lot about boating, and fishing became a relaxing pass time for me." Her voice cracked as memories of Lorenzo floated in her mind.

"This person . . . were they special to you?" Baldric asked. She then realized she must've looked surprised because he continued, "Sorry, it's just, your smile looked sad, and then I remembered you lost your home." His brows curved heavily over his eyes. "I realized you must've lost everyone you cared for in this world."

Salvia smiled weakly as she rested her head on her shoulder. "He was special to me. He taught me many things, as I did him." She closed her eyes, hoping to hide her tremble. "I miss him, and many others, but I can't let their deaths weigh on me. I'm sure they wouldn't want that."

As she opened her eyes again, the two looked at each other, sharing a quiet moment before he smiled and answered. "I'm sure they wouldn't either. You've-You've done so much. Went through—" Baldric took a sudden breath, as if trying to hold something back. "So much. We went through so much, but I . . . How can I move forward if I can't do *anything* on my own? . . . Let me do this part myself, please?"

His eyes pleaded, and she knew better than to argue. Hearing the wisdom in his words, she slid her hand free from his and rested it on her lap. Baldric's life had been forever changed. His path was finally his own. He needed to take charge and make the first step, no matter how inconsequential. She smiled at him warmly and waited patiently for him to do what he needed to do.

Baldric's eyes welled with tears, and he took a deep breath, proceeding to unbuckle the hinges on the back of his greaves. One by one he slid the leather belts away from the buckles, opening the greaves and sliding his feet free. He then straightened himself and nodded for Zinnia to slide the breastplate off as well. She placed the remaining pieces with the rest of the set, nudging the azure cape away with her foot as if it were a diseased thing.

Zinnia stood herself up and crossed her arms loosely over her stomach. Salvia remained knelt in front of Baldric, awaiting his signal should he need help in standing. He remained there for a short time, staring at the floor with one hand on the ground and the other over his knee, his thumb rubbing circles against his index finger as though debating just what his next steps should be.

His shoulders began to tremble. He seemed scared for some reason. Baldric's head fell back, and he stared up toward the dome ceiling. Salvia followed his gaze but found nothing there. A thought then struck her. It wasn't something he was looking at. He was worried about what they might find when they returned to the city above. What exactly would the Finis have done to the shops and homes?

She couldn't recall what Ultor had said. So much had happened over the past couple of days, it all seemed like a blur.

Baldric let out a sudden breath, pulling Salvia's attention back to him, and she watched as he quickly pushed himself off the floor. His fists were clenched at his sides so tight, his knuckles turned white.

Whatever he was thinking, it was clear he wouldn't let fear stop him from seeing what lay ahead. Salvia was about to reach out to Baldric, but Zinnia walked up beside her and stretched out her hand to help her up. She looked up at the copper red-haired woman, and Zinnia met her eyes, gently shaking her head to leave him be. Why, though? Would it really be so wrong for her to take his hand and let him know he didn't have to venture forth alone?

But then it hit her. Baldric had asked to let him do this part himself. It would go against his very wishes if she were to interrupt, even if her intentions were good.

With a defeated sigh, Salvia accepted Zinnia's hand and stood up. The act took a surprising amount of effort. She groaned through gritted teeth, that terrible weight from earlier returning as if the world's pull had doubled, demanding she lay down and simply sleep, but why?

Dizziness crept into her mind and turned her thoughts into a jumbled mess. Salvia took several deep breaths, hoping with every exhale to feel her sense of balance return. Was something wrong with her? It had to be the blood loss. It was the only thing that would make sense and yet, that didn't seem right.

Opening her eyes, she found Baldric still looking up toward the ceiling. His eyes were tightly closed and his brows furrowed. Tears slid down his cheeks. Her heart ached with worry for him, and before she knew it, his name poured from her mouth before she could stop herself. "Baldric?" Surprising herself, she managed to keep her voice soft.

He flinched, then his expression fell into his practiced stoicism. His eyes darted to Salvia, then Zinnia, and then he wiped the tears away from his face. Running his fingers through his silver hair, Baldric returned his attention back to Salvia, seemingly waiting for her to continue.

She noticed a small quiver in his bottom lip. His lips. Salvia found herself looking again at the scar. What once brought on curiosity, now filled her with sadness. Knowing the reality of what had transpired, it was a hard truth. She may now have had a better understanding of Baldric's past, but she also couldn't help but feel regret for having asked about it. It couldn't be easy having a constant reminder of his torment on his flesh.

Baldric's brows pinched together, looking confused by her extended silence. Salvia's heart flipped in her chest. She needed to say something before she gave him more reason to worry. "Um, a-are you ready to go?" She finally said.

He glanced away toward the exit, his gaze hardening, and soon nodded. "Yes, I think so." Baldric was the first to make his way to the stairs, and Salvia, with Zinnia's help, followed close behind. As much as she wanted to know how the two were doing, she was in no state to help them. She wasn't even sure she was ready herself for whatever they were walking into.

She was instantly jostled out of her weariness as the three of them stopped at the base of the stairs. Baldric looked down to his waist. His hands flew to the buckle of his belt and empty scabbard. His sword must've still been somewhere on the ground back in the chamber. He was struggling for a moment, but as he pulled the strap loose from the buckle, he let both belt and scabbard fall to the ground. Baldric then stretched and let out a breath of relief.

Lowering his arms to his sides, he seemed somewhat reinvigorated. His chest raised and fell steadily as he leaned forward and peered into the darkness of the stairwell. After a moment, he turned to Salvia and spoke. "Earlier you held a bit of fire in your palm. Can you do that again?"

"Oh. Um," she shrugged, "I'm—" Salvia paused for a moment, suddenly finding it difficult to find the proper words to respond in the Anglicus language.

"Honestly? . . . Sí,[6] I'm not sure." She raised her hands to her chest and focused on calling the fire. Several long moments went by, but nothing happened. The hollow feeling in her chest grew wider, for some reason feeling flooded with overwhelming sadness. Her eyes began to sting with tears.

"Salvia," Zinnia looked at her with an uncharacteristically soft expression, "are you alright? Is it Ultor? Have you heard from him since you awoke?"

Salvia quickly wiped the tears from her cheeks, confusion wrapping itself around her mind as she mentally called for Ultor, but all she received was silence. Her shoulders sagged and her head lowered to her chest, a realization setting in that she desperately wanted not to be true.

Grabbing at the collars of the fabric of her dresses, she pulled both down, and her eyes shot wide. Besides Lorenzo's golden rose, the only scar now left on her copper skin was the one caused by the spear. Ultor's pentagram was gone.

"Ultor, he-he's gone." Salvia's voice was laced with an unbearable sadness. Grief was too gentle a word. She had lost another friend. Despite knowing that their time together was always meant to be short, it did little to reduce the sensation of loss. His was a bond unlike any other. A part of her was lost.

"Gone? But why?" Baldric asked.

Salvia adjusted the dresses back into place and gently wiped her tears from her cheeks, forcing a small smile on her face. "I must've forgotten when I passed out. I've felt dizzy since waking, and an unusual emptiness inside. 'Salvia, I bid thee farewell, my friend.'" She looked at Baldric. "It was the last thing he said to me as the light enveloped the chamber. That was the last thing he said. He has returned to Infernos with the other demons, I'm sure of it. As I said after we met, the magic

---

6     Spanish for *Yes*

I used was his and his alone. I merely borrowed it." Salvia shrugged apologetically.

"I'm sorry." He replied gently, warming her heart with his sincerity.

She shook her head. "Don't be, his duty was done. I will miss his callous quips, but knowing we aided the ángeles[7] in bringing salvation to the world makes his parting a little easier to bear. If I were to see him again, he would probably be upset. I would likely have to sin to make that happen, and I know he wouldn't want that."

Baldric and Zinnia chuckled. "No," Baldric started, "I don't think he would." Looking by the dome's entrance, he picked up a torch. He then proceeded upward, step by step, with Salvia and Zinnia at his rear.

The light of the chamber diminished, fading into the distance as they ascended the stairway. The climb to the temple's entrance felt shorter than Salvia had remembered. As the group grew closer to the top, a light shined through the rectangular opening, bathing the surrounding brickwork in hues of orange and pink. How long had they been down there? It seemed the sun was now setting on the world. Baldric was the first to emerge from the temple, taking a few steps into the open, then stopped dead in his tracks.

Weariness was finally overtaking Salvia. Placing a hand on the temple's entrance, she leaned against its surface, taking a deep breath and hoping it would pass once more. Just then, the fire from Baldric's torch suddenly went out, as if it were snuffed out by an invisible hand, which seemed to startle her companions but she was too tired to react. They both seemed to go rigid, and as her vision started to clear, her heart fell into her stomach.

The city of Lumen Magnum was now in complete ruin. One would think

---

7     Spanish for *Angels*

this place long abandoned. Once tall buildings had been brought low. The view of the sky was no longer impeded by the looming oppressive structures of man. The alley path they had taken was completely obstructed by rubble and debris. Their horses were long gone. Looking to her right, there was a path which seemed far too clean, as though someone or something had carved it out just for them. Not a single sign of life could be seen around them. No rats scurried through the rubble. No birds flew overhead. Not a single sound could be heard echoing in the distance. There was only silence and stillness.

Salvia's heart thundered in her ears. She couldn't keep her eyes open any longer. As darkness seeped into the corners of her vision, her eyelids fell shut. She felt completely weightless. Any hold she had held on the waking world slipped through her fingers, and she finally succumbed to a much needed rest.

# OUR REST

"**B**ALDRIC!"

The scream startled Salvia back to the waking world. It was a woman's voice, familiar and distressed. Was it Zinnia? Salvia couldn't quite tell. She ebbed and flowed between consciousness. Salvia heard rushed footsteps and what sounded like something skidding across the ground.

Hands suddenly grabbed hold of her shoulders and her body rocked to and fro. Someone was shaking her, calling her name, but the sound was so faint she could barely make it out. A pair of warm palms pressed against her cheeks. They moved her head roughly about, the person's voice growing louder and louder until eventually—

"SALVIA!"

Salvia jumped, opening her heavy eyelids with a jolt. Her body quivered with exhaustion as she blinked away the haze of grogginess clouding her vision. Baldric knelt before her, brows pinched together and lips tight in a frown. He looked . . . worried?

"Salvia, what is it? What's wrong?" he asked in a panicked tone.

"What's . . . wrong?" Salvia looked at him, puzzled. She struggled to keep her eyes open but managed a weak smile. "I'm fine, just . . . tired."

"Salvia you nearly collapsed." Zinnia stated sternly. "Just tell us what's wrong so we can help."

They wanted to help? But how could they when she didn't even know what was going on? Salvia had no idea what was happening to her. "I-I don't really know. It's hard to describe. My body . . . feels heavy, an-and hollow."

Baldric's eyes narrowed, inspecting her up and down, and he eventually pulled his hands away from her face. "Nothing seems to be injured other than your hand. Perhaps . . . Do you remember when Ultor said you died?"

Salvia's chest heavied. The reminder felt like a hand pressing against her heart, squeezing it until she thought it might give out. Looking at Baldric, her smile faded, Ultor's words coming as images in her mind. She saw every moment of that night, the night Lorenzo died.

Baldric's eyes softened into a silent apology. He scooped up her hand and cupped it gently in his, then continued. "Maybe the bond you had with him was what kept you alive, sustaining you, giving you more energy than a body can take. Being bonded with him might've caused your body to become dependent. With his magic gone and the bond broken, your body probably just needs time to remember how to rely on its own strength." He shrugged. "This is just a guess of course. It might also be the blood loss."

Feeling the heaviness swallow her once more, Salvia let her eyes close. Baldric's guess might've been right. She had felt different ever since her resurrection. Her wounds had instantly healed, and she had needed less sleep. After a long deep breath, she nodded and began drifting back into slumber.

"Alright, let's hope that's it then." Zinnia's voice trailed off in her mind. She sounded so very far away. "Come on, let's get her somewhere more comfortable."

Salvia felt something slide under her knees and across her back. Someone lifted her off the ground. Whatever had her had a strong grip. Her head rested over a crook of some kind. She was too tired to open her eyes and see who it was that was carrying her, be it Baldric or Zinnia, she trusted them all the same. Salvia's nostrils filled with the smell of leather and spices. What a strange combination of scents, she thought.

She had no knowledge of how far or for how long she had been carried. In one of her lucid moments, she felt the world itself shake. Her carrier startled and spun around but said nothing. Not even a whisper or gasp to give her a clue of what was happening.

The sound of stone grinding against stone emanated from somewhere a short distance away. Was a building collapsing? Gooseflesh shot down the skin of her arms. Were they in danger and if so, why wasn't her carrier moving? Salvia tried to move, but her body was limp and refused her every command. The sound crescendoed with a roar and suddenly they were left in the quiet aftermath. The person holding her sighed, turned, then continued on.

Eventually the carrier gently placed her down on something hard. She was wedged between something. A stone slab that used to be a portion of wall perhaps. There was no way to be sure. The person adjusted Salvia's position until she was seated upright. She wanted to know what was happening, but it was all she could do to simply remain awake.

"Zinnia, do you mind scouting ahead?" The voice, it sounded like Baldric. Could he have been the one carrying her? Salvia felt foolish for not realizing it sooner. Of course it was Baldric. "I want to be sure the way is clear for us."

"Of course, but don't you think something feels . . . off about her?" Zinnia replied. She was right, of course. Without Ultor, Salvia found herself struggling with more than staying awake. She had been having difficulty with the Anglicus language. Were there more things she hadn't realized yet?

"Well, there's certainly been a lack of demonic magic since we were in the temple." Baldric answered.

Was that supposed to be a joke?

A brief silence followed before Zinnia finally responded. "Was that meant to be a joke?"

Salvia was glad she hadn't been the only one who was confused.

"Yes, was it not any good?"

Zinnia laughed softly. She sounded completely surprised. This clearly wasn't something he was known for doing. "You may need more practice."

Baldric snorted. "Alright. Anyway, to answer your question, yes. I noticed that too. I'm sure she'll tell us once she regains her strength."

"Very well, I'll be right back."

"Thank you, and please don't go too far."

"I know how to scout, Baldric. I'm not a rookie!"

Salvia wanted to laugh, but all she could manage was a small smile. She then heard Zinnia's footsteps as she disappeared into the distance. Now there was only silence, and that made Salvia feel more than just a little unsettled. She still couldn't open her eyes or speak. Her safety was completely in their hands, but they were no longer bound to her. Should either of them still harbor her ill will, she would be helpless, but she didn't really believe they would hurt her. Not now. Not after everything they had been through.

Wait. She realized she had been lost in her thoughts for a time. Was Baldric still around? Where had he gone? Everything was so quiet. She tried to call out for him, but all she could manage was a soft moan.

Salvia then felt the soft caress of skin against her forehead, sliding her hair away from her face.

"Everything that has happened, Salvia," Baldric whispered, his voice difficult to hear, "I just hope all of this was worth it in the end. I'm afraid . . . I'm not as hopeful as you. I don't think I can bring myself to believe that . . . us mortals are truly worth saving."

Her chest tightened at the thought. Did Baldric truly not believe that people could change now that they were untethered to the likes of the Papa Regem, Cardinali Deacon Limus, and others of their ilk? She couldn't help but have faith in them. After all, he and Zinnia had both changed. If he could truly not see that there was good in the masses, then she would try to be that hope for him. Change was coming, she was sure of it.

The hurried shuffling of footsteps drawing closer caught her attention. Zinnia must've returned.

"That was fast." Baldric said.

"It's strange really," Zinnia replied, "but I think this path is a straight shot to the East Gate."

"Really?"

"Positive."

"Alright then."

A hand then squeezed Salvia's shoulder, and for some inexplicable reason, her exhaustion was just gone. She felt the weight of the world rise from her chest. Energy spread as pulses with every beat of her heart, rushing through her limbs and causing her fingers and toes to tingle. Salvia finally opened her eyes. She looked up at Baldric, and he seemed surprised.

"I'm sorry. I meant to let you rest," he said.

She couldn't help but stare at him for a moment, then pushed herself out from the wedge she had been resting in. Now that she could see, they had sat her down between a fragment of wall and cart. She rubbed her eyes with the back of her hand and flashed him a warm smile. "De echo,[1] I feel well rested."

He raised a brow at her, his expression skeptical. "Is that so?" Baldric stood with a smirk which made her stomach flutter. "Then let's test that shall we?" He outstretched a hand to her which she happily took, trying her best not to use her injured hand for balance.

He carefully helped her stand to her feet before stepping away, allowing her a moment to compose herself. Releasing a gentle breath, she patted down her dark violet dress. Rubbing away the dirt and smoothing out the wrinkles as best she could. Salvia took a moment to look around now that her vision had cleared, taking in the destruction left behind by the Finis.

"You know," Salvia grasped her forearm, slowly turning around as she surveyed the broken walls, cracked floors, and statues now laying in pieces on the ground, "I wasn't expecting all this ruin. I wonder if the people's homes can be

---

1     Spanish for *Actually*

recovered?"

"It should be left as it is."

Both Salvia and Zinnia turned to Baldric in surprise. Salvia had assumed he would want to restore parts of the city, build it into something better, but as she stared into his eyes, she saw only resentment for what lay around them. She worried for him.

"The church is said to have been founded on the idea that humankind was chosen to bring peace and order to the world. That our race was *special*." Baldric's hands clenched tightly at his sides as he continued. "I believed in this ideal, bought into the gospel preached and spread by the members of the church. Even after what I went through with Deacon Limus, I thought our crusade was just. I was so very wrong. I see now what our faith has become, and I hate it." Baldric looked at Zinnia, then to Salvia, with a fiery resolve in his deep azure eyes. "They used the teachings to control, manipulate, and deceive the people. They twisted the faithful into believing we were better than the other races, that the world belonged to us, and us alone. Now look at what we, the faithful, brought upon ourselves. We enslaved, persecuted, and murdered. For what? To have the Almighty One call for the Finis and end up as dust in the wind?" Shaking his head, he looked at the city once more. "This place should be left as it is, a reminder of what not to be, of what will happen if we stray from the true path."

Salvia approached Baldric and wrapped her hands around his bicep, causing him to startle. He turned his gaze from the city and looked at her. This wasn't exactly the embrace she wanted to give him, but she hoped it was enough to convey that she was here for him, should he only ask. Whatever he decided to do, she would help him see it through. To whatever end.

His eyes glossed as he hesitantly raised a hand and gently placed it over hers. The corner of his lip twitched, and he looked as if he were trying to hold back a frown. "I'm sorry," Baldric said with a soft croak, "but I wish to take leave of this place. Are you able to walk?"

"Por supuesto,"[2] Salvia replied, "I'm ready when you are."

He nodded once, and his grip tightened. After a deep breath he slid her hands lower, allowing them to wrap around his elbow, as if he wanted to keep her close. Salvia smiled softly and leaned into his arm, enjoying whatever this connection was that the two of them shared. She had never felt anything like it before and she didn't want it to end. They began down the path that Zinnia had scouted, the two of them in the lead and Zinnia following close behind. Just as she reported, the path was fairly straight with only a few narrow turns here and there.

In the silence of the ruined city, Salvia looked about as they walked, wanting to see everything that had been laid low. Homes lay in ruin, shops were toppled, and carts had been overturned. Even the most extravagant of statues now lay crumbled and destroyed, lost amidst the rubble. At least the ground was stable. With the tremors she had felt during the Finis, she had half expected to find the very ground itself had been fractured.

As they continued, something small and furry caught Salvia's attention. The item was wedged in the rubble. She signaled for her companions to stop as she headed over to see what it was. Once there, she knelt and discovered a small handmade black wolf doll. It was completely covered in pebbles and dust, but otherwise undamaged. Picking it up, she brushed it clean as best she could. Looking it over with a melancholy frown, she sighed. It would still need a proper

---

2    Spanish for *Of course*

washing but this would have to do.

"A child might be missing their doll somewhere outside the city." Zinnia said as she knelt beside Salvia. There was a startling amount of hope in her tone and when their eyes met, Zinnia gave her a small smile.

Salvia looked back at the doll, worry gnawing at her heart. "I hope so." She stood, holding the doll close to her chest, and returned to Baldric's side. The group then headed for the edge of the ruined city.

Near the walls that once surrounded the city, the gate they came through had toppled to the ground. The sight looked as if they had been torn from the powerful iron hinges by something not of this world. Portions of the wall around it still stood, though large fissures and slabs of missing stone peppered its remains. The light of the setting sun cast the land in an orange glow. From the other side of the wall, Salvia could hear the sounds of confused and terrified people growing with every step, and steeling herself for what lay ahead, they pressed on.

# OUR DEPARTURE

**P**EOPLE RUSHED THROUGH the panicked crowds, screaming the names of loved ones lost in the event. What remained of the citizens of Lumen Magnum were clustered together, demanding answers for what happened and swarming the remnants of the Cirine order's leadership.

A sudden commotion coursed through the crowd. People screamed and scurried in fear. As the masses parted, groups of angry elves, dwarves, and foreigners who were attempting to leave the city dotted the crowd. A group of elves pushed through the surge of bodies, likely intent on returning to their homes, wherever they may have been. Dwarves were entering the city in search of materials to fix broken-down carts by the gate. Salvia assumed they had claimed the carts to use as transportation. Many of the humans whose origins were clearly not of Marlela were headed for the port but had seemingly met resistance from citizens who were now barring their way.

Salvia stood, mouth agape in stunned silence. The people's reaction to the former slaves of Lumen Magnum was ridiculous. Many of them acted as though they had never even seen an elf, dwarf, or foreign human before. Before she knew it, the confusion started taking a turn toward violence. The citizens of Lumen Magnum began spewing venom at the former slaves, calling elves savages, murderers, and cannibals. They called the dwarves cursed folk and threw out jibes about their short, stout stature. Those who were human, and simply foreign to these lands, were accused of being thieves and scoundrels.

The people were scared and confused, and if this were allowed to continue, no good would come of it. Decades of resentment were about to boil over. Salvia's brows furrowed in annoyance as she tried to come up with a solution.

Glancing at Baldric and Zinnia, she found that Baldric was similarly annoyed by the reactions from his people. Zinnia looked to be downright furious. Her hands were balled into tight fists and her expression was scrunched in outrage. She stomped forward, glaring daggers at each and every person she passed and then bellowed, "What is wrong with you people?"

A hush fell upon the crowd. Elf, dwarf, and human alike turned to her, startled by the sudden outburst. They all wore puzzled expressions, unsure of how to respond. Zinnia then made her way to the elven group and pointed to the people on the other side of the crowd.

"Can you fools please move out of their way? They're just trying to go home!"

The people stared at her, dumbfounded. The elves blinked in disbelief. Having a human of all beings speak in their favor must've been unheard of. Eventually, after several tense moments of gawking, followed by hushed mumbling, the unexpected happened. Some of the people shrugged and moved aside.

"WAIT!" A man rushed forward, his face flushed red and a terrified expression on his face. "If we let them leave, what's to stop them from returning with an army? They'll kill us for sure! The Papa Regem—"

"The Papa Regem is gone!" Zinnia snapped, instantly silencing the fool. "Taken and punished for what he has done to each and every one of us!"

Gasps ran through the growing crowd. Some were steadily growing angry and soon another person stepped forward. They made the mistake of getting right into Zinnia's face. Salvia expected her to drop the man to the floor with a single blow, but to her surprise, Zinnia stood tall and maintained the composure of command.

"How would you know the Papa Regem is gone?" The man spat. "He's guided us—"

"That man guided us to damnation! LOOK!" She pointed to the ruined city, her voice strong and resilient. "Look what has befallen our city. Do you think this was some mere attack? Some accident?" Zinnia shook her head. "This is punishment for what he and his like brought to our faith. How they twisted it. Look what it has done to not just us, but to those whom he deemed lesser!"

The crowd staggered back, looking at each other for answers, and clearly unsure of what to believe. This was as understandable as it was frustrating. They didn't know about the Finis. They didn't understand why any of this was happening. Salvia may not have been on the surface to see all that had happened, but she was sure it must've been quite the spectacle. One moment they were going about their day and the next, everything they had known was in ruin. Even the village outside was gone. Everything they knew was destroyed. The person they had thought had all the answers had disappeared. All they had left was what was around them.

A rumble of commotion ran through the crowd. Something was happening at the gate next, and when Salvia looked, she found a Sacerdotis of all people, escorted by a small group of elves. He looked to be in pain as the elves doted on him, inspecting an injury on one of his hands. Before Salvia could get a better look at the man, the crowd swelled and congregated around the newcomers. The elves quickly placed themselves between the man and the oncoming crowd. They acted as protectors. It seemed today was a day for many firsts.

Zinnia made her way back to rejoin Salvia and Baldric, but Salvia couldn't take her attention away from the group. She wondered what could've happened between the Sacerdotis and the elves for such a bond to form that they would protect a member of the church.

"Give me a moment, you two." Zinnia said, catching Salvia's attention.

"Is everything alright?" She asked as Zinnia stepped past her.

The copper red-haired woman stopped and flashed Salvia a crooked smile, then placed a hand on her shoulder. "Of course, I just need to confirm something with that Sacerdotis. That's all. Nothing to be worried about." She patted Salvia on the shoulder and took her leave.

Salvia's mouth fell open, something about Zinnia seemed . . . different. However, before she had a chance to follow after her, a familiar voice called out. She and Baldric both spun around to find the origin of the voice and then, scanning the crowd, Salvia saw her king, Benigno Dali Cardona, of Cabreo in all his crimson and gold splendor.

A few young men stood at the king's side, which she quickly recognized as his three sons who looked just as baffled as her. Salvia didn't know they had traveled with their father to Lumen Magnum. Why, though? Anxiety crept into her chest.

She hadn't seen them since they had found her in the ruins of her fishing town, and now, she didn't know what to say.

The king waved, welcoming her to approach. Salvia hesitated for a moment, worried that the king might be angry with her for her sudden disappearance, but then again, why would he care? She was just some common woman who baked desserts and tended to farm animals. They were good desserts, sure, but not that good. Glancing to the king's left, to his youngest son, Prince Valerio Ignacio Cardona, he gave her an optimistic smile and nodded, silently telling her that everything was fine.

With a sigh of relief Salvia turned to Baldric, clutching Lorenzo's rose under her dresses. "Baldric, will you, um, be alright? On your own, I mean, I-I think I must—"

"I'll be alright." He smiled weakly and lightly shrugged. "I'll . . . be here."

Her heart skipped a beat. She didn't like the idea of leaving him alone, but she also didn't want to know what would happen if she kept her ruler waiting. King Benigno seemed kind, but he was still a ruler. Salvia exhaled uneasily and acquiesced. "A-Alright." She began walking but let her gaze lingered on Baldric a moment longer. "I'll be here. Right here."

He chuckled lightly. "Go on. I'll be fine. I promise."

Straightening her back and clutching the skirt of her dresses, she gave him a nod and vowed to herself to be quick, then spun around and made her way to join King Benigno. Once before the Cabreoan royal family, she bowed low in a curtsy, resisting the urge to glance back to where she left Baldric. "Su Majestad."[1]

The king placed a hand on his hip and wore a stern expression on his face.

---

1    Spanish for *Your Majesty*

"Nos diste bastante susto con tu acto de desaparición hace casi quince días."[2]

"Lo sé,"[3] Salvia replied, struggling to keep her voice calm. She felt guilty for not leaving anything to let them know where she had gone, especially after everything they had done for her, "y mis disculpas, su Majestad, algo . . . demandó mi atención."[4]

"Hmm." King Benigno went silent. Salvia cautiously looked up to meet his gaze but found he wasn't looking at her but to something behind her. Taking a quick peek, she saw he was looking at Baldric who was now speaking with a group of dwarves busily working to repair a cart.

"Pararse,[5] Salvia."

Salvia jumped to attention. King Benigno had turned his sight back to her. His jaw set and he raised a curious brow. "Debes haber tenido un buen viaje aquí, estoy equivocado?"[6]

Salvia tucked in her chin meekly, shaking her head.

"Entonces, puedo suponer que sabes lo que pasó aquí?"[7] The king continued, tilting his head lightly to one side.

Salvia squeezed the fabric of her dress, shut her eyes, and gave him a nod. A storm of nerves swirled in her gut. Was he upset? What would he think of her journey to Lumen Magnum? Would she believe her if she told him of Ultor, of Hevellum and Infernos? Surely it was clear that something not of this world had

2      Spanish for *You gave us quite the scare with your disappearance act almost a fortnight ago.*

3      Spanish for *I know*

4      Spanish for *and I'm sorry, your Majesty, something . . . demanded my attention.*

5      Spanish for *Stand*

6      Spanish for *You must've had quite a journey here, am I wrong?*

7      Spanish for *Then, am I to assume you know what happened here?*

happened, but still, it was a lot to process all at once.

"Muy bien, puedes regalarnos en nuestro viaje de regreso a Cabreo,"[8] he said, turning away, basically telling her that the conversation was over, however, she wasn't ready to leave just yet.

"Esperar, ahora?"[9] Salvia asked.

"Ahora sí."[10] A look of shock must've been plastered on her face because King Benigno's brows furrowed and frustration burned in his eyes as he moved toward her. He stopped inches in front of her, towering and looking down at her with an authoritative presence perfected from years of ruling. "Nos desapareciste, recibí amenazas de este lugar, incluso he—"[11]

"Padre."[12] Prince Alejandro Ignacio Cardona, the king's middle son, placed a hand on his father's shoulder and guided him back.

Salvia was scared, but she knew he was a kind king. The man was just venting. After all, he was likely used to knowing everything that transpired around him and something like the Finis would rattle anyone no matter how practiced they were at keeping their composure. Then there was what he had said, something about receiving threats. Well, whatever those threats were, if they came from this place, the people who issued them were likely already deeply entrenched in the thralls of Infernos and getting intimately acquainted with Ultor and the rest of demon kind.

King Benigno pinched the bridge of his nose, taking a deep breath, and then

---

8    Spanish for *Very well, you can regale us on our journey back to Cabreo.*
9    Spanish for *Wait, now?*
10   Spanish for *Yes now.*
11   Spanish for *You disappeared on us, I received threats from this place, I've even—*
12   Spanish for *Father.*

exhaled. "Perdón, Salvia, yo solo,"[13] he looked up at the ruins of Lumen Magnum, his gaze hardening with discomfort, "solo quiero irme de aquí."[14]

Alejandro then stepped forward, his chin held in his hand as he too inspected what was left of Lumen Magnum. "I have a proposition."

Salvia was taken aback, having not expected him to speak in Anglicus, and so perfectly at that. She had no idea he even knew the language.

He glanced at her with a smirk, winked, then turned to address his father. "I'll be speaking in Anglicus from here on. You still need practice." King Benigno frowned and looked displeased, but Alejandro simply chuckled with amusement. "I know the language, why don't I stay behind? I could help the people rebuild. Maybe even facilitate a transfer of power." Alejandro said with a shrug. "It would be a start toward healing our countries' relations, which is sorely needed after what they were trying to attempt."

Salvia's pulse quickened again. Just what was Lumen Magnum trying to do? She hoped they weren't on the brink of war, but then again, it didn't really matter.

King Benigno sighed. "A-Are you sure?" His words came slow and uneasy. Anglicus clearly didn't come easy for him and his words were so heavily accented Salvia wasn't sure if the Lumen Magnum people would even understand him.

"Yes, Father. Just leave me some guards and I'll make sure to send letters every fortnight."

King Benigno looked at his oldest son, Prince Miguel Ignacio Cardona, who confidently nodded at his brother. Valerio, the youngest of the three, did the same. With a defeated sigh, King Benigno nodded in acceptance. He then approached Alejandro and opened his arms wide, embracing his son and whispered something

13     Spanish for *Excuse me, Salvia, I just.*

14     Spanish for *I want to take leave of this place.*

into his ear. A chuckle escaped Alejandro's lips, and the two tapped their foreheads together, wishing each other well.

The king then released his son and paused, turning his attention back to Salvia. She stood at attention. King Benigno glanced past her only briefly and commanded, "Say your farewells." He then left with his sons to rejoin his guards, camped far from the people of Lumen Magnum, probably to avoid trouble from the Marlelains.

Salvia rubbed her temples and finally let her shoulders relax. She hadn't expected to be leaving so soon. After everything she, Baldric, and Zinnia had gone through together, she hoped to stay with them a while. Salvia wanted a reprieve, to get to know them better and to maybe even get a glimpse of who they would become. She had noticed the change within them, but it seemed she wasn't meant to watch as they grew and flourished in this new environment full of possibility.

"Salvia?" A hand landed on her shoulder. She turned and to her relief found Zinnia. "Sorry, I didn't mean to startle you. Is everything alright?"

Salvia's mouth hung agape. For some reason she couldn't bring herself to answer. She wanted to tell Zinnia that she would be returning to Cabreo on her king's orders, but that would mean having to explain everything again once they found Baldric, and she wasn't sure she could do so without breaking into tears. So, she clamped her mouth closed, forced a smile, and nodded.

Zinnia's brows pinched for a moment. Salvia could tell she didn't believe her but was thankful she didn't press the subject. "Well, it looks like Soror Fidei Heather came by. Baldric has Rose."

"What?" Salvia exclaimed.

Zinnia laughed softly and stepped aside, pointing in the distance where

Baldric held Rose in his arms. Salvia's heart swelled with warmth. It felt like a flower bloomed to life in her chest. She was beyond glad to see the young girl safe and, as promised, returned to them. Her feet began moving on their own, ferrying her forward to see the young girl before she had to leave.

Just as Salvia was nearing Baldric and Rose, she felt a sudden tug of her dress, causing her to shriek in surprise. Spinning around, she was taken aback to see a young boy staring up at her with tear-stained cheeks. He pointed shakily up to the hand at her side. "That-That wolf is mine."

"Oh?" Salvia had completely forgotten about the wolf doll in her hand. The thing was still grayed from being covered in rubble and dust. She had hoped to clean it before finding its owner, but here he was in front of her.

Raising her gaze to the boy, she was surprised to see the welling tears in his eyes. There was no telling what the child had been through today, but it was plain to see he was scared. It must've been horrifying in the city. She recalled the bells and shaking of the world. Whatever happened on the surface, he had been there and seen it. She gave him the warmest smile she could and knelt before the boy, handing him the wolf doll. "There's no need to be afraid. Here you go."

"Tommen there you are!"

The boy jumped. Behind him was now an older boy of at least ten. Salvia's eyes shot wide with recognition. He was the boy being publicly abused by his father when she entered the city. A few bruises marked his otherwise fair face, but his brown eyes were bright and his dark hair tousled messily.

He gave Tommen a stern look. "I thought I said not to leave my side." The older boy scolded, then looked at Salvia, and bowed. "I'm sorry if he has bothered you, miss."

"Oh! Not at all, I was giving him his wolf back. Here." Salvia poked the nose of the doll to Tommen's, which only served to startle him.

He was stunned for a moment as he stared at Salvia, but then his lips stretched to a wide, beaming grin and his arms wrapped around the doll, hugging it tightly. Wiping away some of the rebellious tears that rolled down his cheeks, he hid the bottom half of his face behind his doll. "Thank you." Tommen said shyly and slowly drew closer to Salvia. She straightened herself, not really sure what he wanted. All of a sudden he leaped into her chest, wrapping his arms around her neck, and sobbed tears of joy. Salvia gasped and let out a fit of surprised laughter. She nearly lost her balance and when she found her composure, she happily embraced Tommen in return, giving him a tight squeeze before letting him go.

Hearing the approach of footsteps, Salvia looked up to see Heather making her way through the crowd, waving as their eyes connected. A smile burst across Salvia's face. She gently nudged Tommen toward the older boy who abruptly told the little one not to wonder again.

Tommen nodded excitedly and squeezed his doll against his chest. "Yes, Petro. I promise."

Petro rolled his eyes with a smirk and took Tommen's hand, walking to join Heather. The old woman gently tousled Petro's hair, and the three continued on, heading in the direction of the Sacerdotis who was now sat by the gate with the entourage of elves.

Salvia was overjoyed to see the boys were safe, safe in the hands of the woman who Salvia was sure would take good care of them and all the children orphaned by the event. She wasn't sure how the little ones would feel having lost their parents: confusion, elation, sadness, anger. So long as they were safe, surely they would be able to move forward and live pain free lives.

"I hope everything went well with your king." A voice said. Salvia recognized it instantly. She spun around to Baldric accompanied by Zinnia, but her smile wavered as she remembered her time here was limited.

"I-I suppose." Her lips trembled. He had clearly noticed her trepidation, and quickly, his smile faded.

"You have to leave, don't you?" He asked, his tone somber.

She swallowed her nerves, her throat tightening. Salvia found it difficult to find her voice and then she noticed Rose. The little girl looked back and forth between the two, then wriggled out of Baldric's arms. She rushed up to Salvia and wrapped her tiny arms around her knees.

Placing a hand on Rose's back, she forced herself to meet Baldric's dark azure eyes and searched for how to answer. Her eyes stinging, she said, "Sí,[15] it seems there are things I must answer for."

"Answer for?" Baldric asked with a bit of a raised tone. His and Zinnia's expressions grew serious and confused. "But you didn't do anything wrong!"

"What? Oh . . ." Salvia slammed her face into her hands, cheeks glowing red and realizing she had messed up her wording. "No, no wait. Um . . . maldita sea,[16] I said it wrong." Removing her hands she took a deep breath and cleared her throat. "Perdón,[17] without Ultor as my translator, it's harder to converse in your people's Anglicus. Fortunately, he taught me much before departing."

Baldric sighed with relief and let out a soft chuckle. "So, what you meant to say is your king has questions that only you can answer. Am I correct?"

---

15    Spanish for *Yes*
16    Spanish for *Damn/Dammit*
17    Spanish for *Excuse me*

Salvia nodded, her heart squeezing in a pang of sadness. She looked down at Rose again and gave the child a weak smile, softly caressing her midnight black hair.

"I see, I understand." Baldric said, a hint of longing edged into his tone. He cleared his throat then stepped to the side, gesturing to the dwarves Salvia had seen him with before. "Salvia, if you don't mind, can you speak with your king about helping these good folk return to their home? They lived in the Buio Forest up north before . . ." His face paled and his jaw abruptly set. "Anyway, your journey should pass there on the way to Cabreo. It would mean a lot to me if—"

"Oh, claro,[18] that shouldn't be a problem." Salvia smiled warmly at the group of dwarves who were all watching with various, unreadable expressions on their faces. She bowed her head in greetings and addressed them. "Cabreo has good relations with dwarves. I'm sure King Benigno will gladly see you home." She then returned to Baldric. "Ojalá,[19] with all that's happened here today, many things will be changing. I'm sure of it."

"Yes, I believe they will." Baldric responded assuredly. He then quickly glanced past her, and when she turned to see what had caught his attention, she noticed King Benigno in the distance. "What is your king planning, if you don't mind me asking?"

Salvia pat Rose on the back, signaling for her to release the embrace. "The king's, cóomo se dice?[20] Middle son, Prince Alejandro, will remain behind with his guards for protection. He knows your language. I think he hopes to act as a bridge between both countries. Please," she tilted her head with a soft smile, "try to make

18    Spanish for *Oh, dear*
19    Spanish for *Hopefully*
20    Spanish for *How do you say it?*

his stay as comfortable as possible. The king agreed to send supplies to aid you and your people *through* Prince Alejandro."

"That's good news, Salvia, thank you." Zinnia said. She then took a deep breath, stepped forward, and hugged Salvia tight. The gesture caught her completely by surprise. "Thank you for all that you've done," Zinnia whispered, "and . . . I'm sorry for how I've treated you." With that, Zinnia let her go and pulled away, standing at arm's length. "Please, have a safe journey home. I hope we'll see each other again." Zinnia placed a hand over her chest and bowed in farewell. Wasting no time, she then stood and returned to the Sacerdotis, undoubtedly to spread the good news.

Baldric and Salvia now found themselves alone, save for Rose who clung to his trousers. Salvia fiddled anxiously with her thumbs, nowhere near ready to say farewell, least of all to him.

"Do you—" They both started in unison. A pause followed and both broke into a chuckle of embarrassment.

"You first." Baldric gestured and grinned.

"Oh, um," she licked her lips. They felt like sandpaper and butterflies filled her stomach. She couldn't tear her gaze off of him. Her cheeks flushed. "You're welcome to come with me, you know?"

"What?" His eyes flashed wide as if he hadn't even considered this an option.

Doubt seeped into her thoughts. Did he not want to come? Had she made a mistake? Salvia cleared her throat and said it again. "You could, si quieres,[21] come with me to Cabreo. It's much different than Marlela. It could be a good place . . . to start anew." The words just poured out. She was afraid of his answer but even

---

21    Spanish for *If you want*

if he said no, at least she could rest easily in the knowledge that she had tried to postpone their separation.

He silently stared at her for a long moment and his expression betrayed nothing of what he was thinking, but eventually, he answered. "I . . . I don't know that I can. Just yet, at least."

Salvia's smile faded, but she refused to let a frown spoil their goodbyes. No matter how disappointed she was in his rejection, she wanted this to be a happy moment. Her silence dragged on for an uncomfortable amount of time. She knew that, but there was a terrible feeling in the back of her mind that she might never see him, or any of them, again. The thought hit her like a cold splash of water, and she quickly forced it away. Salvia couldn't think like that. She wouldn't. She needed to be strong, especially for him—for them. In a way, she understood what he was saying. Though he hadn't directly said it, she knew that he wished to be part of reshaping his nation, and in light of that, her request was a little selfish.

"Alright," she finally said, holding her head high. She filled her thoughts with just who he might become. How he might guide the people of this land. She was proud of him and who he was becoming. When she removed her wants from the equation, focused on what he could do for the people, the hope in his purpose, it helped her summon back her warmth, and her smile soon returned. "Por qué no usamos[22] this time to discover who you are, and what you want. Lead your people well."

"I think," Baldric started, but paused as if figuring out what exactly he wanted to say, "my place is here. For now. I was complacent in my faith, ignoring the wrongdoing of those around me. I need to help my people find the right path,

---

22    Spanish for *Why not use*

set an example of how things *should* be."

Salvia was glad to hear him finally say it aloud. His presence would be a boon to the survivors of Lumen Magnum. She raised her hand to Baldric's cheek and brushed a thumb across his skin. "Do what you feel is right, and take good care of yourself. I know you'll do great things for your people." Her expression softened as she looked into his eyes. "And once you're done, you know where I'll be."

Sliding her fingers away, she looked down at Rose and knelt to her, opening her arms wide for a final embrace. The girl's lips trembled, and she jumped into Salvia's arms. They held each other as tightly as they could. Despite the tears rising behind her eyelids, Salvia promised herself she wouldn't cry. This wouldn't be a sad farewell. This was the start of a brighter future, and she would see them again.

Sliding her hands atop Rose's shoulders, she pulled away and tapped the little girl on the nose. "Take care of Baldric for me, alright?"

Rose nodded quickly and though tears flowed down her pale cheeks, she looked hopeful for the first time since they had met. Feeling her tears about to break her inner walls, she stood up and turned to walk away, but Baldric caught her uninjured hand and as he did, a burst of lightning surged from his touch. Salvia turned to him with a sharp gasp, her eyes wide with surprise.

"Write to me," he said hastily, a yearning carrying on his voice. "Let me know that you are well. I will do the same. I promise."

Salvia's heart thumped with joy. What a wonderful idea, she thought. As she turned to look back at him, she could no longer hold back her sorrow of their parting and nodded in agreement. "Sí, of course."

Baldric then let her go and with nothing left to be said between them, Salvia slid her fingers free and continued on. She wanted desperately to look back as she walked but dared not to. Were she to give in, to look upon them once more, she might not have the strength to leave. For them, she might very well spur a king and that wouldn't be wise, no matter how kind a man he seemed.

As she walked through the thinned crowd toward King Benigno, she raised the hand Baldric had grasped to her chest. The sensation of his touch was . . . odd, but equally wonderful. She was certain, now more than ever, they would meet again one day. It might be months, or even years, but she would relish the day that they would be together again.

Feeling a presence joining her stride, she looked about and found that the dwarves Baldric had introduced her to were now walking beside her. She smiled at one of them, his hair a fiery red and curly to boot. The dwarf grunted at her in recognition. It was clear that he and the others with him had gone through terrible trials to have survived this place. Hopefully, those dreadful days were behind them.

Her mind couldn't help but remain with Baldric, little Rose, and Zinnia. It had been a long time since she had prayed, not since before the fall of Marineros, but she felt a renewed urgency to return to that practice. Looking up at the setting sky with contentment, Salvia whispered to not only Calamar but to the Almighty One as well, to every single deity that she had ever heard of, and asked them to watch over her friends, to guide them as well as they could. Until next they met.

# OUR LIFE

S ALVIA DUG HER HANDS deep into the dirt. It was surprisingly cool despite the beaming sun's warmth in the bright blue sky above. The soil spread between her fingers as she pulled her hands toward her, leaving small trenches in her wake. More and more the dirt piled up. Fall was only a couple of weeks away and she needed to get the crops out of the ground and cured for storage.

After a while, Salvia found the reddish brown rough flesh of the sweet potatoes and grinned. "There you are." Grabbing hold of her gardening fork, she made quick work of the remaining soil so she could easily remove the vegetables, roots and all.

As she took hold of the oddly lumpy thing, she paused, staring at the faded, twelve-pointed, star-shaped scar on her right hand. A wave of melancholy washed over her. It had been twenty years since she activated the Finis on Lumen Magnum, and two anxiety-inducing years since she had received word from Baldric or any of her other friends in the now newly built town they simply called Lumen.

Not a letter. Not a visitor. Nothing.

The last bit of news she received was from a dwarven messenger who she had become quite acquainted with. Baldric had warned her to stay away. That he would send word as soon as things calmed down. But he didn't elaborate on just what was happening, on what the danger was. His message was short and to the point as if there had been little time to say more. Patience was difficult, but she trusted in Baldric. If he told her to stay away, she would.

In the following months she had worried but remained optimistic. However, as time dragged on, she found her thoughts lingering on the endless possibilities as to why he hadn't sent word again. Keeping busy helped to quell the dread looming in the recesses of her mind, and so she toiled away with this and that, hoping that one day a letter would arrive to set her worries to rest.

Her brows pinched together heavily. With the gardening fork still in hand, she dug the teeth into the dirt with a frustrated groan. Again she had forgotten to wear an apron to protect her lavender dress, an increasingly common occurrence she would scold herself for later, and so clutched the fabric in hand. Keeping busy had stopped being an effective distraction some time ago. Her mind was too focused on her friends.

She wanted to know so badly what was going on that she had taken a trip all the way to Zarago, the capital of Cabreo, to speak with King Benigno, hopeful that he might know something, anything about the state of Lumen and their council leaders. It was a wasted trip. All he said was that his son, Prince Alejandro, had sent no word of trouble and thus assumed all was well. He instantly ended the conversation there and went about other tasks. He had been doing that a lot lately.

With a sigh, Salvia pictured what each of her friends might've looked like now. Rose would've grown into a woman. Would she even recognize her now? Baldric, likely having perfected the look of a stoic, strong leader, might've grown a beard. Zinnia was probably still the most imposing visage of strength but had hopefully softened some in her intensity. Heather had died some years ago, but she had a full life and helped so many children over the years. In one of his letters, Baldric had simply said it was her time.

She was then surprised by a pair of familiar voices, raising arguments she had heard countless times before. They belonged to a pair of twin dwarven siblings, brother and sister. To her right, to the edge of the Buio Forest which skirted her home and that of the Ringiovanire Lake several feet behind her, were the two dwarves.

They looked so similar it would've been difficult to tell them apart were it not for the brother's long, distinct beard that ran down his chest and his sister whose sideburns were always neatly brushed and curled beautifully. Both were a little over four feet tall and had the stoutest of builds.

They were arguing about whose turn it was to cook the evening dinner. The siblings always brought a smile to her face, and she was happy to have their company.

Eomir, the brother twin who swore he had seniority due to being born a lofty two seconds first, raised a hand and pressed his index finger firmly to Eowyn, his sister's lips. While the gesture stopped her from speaking it was clear upon her face that he would pay for it. He paid her no mind, instead looking at Salvia with a wide grin and clearly enjoying his sister's frustrated pout. "Oi, Salvia, how ye be?"

Salvia laughed and turned to face them while still knelt on the ground. She then noticed the sizable wooden wheelbarrow Eomir was pushing. "I'm good. Just tending to the harvest. Are you here to pull the fish net from the lake?"

Eowyn shoved her brother's hand away and swiftly kicked him square in the backside, then smiled mischievously. "Ye know it. We'll make sure not to cause *too* much trouble for ye." She gave Salvia a wink just as Eomir countered by pushing his sister's arm away, picking up the wheelbarrow, and continuing toward the lake, grumbling all the while.

Salvia shook her head and stifled a laugh. If the two had heard her react, their rivalry would've become a competition, lasting long into the night and there were still things to be done. She returned to pulling her vegetables from her small garden. As much as she was worried about her friends in Lumen, there was little she could do about it. The best she could do for them was to take care of herself, and that meant getting these vegetables pulled before the Fall snow fell.

Just as she bent forward to continue her work, a golden glint caught in the light. Her rose slipped out of her dress. Salvia startled, thinking her necklace would fall into the dirt, but the gold chain still held after all this time. She slowly spun the intricately crafted rose between her index finger and thumb. The memory of Lorenzo washed over her like a warm embrace.

An old song she hadn't heard in ages drifted through her mind, and without realizing when she had started, Salvia hummed the tune. She dropped the necklace back inside her dress and then returned to the vegetables and herbs of the garden. It could've been a peaceful afternoon. Unfortunately, she had made the mistake of ignoring the twins. The longer she tried to keep to herself, the louder it seemed their arguing became. She finally glanced behind to see what the fuss was about when she heard yelling.

"Will ye stop pulling!" Eowyn exclamed. "It's stuck on something, ye'll break the net if ye keep that up."

Eomir rolled his eyes with so much exaggeration it was a miracle he didn't completely topple over. "Da made this net. I doubt a simple twig could break a rope this thick."

The rope looked to be straining against something near the water and as Eomir braced again to pull, Eowyn grabbed at the net and yanked in the opposite direction. "When I said break, I didn't mean *break*. I meant it'll come undone ye dolt!"

"Don't call me a—"

Salvia giggled as she stood up, brushing the dirt from her hands and wiping her palms on the lavender skirt of her dress. "Honestly, if you put as much effort into working as you do arguing, you two could accomplish anything." She then made her way over to them, tying up her skirt before wading into the lake. "I've met deities that are more cooperative than you."

The siblings looked at each other for a moment, brows raised as if pondering what Salvia was suggesting, but quickly turned their heads away in frustration. The sheer determination in their opposition made her chuckle.

The water came up to her knees. Salvia bent to one side and saw the rope became more taut the further into the water it went. Ignoring the flopping fish caught inside the net, she spotted the problem.

"Ah, here it is." Salvia said as she reached inside the water, grabbed hold of what felt like a twig with both hands, and snapped it. She pulled both pieces from the mud and water and held the stick to the twins. "There, that should do it, go ahead and—"

Eomir immediately pulled an ax from his belt, face snarling, and looked as if he were preparing to attack. Salvia and Eowyn startled, but as they turned, Salvia's entire being went rigid at the sight, her eyes panning to a figure only a short distance away. The man's face was hidden within the shadow of his hood but seemed incredibly familiar.

"Please wait!" The man pleaded. Leather-gloved hands flew into the air to either side of his head. A deep violet cloak billowed in the breeze, revealing glimpses of a sword and dagger firmly sheathed in holsters at his waist. "I'm a friend."

Everything suddenly went silent. The moment seemed to stretch on for a lifetime as if time simply stopped. Salvia's heart didn't beat. The ripples in the water's surface went still. Even the twins had gone uncharacteristically silent. Then, as the sands of time began to correct themselves, the man's bright brown mare nickered and lazily trotted to the water and began to drink.

Salvia's breath refused to return. Her eyes were wide, and she stared at the man. He couldn't possibly be—No. She refused to even allow herself that spark of hope because if she did and she was wrong, she couldn't bear it.

The man's posture relaxed, his fingers curling in and out as though his hands were sore from a hard ride. He then slowly raised his hands to his hood and slid the fabric back. Silver hair caught in the wind, tied back at the nape of his neck save for a few loose strands brushing against the side of his face. He had a rugged face, worn from years of harrowed experience. He had a beard, neatly trimmed, surrounding a bare patch where hair couldn't grow over the scar crossing over his thin lips.

Salvia's breath hitched. If it were possible for her heart to punch a hole in her chest, it would've. "Baldric?" She whispered.

His lips stretched into a wide smile. "It has been awhile, hasn't it, Salvia?"

Her eyes burned with tears. She lifted large handfuls of her skirt out of the water and rushed to him, stumbling as she did, but Salvia didn't care. Baldric was here. He was actually here, of all places, standing right in front of her. As soon as she reached the dry land, she ran and nearly crashed into him with excitement. Her arms wrapped around his neck, tears streaming down her cheeks. His arms felt warm and strong as they wrapped around her waist. His face buried into her neck.

"I can't believe it." Salvia croaked as she stared into the slowly graying sky. "Baldric. You're here. You're really here!" Her hands tangled in his cloak and gripped the fabric tight, trying and failing to hold back her sobs. "Why—" Her throat tightened. "Why did you stop writing to me? I was so worried when Balin came with your message." Salvia slid her hands up his back to his shoulders, holding him tightly as she pushed him back to arm's length, eyes wide and staring into his face. "Baldric, what happened to you these past two years?"

He didn't meet her gaze, his eyes instead locked on the ground almost as if he was unable to look at her. Her brows curved, desperately trying to understand just what was wrong. His shoulders trembled under her palms, catching her by surprise and sending a bolt of dread into her chest. Before she could react, he grabbed at her dress and pulled her back into the embrace once more.

Salvia let out a sharp gasp, startled by his dejected silence. Something terrible had happened, she knew it. She was terrified of what could've possibly caused him such anguish and desperately wanted to know, but the last thing she would do would be to force it out of him. When he was ready to talk, she would listen, so in the meantime, she slid her hands up his back and latched onto his shoulders, focusing only on this moment.

Something moved in the lake behind her. Salvia then remembered the twins and their net of fish that they had been working at freeing. Water splashed and the sound of heavy boots sunk into the ground with wet squishes. A series of grunts were followed by a loud thump. She assumed the siblings had managed to get the net out of the water and loaded onto the wheelbarrow. She should've probably said something to them, but Baldric hadn't yet let her go so she would patiently wait.

"Oi, Salvia!" Eomir bellowed, completely ignoring the moment they were having. "We got the fishes out. Come grab your share when you and your friend are—OW!"

A giggle slipped from Salvia's lips. As Baldric's grip on her lessened, she let him go and slid back to find a crooked smile on his face. Turning to the siblings, she shot them a grin. "Thank you, I'll come by early this evening." She curtsied in farewell to the twins who both bowed with smiles of their own.

Eomir grabbed the wheelbarrow and pushed it into the forest, letting out a tired groan as Eowyn scolded him. Salvia shook her head and laughed sweetly at the pair. Those two wouldn't change anytime soon.

"You've done well for yourself, haven't you, Salvia?"

Salvia turned to Baldric and her heart began to flutter. She felt the heat burning in her cheeks as she bashfully fidgeted with her hands. "Yes I have, thanks to his Majesty, of course."

"That's right, you're an ambassador now for Cabreo. I should greet you properly for one of your station." He took a step back and bowed with exaggerated flair.

Salvia was so taken by surprise that her laughter came out as snorts. He had never been so playful before. It was a nice surprise. Shortly after she had returned to Cabreo and recounted everything to King Benigno and his sons about her travel to Lumen Magnum, Ultor, and the Finis, the king appointed Salvia as an ambassador of Cabreo to the dwarves that now lived in Buio Forest. Before the day of the Finis, she and King Benigno had no idea that the Papa Regem had enslaved all the dwarves of the region before Atabey's Mountains just north of the forest.

Lightly pushing Baldric's shoulder, she was barely even able to get him to budge and exclaimed with embarrassment, "Oh stop, it's not like I'm a noble or anything."

Baldric laughed, and the sound was like sweet honey to her ears. Gently locking her fingers in his, she stared into the pools of his eyes, and as his laughter quieted, they fell into each other, their foreheads touching. Her heart wouldn't stop pounding against her chest, but she didn't care, it was exhilarating. She wanted to enjoy his company for as long as possible.

"Come, sit with me." Salvia pulled Baldric toward the edge of the lake as he patted his horse's back. The creature neighed happily and trotted by the water.

Once Salvia stopped, she took a deep breath and took in the vastness of Ringiovanire Lake before her. It had been a long time since she heard from him, and there was no telling what had happened to him in those years, but she hoped to make this meeting as relaxing and pleasant as possible. Letting go of Baldric's hand, she knelt, spreading the fabric of her dress so it wouldn't bunch, and softly fell backward onto the soft green grass.

Gently closing her eyes, she focused her breathing, deeply inhaling then exhaling. She couldn't let her excitement get the better of her. It was best to let things progress one small step at a time.

Opening her eyes once more, Salvia turned to Baldric and caught the briefest of smiles as it faded from his face. He was staring out past the lake. Propping herself on her elbows, she followed his gaze and saw massive storm clouds gathering over the horizon. It was a strange sight for this time of year, but if there was to be rain, it was still far off.

Baldric's expression turned troublingly dour. His hands shook at his sides. Something had him worried, that much she had already gleamed. Swallowing, Salvia mustered up her courage and asked, "Baldric, why did you suddenly stop writing to me?"

His gaze never left the horizon. The stoicism he once wore in youth had softened with the many years they had been apart. He sighed with his entire being.

Eventually Baldric sat down beside her and began to answer. "After you departed with your King to return to Cabreo, things . . . actually went well for a time. You remember that Sacerdotis who exited the city a bit after us? He was accompanied by a group of elves."

Salvia tilted her head to the side, trying to recall that chaotic day, and the man's face slowly came to mind. "Vaguely."

"His name is Osgar Gentile Nardovino. He's like you."

"Like me?" Salvia sat up, unsure of Baldric's meaning.

He grinned and chuckled expectantly, then finally turned his head to look at her. "Yes, he had been a host for a demon as well."

"Oh. Hmm, I think I had my suspicions at the time, but I hadn't really thought about him much since."

"How so?"

"Before the crowd surrounded him, after Zinnia told them what for." She chuckled softly but stopped as Baldric's face fell sullen. "That man, Osgar, looked to be in pain and had a bloodied hand like mine." Salvia looked down and brushed her fingers through the blades of grass. "I was told there were other hosts but didn't expect to see any once I'd entered the city. We all had our own goals. Our own paths to take, our own temples to reach."

"Mhm," Baldric nodded, "Osgar said something similar. It was through Zinnia that I got to know him. As you know it was also thanks to him that we were able to move past what happened and created a council to run the town. He's surprisingly quite the patient man. Everything went well, for a time." His eyes narrowed briefly, but there was a strange air of relief about Baldric. Salvia wondered if he had been glad there was someone from the original order that he could actually trust after all. His eyes then hardened. "Sadly, a massive group of Templar Equitums who'd been stationed at the northern border came down and changed everything."

Salvia's heart stilled. How could she have forgotten about the soldiers stationed at the Cabreo checkpoint? "Did my letter not find you before they arrived?"

"What do you mean?" Baldric asked with a look of shock.

"Th-The king and I both sent letters. Mine to you and his to Prince Alejandro, warning of what might be headed your way. When a few months passed with no response, I sent a letter with Balin to make sure you were alright."

"I met with Balin briefly, but he couldn't have arrived at a worse time. Fearing for his life, I asked him to leave." Baldric paused for a moment, then looked away. "I was afraid of what those knights might do if they found him. So I rushed him away so quickly he must not have had time to give me the message. All I had time to tell him was to not worry you, that things were growing complicated, but I would send word when the situation resolved." His fingers curled into a tight fist, leather gloves screeching. "Unfortunately, that time never came. As for the letters from you and the king, we received none."

All the air left Salvia's lungs. Her head felt dizzy. What happened to the rider who was carrying those earlier letters? She clenched the rose under her dress, struggling for what to say. "Baldric . . . I'm so sorry."

He snorted. "Why are you sorry?"

"Because . . . those knights came down from the north because of King Benigno. He demanded they leave their post at the border. Due to his experience with the Papa Regem and everything that transpired on the day of the Finis, he didn't trust them to remain within his lands. He demanded they leave immediately. They refused of course, and a small skirmish ensued." She fidgeted, finding it impossible to sit still as she recalled the battle. Blades clashed. The world was painted crimson with blood. Battlecries echoed through the valley. "Their numbers were great, but they were no match for the might of the Cabreoan army. As they waited for reinforcements who would never come, we quickly overpowered them. King Benigno commanded the survivors to disperse. He *hoped* they would leave to live out normal lives. That's when we wrote to you both, hoping our concerns would not come to pass, that they wouldn't return to Lumen." She sighed, troubled by the possibilities of what those men did when they returned home. "When we received no word of trouble, the king thought his hopes had come to fruition. . . I didn't hold the same sentiment, but alone I could do nothing."

Baldric was quiet for a moment. Salvia grew increasingly anxious the longer he said nothing. When she looked at him, he watched the waters gently roll up the muddy bank, his only movement an index finger tapping at the bottom of his knee. "That explains it then."

Salvia startled. "What? Explains what?"

He turned to her again, and it seemed he found his familiar stoic expression that until now, seemed lost. She must've looked utterly terrified because he reached out and took the hand that was clutching Lorenzo's rose and held it gently in his. "The General that led them, when he arrived, he personally sought for *me*. He knew me by name, but the man never disclosed how. I believe your message did make it to Lumen, just not to me."

Finally finding her breath, Salvia let out a gasp while shaking her head. "I'm . . . I'm so sorry I—"

As she cupped his hand in hers, Baldric gently placed two fingers over her lips, silencing her apology. His dark azure eyes glanced down to her lips, stilling her breath once more.

After all this time, all these years, Salvia knew her feelings for Baldric had only grown. This was unlike anything she had ever felt for Lorenzo, or anyone else for that matter. It was as if every letter nourished her soul, feeding a part of her that knew, despite their distance or chosen paths in life, they were meant to be together, and these last two years of silence left a hollow ache that nothing in this world or the next could fill.

Baldric withdrew his fingers from her lips. She felt silly. It wasn't the time to dwell on her feelings. There would be time for that later. He then slid his knuckles against her cheeks. His touch was as delicate as it was intoxicating, and she could've gotten lost in that moment for hours.

"Don't apologize," he said softly. "There's no need, there never was. I'm glad you tried, I really am."

Unsure of how to respond, Salvia chose to remain quiet, looking at him with shaky eyes. She needed to know what happened in Lumen, and why Baldric was here now.

"Two years ago, when they showed up, they demanded answers. They wanted to know what happened to the Papa Regem and to their city." He slid his hand from her face but left the other wrapped between her palms. "The people were understandably terrified. Osgar, Zinnia, and the rest of the Council ran the town and did their best to quell the soldiers' anger, but that damn General would hear none of it. We had even just brokered peace with the elves and established trade." He paused, his frustration and sorrow showing heavily on his face. "Fights broke out. Few at first, but with increasing frequency as time passed. The people were growing scared. Some even suggested allowing the knights to run things, hoping the violence would finally stop if only we gave them what they wanted, but others opposed, saying that would only make things worse. Those arguments happened quite often, actually. Words turned to yells, then became something else entirely . . ."

Baldric went quiet. Salvia's heart pounded as his eyes glossed with tears. She raised a hand to his face, gently wiping the tears away from his cheeks with a finger. His head hung low, his eyes staring unfocused at their hands held within each other.

"Civil war broke out . . ." he started quietly, his lips pulling back into a pained snarl, "just as that bastard thrust his sword into Zinnia's stomach."

Salvia's breath hitched in her throat. Zinnia was . . . dead? No, that couldn't be. Eyes welling, Salvia could just barely remember the copper red-haired woman's form. Her strong posture. Determined emerald green eyes. Zinnia had ever been silent in their time together, but in Baldric's letters, she became so much more. She was always resilient and reliable, but in those twenty years she became caring and levelheaded. How could she be gone? No way did they endure so much to end so suddenly, so violently. Tears fell freely from Salvia's eyes.

Fear then struck her like an arrow to the heart as another name entered her mind. A little girl whose world was taken from her all those years ago, who found a new family in Heather and the orphans turned brothers and sisters. Salvia flew to Baldric, grabbing onto his shoulders. He must've known what she was about to ask as before the words could pour from her mouth, he turned his head with a look so cold and sorrowful it could've made the dead shiver. Her heart sank, but he hadn't answered her. She clung to the tiny spark of hope that perhaps she might still be alive. Maybe Baldric's visit was a plea for aid. "What of Rose? What happened to her?"

Baldric remained silent.

Her pulse thundered in her ears, muscles tightening and throat scratchy with anxious anticipation. With a trembling breath, he finally answered. "Two years . . . two long years we tried to fight them. To hold them back, but not everyone was a warrior. Not everyone knew how to fight."

Salvia could hear the tightness in Baldric's voice. This must've been hard for him, recounting the horrors he'd had to suffer after spending so many years trying to pick up the pieces of that fallen city. Moving her hands to his cheeks, she cupped his face in her hands, gently wiping the tears from his skin.

His eyes remained closed as he took a breath and continued. "Eventually, Osgar made the difficult but practical choice to flee Lumen. To flee north to the safety of Cabreo with Prince Alejandro and as many survivors as we could find. Just before we left—as we were finishing preparations—Rose . . . she came rushing, trying to warn us of the knights headed our way." He took a sharp breath. His voice and body trembled violently. "Just as she reached me. Just as I saw the panicked look on Rose's face and tried to hear the fearful message she'd bravely rushed to deliver—" Baldric clenched his hands and teeth, sadness and regret clear on his troubled brow. "That moment will remain with me until my last day." His voice was so soft. "I heard the twang of the arrow as it was loosed, but I wasn't fast enough to stop it . . . it struck her in the back!"

Salvia could no longer find her breath. Her body went rigid and the little sliver of hope that she had been holding on to turned to ash. This—This was more than she could bear.

"An endless hail of arrows followed," Baldric continued, "raining down and cutting off any chance of reaching her. I watched as the fear on Rose's face turned to confusion and then a blank horrible stare. Her body went limp. And I was powerless to do a thing." His voice cracked and quieted to little more than a whisper. "The color drained from her face, and I saw the moment her life vanished from her hazel green eyes. I couldn't even take her with us. To give her the funeral she deserved. She trusted me to keep her safe, and I-I FAILED HER!"

Baldric bent forward, curling in on himself and head lightly touching the ground as if seeking forgiveness. His face slipped from her hands. All she could do was stare at him in pained disbelief. Silent. What could she possibly say to him? This wasn't how things were meant to end up. The whole point of the Finis was to put an end to such heartaches. Perhaps she was foolish for thinking removing one rotten egg would stop the whole basket from going bad.

"Salvia," he sobbed, "I'm sorry—So very sorry. I couldn't keep them safe!"

A whimper escaped her lips. She grabbed Baldric's shoulders, lifting him up and pulling him close to rest his head on her shoulders. Her arms wrapped around him, and she held him as tightly as she could. The two sat there, grieving for a long while. She could only guess how long Baldric had to hold in his sadness and anger, keeping his grief from prying eyes to appear strong and reliable for all those who counted on him. Without Zinnia or Rose, he likely didn't have anyone to turn to. To be vulnerable. Baldric needed this, to allow the sorrow to flow from his being. She would remain in his arms as long as he needed.

His arms wrapped around her waist. His cries eventually began to soften. She ran her hand across his back in a circular motion. Her other hand cupped his neck, and despite the lump forming in her throat, she managed the only words of comfort she could find. "Baldric, please, you have to stop blaming yourself for what was clearly out of your control."

Baldric jolted and raised his head, looking her in the eyes. She forced her lips to form the warmest smile she could and held his gaze. "There's no way Zinnia, Rose, or any other person who was lost would blame you. They know you did everything you could to save them. To help them. And I'm sure you saved far more than you lost. Right?"

He stared back in stunned silence. She wiped away the stubborn tears still falling from his eyes and continued. "You did all you could for them. There's no way for you to know what the future will hold. All we can do is try our best to bring good to the world. To live each day and take on the challenges as they are presented. We do our part, but we can't stave off every tragedy and shouldn't blame ourselves in moments like this." Her voice strained by the end, not sure where the words were coming from.

Feeling her calm facade about to break, Salvia rested her head against his neck and placed her palm to his chest. His heart beat rapidly beneath his white tunic, but the tension was leaving his shoulders. Salvia sighed with relief, glad that her words were getting through to him.

Baldric raised a trembling hand. She watched as it hung there, as if he wasn't sure what he was doing, and slowly, he placed it on the back of her head. "How is it that you always end up encouraging me?" He asked, more a statement, than a question. "Always bringing me hope."

Salvia let herself relax. Closing her eyes, she breathed in the familiar scents of spices and leather, and let her mind wander back to the letters they had written to each other over the years. She'd told him of her adventures throughout Cabreo and her interactions with the dwarves of Buio Forest and the Atabey's Mountains. She spoke of her love of sailing and gardening. It was through their letters that he started to open up, telling her of his hopes, his love of reading, and even cooking.

Gently caressing her umber brown hair, Baldric tucked a loose strand behind Salvia's ear, and slid a finger across her jaw, sending goosebumps across her skin. "With everything that has happened, I . . . I wanted to see you, Salvia." He spoke in a whisper, his words making her heart flutter wildly. "I needed to know you were well. To see you with my own eyes."

Her cheeks burned, a bashful smile growing on her face. Wiping her tears away, Salvia sat up, chuckling softly. "This isn't the meeting I was expecting, and despite the pain I feel for our losses, I am glad to see you safe as well." She returned her gaze to him and asked sweetly, "Baldric, would you like to stay here with me? I have plenty of room in my home. You can even settle here, if you want. You need not return to a life of hardship."

After wiping his sleeve across his face, Baldric answered. "Y-Yes, if you don't mind having me."

"Of course not." She wrapped her arms around his neck and smiled.

It was a nice moment, but it wasn't meant to last. Thunder suddenly boomed in the distance as if the sky itself had cracked open. Salvia startled and released Baldric. The two looked to the east across the lake. Dark clouds hung heavy on the horizon, stretching far across the grasslands and treetops of the forest. A red haze glowed in the air as lightning flickered within the darkness. Thunder broke again and again, echoing through the valley.

Concern wrapped its claws around her heart and squeezed. "What in Eldara is going on?" She whispered, trying to hide her panic.

Baldric was quiet for a moment. He then took her hand from his arm and brushed his leather covered thumb over the scar she received from the Finis.

"Salvia, what happened to your hand? It doesn't look like it healed right?"

Glancing back to Baldric who stared at the back of her hand, she couldn't help but feel . . . it wasn't melancholy, but something akin to it. Sorrow, anger, regret, longing, and a hollowness in her chest that threatened to devour her whole, all cobbled together into a sensation that felt like icy spiders crawling just beneath her skin.

She glared at the misshapen scar. It was larger than it should've been and much lighter than the rest of her copper skin. Her memory of that night was clouded in a blurred, fever induced haze.

"It was my fault." She raised her hand between them. "I was so preoccupied with everything that was happening, and that had happened, that I neglected seeking out a healer. I think it was only a day or two before I started to feel sick from infection. It was light at first, but the pain grew immensely. One of the king's sons, kind as he was, sought out anyone who had medicine that could treat the wound. It was one of the dwarves who had been traveling with us that came forth. She did the best that she could, but medicine was in short supply. She sanitized the wound, stitched it closed, placed a healing ointment over it, and renewed my bandages when they needed changing."

Baldric's brows twitched and he took her hand once more. "Salvia, what's really on your mind?"

Such a simple question, but so complex was the answer that she wasn't sure where to start. A lot was on her mind. Not necessarily a single thought, but a tangled web that grew and grew and the seconds drifted by. She remained quiet for a long moment, staring intently at the scar before suddenly blurting out, "Baldric . . . do you think what we did in Lumen Magnum was worth it?"

His body went taut, no doubt startled by her question. Baldric gently grabbed Salvia's chin and guided her gaze to his.

The silence between them was deafening. She didn't know what was going on in the world now, but it scared her. It had been a while since she was last in Cabreo, in any of the major cities. Salvia was so far removed from society that if something major happened, she would've been no more aware of it than she would a whisper lost in a howling wind.

He opened his mouth to say something, however, at that exact moment, a strange, deafening tone, sounding like the blare of a lituus, blared out in the far distance. It echoed on for what seemed like an eternity, calling their attention to the ever-darkening sky.

Her eyes widened with confusion, her heart aching in her chest. She would never forget that sound. She had only ever heard it once before, on the day of her death. "So . . . it was all for nothing." Salvia said softly.

"That isn't true." Baldric grabbed her arm, turning her to him. She was taken aback by the resolve she could hear in his tone. His brows furrowed heavily as he continued. "What you did wasn't for nothing. I'm sure there's a reason for this; maybe another city needs cleansing. That has to be it. I lost so many good people, I can't lose you too!"

Salvia let out a sharp breath. He then cupped her cheek and tapped his forehead to hers, his hot breath lightly brushing against her lips. "I'm sorry, I just-I just don't believe that everything you went through—what *we* went through—was for nothing. I won't lose hope, and neither should you. Remember what you said in your letters. Have faith. Have faith and believe that all will be well." A gentle smile grew on his face.

Salvia forced a smile as well and the two of them held onto each other tightly. Baldric gently ran his fingers through her hair. Slowly closing her eyes, she prayed that he was right. Her actions had to have brought on everlasting change, she thought. The alternative was just too much to bear because if she was wrong, if the foundation they had worked so hard to build was faulty, it would spell the end of their world as they knew it.

# Acknowledgement

Ok, here we go again! Like with this manuscript, I've redone my acknowledgements too. After completing The Call for Finis: Lust, book 2 in this series, Pride read very differently. It was originally written in several perspectives and as it was, it could've been a little confusing as a first entry, so I wanted to fix it. The fix was meant to come after the series end, but because of the different writing style, I was worried Pride would be ignored and skipped over by newer readers. So, here we are, a whole three years later with an updated manuscript and I've never been so happy with how it turned out.

Now let's get on to the thanking. First up, I want to thank my Alpha Reader, my husband **Marcus**, the very special person who was there from the story's very first inception. Without his encouragement, I don't think this story would've ever been written. Next up I want to thank my Beta Readers: **Ellis** and **Briana**. I also want to thank **Chely** who helped looked over the Spanish to make sure each line said exactly what I wanted it to say.

Of course, my acknowledgements wouldn't be complete without thanking my awesome cover artist **Odette A. Bach** and the text designer **Milica Popović** for creating this gorgeous cover of Salvia and Ultor, I can't wait to see what you will do for the rest of the series. My editor, once again, **Jennifer Jarrett**, gets a shout out for coming back to working through this manuscript, and I'm so happy you enjoyed it so much this time around. You've been incredibly encouraging and I really appreciate that.

TCfFP has come a long way, and I also want to thank YOU for making it this far. Please don't forget to leave a review on places like Amazon and GoodReads, reviews help indie authors like myself, and my books, get noticed by other readers. Again, thank you so much for reading, I hope you give my other stories a chance, please stay tuned for more to come.

~A.J. Torres

# TEASER FOR

# THE CALL FOR FINIS: LUST

## AVAILABLE NOW ON AMAZON

# THE HOST

FIRELIGHTS DIMLY FLICKER INSIDE LANTERNS, chasing back the encroaching darkness of night. The salty scent of ocean waves mingled with the putrid stench of the recently deceased. A large wooden cart creaked as the wheels sank and stuck in the sand underneath the Lumen Magnum harbor. Two men struggled onward toward the waters.

"Dammit, I can barely see the water," one of the men exclaimed.

"Shut it! Do you wanna get caught? Come on, let's get this over with."

Both men hung their lanterns on the cart and grabbed hold of a linen wrapped body. They pulled it out and tossed it to the sand, landing with a soft thud.

*Tsk! How dare they treat him so.* A feminine voice whispered angrily from within the confines of her host's shadow. Though the elf's reawakening was a certainty, life had only just started to return to him and so the portal between worlds was at this point no more than a crack. Safeguards would need to be put in place should the host's second chance at life be threatened. As the two men turned back to the cart, a tiny spider birthed into existence from the depths of the wrapped body's shadow. Another body landed on the sand with a soft thud. The arachnid wriggled and stretched its limbs, taking a moment to acclimate itself to the mortal realm, and shifted its body left and right. *Go on, my child, we haven't much time.*

The spider took a few steps toward the body, then quickly scurried onward. Another body thumped to the sand as the spider climbed the folds of the cloth. Searching for an opening, the spider found a small tear in the cloth covering the corpse's face and crawled inside. Claws skittered over soft cloth as the spider squeezed its way between the wraps, until finally touching skin. It made its way across the body's still face, up to the ear, and entered.

*Careful my little one. Latch on to his optic nerve without damaging it.*

The little spider trod cautiously along the body's cold insides, mindful not to push anything out of place or puncture the soft tissue. As the last body flopped to the ground, the tiny spider reached the eye and wrapped its eight legs around it. The claws latched to the whites and its fangs sunk into the optic nerve.

*Now my dear vessel, open your eyes, it's time to wake. I cannot act without confirming they've sinned.*

The corpse's eyes opened to a faint gray blur obstructing his vision. A loud gasp escaped his bandaged mouth, startling the two men as they reached down to grab him.

"What the fuck!? I thought these elves were dead!"

"Oi, keep your voice down." The other hissed, shooting him a glare.

"Fuck you! Is he still alive?"

"How should I know? Give me your knife." He knelt beside the body and pulled open the cloth, revealing a youthful, olive-skinned face. His dark brown hair just barely protruded from beneath the wrap. His throat was split wide, surrounded by crusted blood and bruising. Both men stared down at the elf, his green eyes, wide and unmoving, stared into the night sky above. Thanks to the little spider who now served as a conduit for the mysterious voice, she could see through her host's eye. The bodies of the two men began to glow with the color of their sins.

*Gray. Sloth is so unpalatable.*

The two men stared trembling and wide eyed at the body. Soon, the kneeling man released a soft sigh. "There, see? Nothin' wrong here, just a dead elf— heathenous shit. Now give me your knife." He reached a hand out to the other man, waiting for the blade.

"Why?" The standing man drew his dagger and handed it to the one kneeling.

"To make sure, what else?" He raised the dagger high, ready to plunge the blade into the elf's chest.

*No! You must breathe. BREATHE!*

The elf sucked in a deep breath, wheezing as his lungs stretched with life, his body slowly reanimating. The wound on his neck began to heal, the skin weaving back together, leaving only a thin faint scar over his olive skin. The kneeling man jolted, nearly dropping the blade, and fell back onto the sand.

"What the—"

"*Oh my, this just will not do.*" A feminine voice bemoaned from the shadows.

The two men turned, scanning, eyes darting left and right as they searched for the source of the voice. Sweat slid down the men's brows. The man with the knife held it forward, his grip tight and jaw clenched. The other man stood completely still as if frozen in place, save for the shaking of his knees. Valdina watched with anticipation as life returned to her host, and thus her pathway into the human world opened. Terror grew in the two men's hearts, and as their fear crescendoed, two pairs of blue eyes, one set just inches above the other, fluoresced from within the vessel's shadow.

"*You tried to kill my host.*" As the shadowed voice spoke, two spiders the size of horses, her children, answered her summons. "*Sinners of sloth aren't really my thing, so you'll feed my children instead.*"

Her two children leaped through the opening into the mortal realm and wrapped their legs around the men's bodies. Only a quick shriek escaped their lips before the spiders' pincers bored into their necks, cutting short the last sounds either man would make. As her children devoured the men, she stretched her arms out from the elf's shadow and pulled her torso through, feeling the weight of the mortal realm pushing down on her.

*Damn this realm's pull! It's stronger than I expected.*

Valdina hovered over the elf, her white hair cascading around his head. With labored breath, he gasped as tears flowed down the side of his face. He moaned weakly, sounding like the croak of a toad full of sorrow.

"*Shh. Shh. It's alright, my dear Willka.*" She slid an arm beneath his neck and pulled him tight, cradling him as a mother would a baby. Rocking him gently back and forth as she wiped the tears from his face with her long, stone-like claws. "*We'll make them pay for what they did to you.*"

# THE PREPARATION

W ILLKA STOOD BEFORE A DARK STONE TUNNEL located deep within Dispessore Forest, a fair distance to the south of the city of Lumen Magnum. His brows furrowed as he recalled the stories his mother would tell him before they were parted, of a forest home where she lived before being stolen as a child. There was no way to know if this was truly the home she spoke of, but of all the forests within the borders of Marlela, it was the closest to the city. If any place had a high probability of being the home she had spoken of, this was it. With no way to know what became of his mother, those stories were all he had left to remember her by. The magical totems of her people had to be here.

A chill shot up his spine. The night air was cold, but thanks to Valdina, he felt the warmth of a summer's day across his skin. She channeled the flames of Infernos, the demon realm, throughout his body to chase away the chill.

He raised a hand to the side of his head above his long, pointed ears, running his palm across the recently sheared, dark brown bristles of his hair. The hair on the rest of his head fell long to his shoulders and was brushed to the side. It felt odd but was somewhat refreshing. This hairstyle originally belonged to another, his now deceased lover. The physical trait they now shared gave Willka some comfort, though he wore it just a little differently, parting it to the opposite side. It felt as if a part of his beloved was still with him in some small way, reminding him of the vengeance he would soon wreak on those responsible for what happened. He struggled to force his nerves to settle and began forward into the tunnel, his bare feet digging lightly into the soft earth with every step.

Coming to terms with the events of his life, death, and reawakening would have been too much to bear were it not for the fury driving him to continue forward. Everything had been taken from him. His last moments seared into his mind forever, haunting his thoughts every time his eyes shut, clawing at the back of his mind. Then there was the fact he had been brought back, the feeling of his wounds closing just as excruciating as when he had received them.

Valdina's very existence horrified him. Her love of punishing the wicked was only matched by the care she showed him while he was recuperating after his awakening, somehow making her all the more terrifying.

On the journey here he had come across a small band of rogues. He had not seen them approach. Their footsteps were quiet and thanks to the clouded night sky, he could only see the short distance in front of him. The men descended quickly and tried to rob him. Finding he had not a single coin to his name, that's when it happened. Willka could see the men's sins as clear as a candlelight in the darkness. As Valdina emerged they tried to flee, but their attempt at escape was in vain. They were dead the moment she saw their sins, but they didn't know it yet. Her wicked laughter rolled across the plains. The strange thing was not that she reveled in her duty as a demon, but that when she returned and found Willka scared, she comforted him as a mother would a frightened child.

Shaking the memory away, Willka rolled his shoulders back and forth. It had been a week or so since his reawakening, but his body didn't yet feel familiar. Willka looked down at his hand, curling his fingers inward and then opening them up, again and again. Valdina had told him that the body he reawakened in was his own, and yet, it didn't feel like it.

*It is yours, my dear Willka.* Valdina answered in his mind. *Coming back from the dead is not something everyone gets to do. It's unnatural to your kind, a gift only meant for a few. It won't be easy, but you'll eventually grow accustomed to it.* Valdina's words were sweet as they washed through his mind, reminiscent of a clamoring of voices from that of a small child to an elderly woman all speaking in perfect unison. It was usually rather unnerving, but at this moment, it felt somehow oddly tender.

"If you say so."

*Shush, my dear, I hear voices ahead.*

As Willka drew close to the end of the tunnel, he glimpsed the glow of a huge fire. His heart raced nervously within his chest. Willka cautiously peered around the end of the tunnel to search for a place to hide and spotted a sizable boulder just to the right and scurried to it. Kneeling low, he peeked over the boulder. The chamber was enormous with a dome shaped ceiling. A large campfire blazed brightly at the center while smoke billowed upward and out through a circular opening at the ceiling's peak. Around the flames were nearly two dozen elves kneeling atop colorful intricate tapestries, arguing in another language. Listening, Willka recognized a few words here and there as Elvish, a language he hadn't heard since being separated from his mother. Brought up in slavery, he hadn't been permitted to learn the language of his ancestors. Willka's hands tightened into fists, his knuckles turning white.

*Relax, my dear Willka.* Valdina's words came as a seductive whisper in his mind, making his spine crawl.

*I'll relax when Lumen Magnum is nothing but rubble,* he bit back, but instantly regretted doing so as she didn't deserve his ire.

She knowingly giggled in reply. *Once we've retrieved the totems so that you may protect yourself, we'll set off for Lumen Magnum. As we agreed, the Finis will see to the sinners and thus, you will have what you truly need.* Valdina fell quiet for a moment, her cryptic words lingering in Willka's mind before she continued. *Now, to the task at hand. Ten of the elves are chieftains. The ones behind them are their protectors.* Valdina suddenly went quiet, which caused his brows to twitch nervously. After a moment, she broke her silence. *I can translate for you, if you'd like.*

*You could translate what they're saying this whole time? Why didn't you do so already!?* Willka's teeth ground in frustration.

She replied playfully, *I was just waiting for you to ask my dear.*

He let out a soft groan, his head fell forward to rest against the boulder's cold surface. *Valdina, can you* please *translate what they're saying?*

*Of course, my darling. One moment, some of them are quite agitated with a few of the chieftains present.*

Willka quickly raised his gaze to the elves, intently listening to Valdina's translation.

*You see that large elf at the top of the circle?*

Looking to the side of the campfire, he spotted a muscular elf decorated with many feathers about his headdress, neck, and hair.

*He and the one beside him are dismissing the others' concerns, arguing they should forget about the enslaved elves currently held in Lumen Magnum, and to abandon those who have been recently captured.*

*WHAT!?* Willka's eyes narrowed with anger. Many of the elves' bodies suddenly shrouded over in hues of various colors, catching him by surprise. He had accidentally triggered Valdina's gift of second sight, an ability that allowed him to see the souls of others who have committed great sin.

*They're suggesting strengthening their borders to protect themselves from Lumen Magnum. The large one is glowing brightly in yellow, meaning Greed has overtaken him. I'm guessing he's made a deal with the human city.* She sighed, boredom clear on her tone. *He wouldn't be the first to sell his people to make his own life more comfortable.*

Willka's eyebrows twitched in aggravation.

A chief to the far side of the circle stood in outrage. She was somewhat taller than Willka and had an athletic build. The feathered chief, however, dismissively waved her away.

*She just accused the feathered muscly one of being deplorable for his willingness to abandon their kin. Many agree with her, but the chief to his side retorted that they simply don't have the means to face off with the likes of Lumen Magnum. Hmph, I suppose I understand their hesitance, but if they play it smart, they have a chance of success.* Valdina snickered sinisterly.

"I've had enough of listening to cowards." Willka growled.

The chieftains startled, hearing the unfamiliar voice. They looked warily in

Willka's direction as he stood and stepped out from behind the boulder, careful to remain mostly hidden in the shadows.

"It must be easy for you to sit idly by, here in the safety of your forest while those monsters in Lumen Magnum abuse those elves unfortunate enough to have been caught, hauled off and forgotten. Toyed with. Used. Punished for petty grievances." Able to now see all in attendance, Willka scanned the room and several more began to glow. Two yellows, an orange, a gray, a purple, and two reds. "Killed for sport. Many have never even known what it is to live like you do, instead born into bondage. You turn your heads without even considering what they live with on a daily basis. Those of you comfortable with that, well, today you get what you deserve."

*Clear enough for you Valdina?* Willka mentally asked.

"*Oh, this suits me just fine.*" She laughed hungrily as worry began to spread through the elven congregation, her laughter echoing in the chamber. Her hands emerged from Willka's shadow and slammed down at either side of his feet. He felt her presence rise and loom behind him. "*The greedy ones are some of my favorites,*" Valdina moaned as the strange chatter of her children surrounded them both.

With a flick of her ebony, stone crusted wrist, her children pounced on the elves. Those lucky enough to be spared in the initial attack went for their weapons but were too slow. The waist-high, deep blue and ebony spiders shot out bundles of sticky webbing, trapping the elves inside. They tried desperately to push their way free, but their efforts were in vain. The spiders dragged the captured elves to the back of the cave. Some of the captives hung from the ceiling while others were piled on the floor. A few disappeared into the darkness, to a different corner of the cave, kicking and screaming all the way.

Willka walked forward to the dancing flames in the pit. He stared down at the large fire before him, watching it sway left and right, his mind traveling to memories of his beloved. They had laid on the floor together beneath a thin blanket, bathed in the warm light of the torch hanging from a wall nearby. His partner's golden blond hair shimmered, the sweat covering his golden-brown skin glistening, and his amber brown eyes twinkled against the firelight. A pang of longing swelled within his chest, thinking of the night they shared his cot for the first time. Anguish washed over him in waves, an unbearable ache spreading throughout his body and down his limbs, causing his body to tremble. A deep frown formed on his face.

A loud thud startled Willka. He glanced up as Valdina's eight ebony legs stabbed into the earth, one after the other, stopping beside him. A dense, black exoskeleton covered her entire lower half and partially spread up her humanoid torso, resembling a corset. It also spread from her hands, up just past her elbows and gradually gave way to the pale, bluish skin covering her shoulders, neck, and face.

Her four, glowing aquamarine eyes blazed with hunger as her children brought the muscular, feathered elf to her. The elf chief tried to fight them off, but the web binding was too much for him.

*"Oh my, he looks so scrumptious."* She wrapped her clawed, ebony fingers around his thick throat, and lifted him as though he were as light as a flower petal.

Higher and higher he rose as she straightened to her full height, the chieftain's feet dangling just above Willka's head. She licked her azure lips in anticipation. As her mouth opened, two sharp fangs emerged, seemingly growing larger as her maw widened. Her bright blue skin stretched tight.

The elf chief screamed out as he stared wide eyed into the abyss. Terror was clear on every fiber of his being. The yellow hue of his soul shrouding his body, slowly ignited and was enveloped in a fiery storm of crimson and orange.

His heart sank into his chest at the sight. As her mouth stretched with seemingly no end in sight, her fangs sank deep into the chief's skin. Willka looked away, trying to ignore the horrible slurping sounds he was sure he wouldn't soon forget.

Glancing to his left, he counted nine spiders crawling toward him, clutching bags between their chelicerae. Their bodies bounced up and down in excitement. He tilted his head and raised an eyebrow in intrigue. Willka knelt and hovered his hand under one of the bags. Just as he did, the spider dropped it onto his palm, clapping its chelicerae.

Willka placed the bag on the floor, making sure it was visible in the firelight. Opening it, he found many tiny wooden figures within. His heart jumped with triumph at the sight. "This is it, the totems my mother spoke of!"

He jolted as a loud thud sounded behind him. Willka turned and saw the body of the feathered chief lying on the ground before Valdina, now shriveled and gray. A horrified look was frozen on its now darkened face. Willka's stomach churned.

Valdina smeared the blood over her mouth, savoring every moment as she ran her tongue over her now crimson painted lips. "*I love wrath but trust me when I say greed holds a special place in my heart.*" She moaned a satisfied hum and hungrily eyed a group of tied up elves nearby. "*Now, where's the other one?*" Valdina quickly scurried over to the other elves whose souls were awash with sin, piled in a different corner of the cave. Her white hair, both loose strands and braids, fluttered behind her. A few of her children followed.

Willka's eyes glanced down to the body of the elf she had devoured moments before. His thoughts drifted to his beloved, wondering if his once beautiful being now had more in common with the corpse before him. His jaw muscles slowly clenched, vowing that the human slavers would pay for what they did to Willka and his beloved. His eyes blurred as he fought back tears, taking a tight breath. Willka then noticed a bag hanging from the corpse's waist.

He quickly looked away, the carnage bringing back memories of his death, and that of his lover. Taking a moment to calm his nerves, Willka glanced at the spiders before him, their many eyes staring back at him, seeming almost as if they were watching with curiosity.

"Ca-Can one of you bring me his totem bag?"

The spider who handed him the bag lifted its body up, clapped its chelicerae eagerly, and scurried to the body in compliance. The other spiders left their bags by his feet. He thanked them and turned to the fire, dumping the totems onto the earth to examine them.

Each totem's appearance was unique, representing a lost loved one. Sifting through the pile, he eyed the symbols etched into them, some on their bases and others on their backs.

Soon, the spider returned from the shriveled elf with the totem bag held high and placed it at Willka's feet.

A group of bound elves, those free of sin and spared from Valdina's devouring, yelled at him in their language. He glanced at them with squinted eyes, noticing their rising agitation, unsure if their anger was solely due to the havoc he and the demons had wrought or if it was something more.

He looked back to the pile of totems, recalling something his mother once said. These elves see the totems as sacred items, meant to be treated with respect as one would their own family. Dumping them discourteously on the ground likely provoked their increased agitation. Although he felt a little guilt for how he was mistreating the totems, he didn't have time to be tender. Willka renewed his search through the totems, ignoring the elves' vitriol.

Totem after totem, he studied the symbols carved into them, each symbol differed from the last, but none were familiar to him. "Damn, what did Mother say again?"

Revealing another totem's base, this one marked with a triangle embedded within a circle and a diamond at its center. "This looks familiar. Is this the symbol?"

Willka buried his face into a hand, thinking carefully on his mother's words. "The square with a circle within and another square is . . . earth, I think. A diamond with a circle was wind, or maybe it was the triangle whose points pierced the circle . . . Or was that water? Damn."

He returned to the triangle with a diamond within. "If so, that means this one should be fire." Willka gripped the totem resembling a feminine looking elf, picturing a small flame in his mind, and hoping the totem would respond. Then a strange warmth crawled its way through his fingers and up his arm. His heart raced, his hand trembling lightly. "Yes, this is it."

Grabbing one of the empty bags, Willka stuffed every totem with the fire symbol into it, leaving the rest. The other totems as he understood them were powerful in their own rights but fire, destructive and chaotic, would suit his needs. He wouldn't need precision for fire. It would spread and destroy all in its path until there was nothing left to burn. It was the perfect weapon to bring ruin to the city that harmed him. Tying the bag to his worn leather belt, he made his way back to the tunnel. "Time to go."

*"Alright, come children, where we're going there will be plenty for you all to devour."*

The pitter patter of their many legs filled the tunnel with a soft hum. Making his way through the tunnel, the hum slowly softened as the demons disappeared into his shadow, passing back into the realm of Infernos, leaving only the thump of his footsteps, and the distant cries of the bound elves remaining in the cave.

The smell of oak and damp moss filled his senses as he stepped out of the tunnel. The moonlight struggled to breach the canopy of the trees above. He breathed in the earthy scent of the forest, finding a momentary pleasure in the calm.

"These people should consider themselves lucky. No chains, no leather leashes, and not a stone cell in sight."

*Soon, no one will ever have to worry about such woes as you've endured,* Valdina responded softly.

Willka flinched at the comment, finding it unsettling that such sincere, heartfelt concern existed within the same being who delighted in devouring sinners. He took a deep breath and exhaled. *With luck, Valdina, we will slip out unnoticed, as easily as we came in. I think I've had enough death for one night.*

The sound of rushed footsteps suddenly drew close from behind. He stopped and looked back into the tunnel. The chieftain who had protested against the feathered elf, appeared with labored breaths. Her braided black hair was disheveled and now hung over one side of her olive-skinned face. Worry shone in her amber brown eyes.

He stared at her, bewildered, wondering just how she was able to break free of the spider's webs.

*She must have a finely forged dagger to have broken free,* Valdina remarked. *Poor thing was probably working at it since my little ones bound her and the others. I like her.*

Willka glanced down to the elven chief's outstretched arms and saw a fresh set of clothes in her hands, looking similar to her garb. A beige buckskin shawl and moccasins with simple white and blue stitching going across them, white top and beige trousers, a blue sash, and a leather belt.

"Only attacked bad chieftains. Here, take," the woman said in broken Anglicus,[1] the common tongue of the humans and their slaves.

His eyes narrowed, a bit wary of her intention.

She took a step closer. "Take. You like us. Like me. Want to help. Take, please." Her posture softened.

His lips trembled lightly. "But I don't know if I'm even one of you. My mother, she . . . she was taken when she was very young, before I was born. She didn't even remem—"

"Does not matter. You know totems. You us." She pushed the clothes to his chest, forcing him to take them, and gently patted the buckskin shawl.

Willka clutched the bundle of clothes, keeping his eyes fixed on hers, baffled by her insistence. He then glanced down at the clean clothes in his arms and then back at her, wondering just how she came to learn Anglicus. "How—"

"Another time. Here." She slid the strap of her satchel off her shoulder and handed it to him.

---

1    This world's version of English

He tucked the clothes under one arm and accepted the satchel. Looking inside, he found a large buffalo bladder, probably filled with water, a piece of thin meat sticking out of one of several parfleches, and the totems he had left behind. "Wait, I don't—"

"You do. Healing totems will help." She pointed to his dirt ridden feet, looking rather worse for wear. "Other totems for . . . vengeance."

*Take her kindness, Willka. The nights are cold, and your feet could use the protection.* Valdina encouraged.

He looked at his torn and sullied slave clothes, and his blood burned. Placing the gifts on the ground, he began to disrobe so that he could change into his new clothes. When he glanced up at the elven chief, he saw a small smile break on her face. With a bow of her head, she turned away, allowing him privacy.

Slipping on the clothing, belt, and sash, and next the moccasin boots, he took the straps, and tied them about his shins and ankles so that the fitting was snug. Willka then reached into the bag he had stuffed the fire totems into and took one out. Pointing it down to his slave outfit, he thought long and hard on his mother's words: *Ask the spirits within for aid, and with the right totem in hand, they may answer. Light a fire, heal a scratch, quench your thirst, whatever you need. Just ask.*

He took a deep breath and focused his thoughts on the old clothes—*Burn.*

The wooden totem of what looked to be a wolf glowed faintly orange. A spark flashed and quickly flew out wildly. As the spark touched the tattered fabric, his old clothes burst into flames. The fire danced wildly and consumed the linens. He watched as the last remnant of his time as a slave was burned away. Watching the pile of cloth reduced to ash, he felt the weight of his burdens lessen slightly.

"What's your name?" Willka asked softly.

She was quiet for a moment, watching the clothes burn. "Meztli. Chief of . . . this forest. You?"

"Willka." He stood and dropped the totem back into the small bag. Stuffing it into the satchel with the other totems, he slipped it over his shoulder, and began to walk away.

"Come back."

Hearing this Willka stopped, confused, and looked over his shoulder.

"After task done, come back. I take care of you. Promise." She crossed her hands over her chest and bowed her head.

He stared at her for a long moment. The sentiment touched his heart, but the comforting thought was quickly chased away by the uncertainty of an after. "We'll see."

.

# ABOUT THE AUTHOR

Adlin(A.J.) Kennedy Torres is a writer who likes to dabble as an anime artist for fun. She enjoys Fantasy and Science Fiction stories. Adlin particularly loves to write Fantasy and easily gets immersed in books like The Goddess of Nothing at All and Aletheia. She's loved Fantasy stories ever since she was a kid picking up The Lord of the Rings and Eragon for the first time.

Nowadays you can find Adlin in the hot and horribly humid sunshine state of Florida, hanging out, playing video games with her husband, and chasing her son around the house with two needy dogs and a very chill cat.

Instagram and Twitter: @A_J_Torres0